CW00968862

A Sharp Scratch

A Sharp Scratch

HEATHER DARWENT

PENGUIN
VIKING

VIKING

UK | USA | Canada | Ireland | Australia
India | New Zealand | South Africa

Viking is part of the Penguin Random House group of companies
whose addresses can be found at global.penguinrandomhouse.com

Penguin Random House UK,
One Embassy Gardens, 8 Viaduct Gardens, London SW11 7BW

penguin.co.uk

Penguin
Random House
UK

First published 2025
001

Set in 12/14.75pt Dante
Typeset by Falcon Oast Graphic Art Ltd
Printed and bound in Great Britain by Clays Ltd, Elcograf S.p.A.

The authorized representative in the EEA is Penguin Random House Ireland,
Morrison Chambers, 32 Nassau Street, Dublin D02 YH68

A CIP catalogue record for this book is available from the British Library

HARDBACK ISBN: 978–0–241–74045–3
TRADE PAPERBACK ISBN: 978–0–241–74046–0

Penguin Random House is committed to a sustainable future
for our business, our readers and our planet. This book is made from
Forest Stewardship Council® certified paper.

For my family

'think little of thy flesh: blood, bones, and a skin; a pretty piece of knit and twisted work, consisting of nerves, veins and arteries; think no more of it, than so'
– *Meditations*, Marcus Aurelius

Preface

For many years, I heard stories. A girl in HR hinted at something unsavoury as we hovered around the kitchen in our break. Snippets of gossip to mull over as our lunches spun in the row of office microwaves: outsides crusty, insides boiling away. A long beep and we'd poke with a finger to check the leftovers were hot. The conversation ended.

There were other things too. A friend of a friend would be off the radar for a while. I'd email and there would just be . . . nothing, or a cheerfully worded if vague bounce back. And then there were the rumours that followed in breathless whispers.

Couldn't hack the pace . . .

Fucked-up nose job; then a complete and utter breakdown – maybe they've gone self-employed, freelancing in Portugal, I think . . . digital nomad. I know, so predictable – they always said they'd do that, but I haven't heard from them, not in ages! Too long.

An ex-colleague said a neighbour returned from *God knows where* . . . and she was a bit *different*. It was just an offhand comment, our eyes meeting above our screens, and I didn't press her for more.

The word 'agitated' came up and 'paranoid' too. But then there were the girls who came back better; somewhat revived, apparently.

I must emphasize that none of these stories were serious. It wasn't like they were missing girls on the news – their full names, their former jobs, their desperate, crying spouses imprinted on our minds forever. It wasn't like that, because these girls came back. So, there was no reason to probe. They were just people who'd gone off-grid for a while.

I was focused on my own problems, which felt entirely

unrelated. Though the word 'agitated' stayed with me for some time after I left the office. A cramped, prickled word. A ball of barbed wire cutting the throat when I repeated it to myself, even though I didn't know these girls, and I didn't know where they'd been, and I didn't know what had happened to them.

Before Carn

I.

It was the beginning of a long heatwave in Edinburgh. Hot for May, when the late-spring days were usually pinched with rain. Oh, how *lucky* we were to have it on my – or our – big day! Something we'd planned for so long, until it snuck up on us in the end.

We had breakfast out on the balcony because that was a nice thing to do, and the room was stuffy anyway – filled with a warm haze of coconut deodorant, it was like we couldn't breathe. Up above, blue as far as the eye could see and not a single cloud.

Eggs for breakfast. The hollandaise hanging off them was thick at first, until it wept across the plate, flattened by the heat. I was rarely hungry back then, and it was too hot for flabby eggs, but we picked at them anyway. The thought came to me that I could crack an egg on the ground, and it would fry and sizzle on the paving stones. I'd seen it happen once on TV, on the strip in Las Vegas.

When I mentioned it to Siobhan, my only bridesmaid, her eyes widened. 'Betsy,' she scolded. 'Why are you saying things like that today of all days! Just . . . chill out about the eggs!' Siobhan did not respond well to odd comments. They seemed to puzzle her – her voice went all high and confused, her lovely face screwed up tight. I suspected Harry would have told her to keep an eye on me, and she was right to keep me in check.

We drank from those blocky little hotel cups that never have enough room in them for a proper amount of coffee, both of us playing absently with the sugar sachets. When the time came to get ready, we'd emptied them out on the table, ordered them into gritty little lines and then torn the paper into pink shreds.

I went for a bath.

'A hot bath is an . . . unusual choice,' Siobhan said.

I lay there, very still, waiting for it to start. The urge to duck my head under was strong.

Wizened relatives said it would be the happiest day of my life. They whispered it when I was young, but it formed a more frequent whine as I grew older. Like if they didn't tell me enough times, I wouldn't get round to it. But I did, and the day had arrived. All the months of planning, everything leading up to that one day. I repeated their tips to Siobhan, mockingly, their words of wisdom lifted from magazines and parcelled into neat soundbites: *Hold your husband's hand all day so you can enjoy the day together* – that's what they all said.

It will go so quickly you'll hardly even know what's happening – singsong advice that suggested some kind of blackout.

You're so lucky to have him – and by that, they meant Harry, and by lucky, they meant because he was aesthetically pleasing, and he put up with me.

Then came the horror stories: *What if you're on your . . . period!?* Imagine! A deep red stain spreading on silk. Something secret there for all to see.

And the *weather* – the most mercurial of villains, with the power to destroy everything. Even though the skies were clear, Siobhan (never one to trust nature) sat on the toilet seat scrolling through meteorological apps on her phone with a shaking hand while I soaked.

'I hope it doesn't rain,' she said. I couldn't quite read her expression.

'If it rains, it rains,' I replied. And I wanted to tell her that there were things far worse than a brief shower.

2.

I was sour under the arms, flyaway hairs frizzing around my temple. Still, there was no time to waste, and we were running close to the outer allowances of the schedule. With Siobhan's help, I pulled out the dress – *so heavy; you should have had more bridesmaids!* – so the photographer could take pictures of it hung up against the window. The light shone through the bloated layers of lace, exposing all the different parts like a frilled X-ray.

Siobhan helped me pull it on and do it up tight at the back. And it all came together. That was when it hit me. The day had come, and I was finally going to allow myself to look forward to it. I hadn't really imagined that it would get to this point, but it had, and it was breathtaking. They'd all been right. It was going to be the best day of my life.

'You look *amazing!*' Siobhan said. 'How do you feel?'

'I feel fine?' I said, unsure. 'I slept okay. I'm excited.'

'Of course you're excited! It's going to be perfect,' she trilled, and the words were right, but something was off with her face, her brow knitted as she stood in front of me and fiddled with my hair and veil.

Siobhan was all I had that morning. I reached out to squeeze her wrist. As I've said, she was lovely, but maybe not to everyone. Her face was dominated by a vast smile and her features were all big, even overwhelming. Siobhan was an expert at 'making the most of herself', as she called it. Wonderful in a long orange dress we'd chosen together. It swished against the floor and clashed, in a way that worked, with her long orange hair. Wonderful with gold bangles snaked up her wrists and arms. Then, the final touches. The hairdresser tried to convince me to add in some fake hair and glue some eyelashes on but I declined. Siobhan was up for it, and they sewed in more slippery auburn strands, so it fanned out around her back. Someone had hinted that I might be worried that she'd outshine me on *my* day. *Put her in something plain!* they'd said. But we were so different. And I didn't even think of how we compared to each other.

Down below, out of the window, we could see the marquee being set up.

'I don't think it's going to rain,' Siobhan proclaimed with finality. 'Shall we?' And she grabbed on to the back of the dress to steer me out, like a parent manoeuvring the reins you attach to toddlers.

We made our way to the outdoor aisle. My father swooped in next to me and held my arm at the elbow. I had hoped for a kind word from him, but it didn't seem forthcoming, so I looked around at our guests. They wore sunglasses so I couldn't see their eyes, a crowd of tiny mirrors. I could just about make out Harry's parents in the front row. His mother wasn't wearing *pure* white, her dress had a hint of lilac to it, but I knew Siobhan would find it a little too close to white to be acceptable.

The men were sweating. And the women fanned themselves with the orders of service, their hair in complicated arrangements, their bags on their laps. The buttery biscuit smell of fake tan was in the air.

I noted the gang from work, friends from university, from school. As I proceeded down the aisle, I saw my brothers. All three of them sat in navy suits; bulky and jovial. My mother was tiny next to them at the end of the row – in awe that the day had come, and that I was actually getting married.

Then Harry turned around and my *heart* when I saw him! Like it had wormed its way to the surface and surely everyone could hear it beating because it was him, there and then, how he'd always been. It was everything in that moment. Every date we'd ever had, every second together, flashing in front of me. How could I possibly not cry? I couldn't not cry, and I hoped that they were pretty tears.

Harry wore a green linen suit – *It's chartreuse, Bets, that's what the guy in the shop said*, he'd snapped at me. He had a tear in his eye that must have been there before he turned to look at me, because how could it have flowed so quickly? He watched me intensely as I made my way down the aisle. When I reached him, he took my hand in his firmly. 'Are you good?' he mouthed.

Whatever had happened before, the day was bigger than all that.

I nodded.

I stood there; we did the vows.

You'll feel like the only two people in the world, they had said, and they were right! Just me and Harry, and our vows, which were quite prosaic really, and his smile which said, *I know, I feel the same way as you do. I feel like it's just the two of us right now, and it doesn't matter about anyone else in the world.*

I don't know if I saw him flinch when we recited *in sickness and in health*.

We both said 'yes'.

The meal was in the marquee and our guests mingled. They pretended to be satisfied with talking to each other, but really, they wanted time with us. We were the stars. *Bride time*, Harry always said when we went to other people's weddings, *they fucking love it, look at them crowding round her.* They did crowd round me, and Harry and I were photographed in different positions. Mostly in front of a huge rhododendron bush with dark leaves the size of my palm.

Harry had some pictures taken with his groomsmen, and they pushed each other around a bit. *Joshing*, Harry said, *just joshing, get in the picture, Bets.* They tried to lift me up.

The flowers didn't seem real, and I reached out and pressed one between two fingers, and then Harry's hand was on mine.

'Don't do that,' he said, quite pleasantly.

Hold your husband's hand so you can enjoy the day together.

★

'Is it everything you thought it would be?' Siobhan asked.

'Yes,' I said. 'I think it is.'

Everything and more. But it was brighter, somehow less kind than I'd expected.

She nodded, and then she was gone.

The sweat was gathering in my armpits, on my legs. And that was what the whole day was like: bliss then tight discomfort – some moments were unspoiled and in others my world was too close and too bright.

Harry's suit choice was ill-judged. It looked radioactive when he stood up, commanding the crowd as he told the story of how we'd met.

The tale was supple as he moulded it for our audience. It was almost a love story, but he talked about how I'd reminded him of a hamster. Not that I was rodent-like all the time, but I just seemed like I wanted to curl up in a ball and hibernate for a while – leave everyone else to real life and join in later. Like I'd found myself in a room with no idea how I'd got there.

He said *like* and *hamster* many, many times. Still, our audience smiled dotingly as he merged three different and true anecdotes into one slick tale involving punting in Cambridge on a weekend break and the fortuitous retrieval of a straw hat from the water.

Scrambling like a horrible little hamster.

A kindly old man and a missed train.

A rodent, cheeks bulging.

Crossed wires. Young lovers.

I listened. Everyone laughed. There were more glasses of champagne.

I rarely drank, but that day I gulped down the champagne, lifted the glass to my forehead to cool myself down. My brothers were red in the face with beer, bellowing away. My parents seemed concerned and I smiled to show them that all was fine.

Then the remains of the day became patchier, stickier too. All the courses came with sweeps and dollops, little squares of smoked salmon on soft, buttered bread, then lamb rump, all of it a mess as our guests picked away. By the end, we were coming apart with make-up running down our faces. Too many coupes of champagne and not enough water.

It felt hotter than the sun in that marquee by the time the cake-cutting ceremony happened, with Harry forcing a long, sharp knife down through the yellow sponge.

After, I went outside to the rhododendrons. Harry was there.

I staggered back inside the marquee, and then his hand was on my arm, guiding me through the swarm of guests. I wanted to say something; I could have said something right then, but I didn't. He led me into the hotel and up the stairs, and then we were in our room, where I'd got ready.

'Stay in here,' he said.

I was only half aware of what was happening. I lay on the bed. He closed the door and, at first, it was like he was going to come closer, but when I stood up, he was gone.

I rushed to the door, but it was locked, and so I shouted and pulled at it, but there was no one there on the other side. I kind of understood what he was doing, but it was too difficult to wrench through it all, so instead of fighting the heat, I let it in. I thought of how long we'd planned for this day, thinking about the seating arrangement and noting each dietary requirement. I had matched colour to colour to colour until tasteful swatches swam against my eyelids. Lying there on the hotel bed, I added it up in my head and divided it: every minute of our wedding cost eighty-three pounds.

With the number settled, I allowed myself to sleep. The room became a little cooler and eventually it was dark. The rest of the night has very little shape to it when I try and wrangle it back into the forefront of my mind. Harry returned. It was violent. We had coffee together the next morning in silence. I went back home, and I was married.

3.

After the wedding, a few days passed, and then Harry turned up at our flat. He didn't speak to me much, but then it was like he'd made a decision that we were going to work it all out. We flew long-haul for the honeymoon; a beach holiday, even though we both knew I wouldn't go into the sea.

There were points on the honeymoon where Harry was like he'd been when we'd first met, and I enjoyed him. He swept me through customs, going through my bag for liquids because he knew I always forgot something. He hailed us a taxi. He'd sorted everything, every aspect, and though a beach holiday wouldn't have been my choice, he had made the effort to plan it all. We shared some jokes at the beginning.

'Seen them?' he said, laughing at another couple as they battled through the departures lounge with too many bags. He was being cautious with me. We joked and we joked, and it all started well but it spilled over, and I became the joke.

At the end of the week, we discussed my character defects over limp and fishy starters.

'Always perhaps and maybe,' Harry said with a sigh. 'A bit more force, a bit more oomph.'

He acted out the oomph with a punch of his fist into the air.

It was a fair point. I was fond of the non-committal, but I wasn't biting, not on the honeymoon.

He raised a glass to me. 'I'm Betsy and I'm an insomniac,' he said in a funny voice. He laughed and, as his face split open in a smile, I thought I glimpsed a scratch to the side of his cheek, below his ear.

His 'bit' was pitched as comedy, a light dig, not quite cruel enough that I could say anything. He preferred to go down the insomnia route when he spoke of me, or to me.

Insomniac.

Not quite, I thought. *Not quite right and you know it.* I had no appetite, but I forced down some of the calamari as we watched the waves lick over the black sand.

The holiday ended not with the bang of an argument, but in a muttered strand of minor irritants. Things had not been good, and I felt that I needed less stress, and so I quit my job while we were away and started my search for employment from the loungers, scrolling through adverts and imagining a new me.

I started a new job at a bookshop within a week of returning from the holiday, and I was proud of myself for finding something so quickly. It was still a difficult time in the weeks that followed. I had palpitations during the night, and the days were long.

I preferred to avoid mirrors, skirted round them, and stayed away from the reflective surfaces of shop windows. Imagine the most brutal of make-unders – that was me. I had a crawling feeling of being covered all over in a flaked crust, and when I did slap on some make-up, it sat in a grimy layer. My skin was all white and yellow. The crimson thread of my bloodshot eyes stood out like knotty little pieces of crochet. I couldn't think what to wear, and when I dressed, all my clothes looked stained and stretched; none of them quite fit. I was rumpled, constantly, and everyone outside was talking about how hot the summer was, how lucky we were, but the summer was torture for me, hot days stretching on and on.

I didn't want to see anyone, but I could not escape a dinner with Siobhan and Spencer that we'd rearranged, then rearranged again. I was busy with the new job and, in the end, over a month passed after the honeymoon before I saw her. I had no desire to go. It was a test for all of us. Could we be normal? Certainly, I was willing to try.

The evening did not start well. Harry had had a bad day at work and was already annoyed. The time they asked us to come made him irate – *who the fuck invites someone to dinner at 6.15 p.m.?* – and the lack of any details about the meal was also an issue – *you know I'll have a bit of gluten, but I'd like the transparency of knowing when it's in the meal in advance.*

'Are you okay?' Harry asked me on the way.

We hadn't spoken so much, not for the previous few weeks. It had all been quite bad.

'Fine,' I said, with a lump in my throat.

'Really?' He swapped from irritation to a questioning pity.

'I'm tired,' I said, hating the sound of my voice.

'Hmmm. Can you turn the radio off, please?' he snapped at the taxi driver.

All was quiet.

We arrived, and Harry pushed through the tangle of bikes stacked in the stairwell with a groan of exhaustion; he hated clutter with a passion. We went right to the top of the block of flats where Spencer and Siobhan lived. Our greetings were stiff. Spencer and Harry shuffled round each other, and they ended up deciding on a nod and a kind of tap on the shoulder instead of a hug. Siobhan kissed my cheek.

'It's roasting outside,' I said.

She cocked her head. 'Oh, really? I didn't think so, I thought it was cooler than earlier.'

I shrugged. 'How's work?' I asked. Siobhan and I had worked together for a few years before I'd quit.

'Oh, you know . . .' She led me through to the kitchen, and I watched her take the meat out from the oven to prod it. Beef. It yielded too much, and she wrinkled her nose, shoving it back in.

She turned to me, giving me her full attention. She glowed, and it made my insides churn even though I didn't trust it. With Siobhan, you could feel like you were having a lovely time in the moment, but on reflection, it was clear that she was counting down the minutes until you left, the task of hosting completed.

'There's so much to catch you up on with work, but I promised myself I wouldn't bother you with it. After all, you've escaped! You look great, Bets! Anyway . . .' she said, peering into her oven. 'We miss you at the office!'

'Do you really?' I asked. Needy, suddenly.

'Massively. It's not the same without you.'

She didn't ask me about the bookshop. The conversation halted, but it wasn't so awkward. I had been worried about the evening, but I found that I could take the problem of Siobhan and fold her away into a crevice at the back of my mind. This became easier with practice.

Harry came into the kitchen.

'HarryHarryHarry!' Siobhan said, arms stretched out towards him.

They embraced and she took the wine.

'None for me,' I said. 'Just water.'

Harry wandered away to the toilet.

'You okay?' Siobhan asked. Still, she couldn't break the habit of constant, grating concern.

'I'm fine,' I lied. 'The new job is good. It was the right decision. I need to get better. Be better.'

She nodded. 'And how are things with him?' she said in a low voice.

'Not great, not terrible.' The words wavered; I caught them early and steadied myself because I never cried. 'I'm exhausted, so I get back from work and I'm not the best company, and he's always so angry about it.'

She was nodding like she understood.

I decided to ask her. 'Shiv, the wedding . . . Did I leave early?'

'What do you mean?' she shot back, flustered.

'Well, did I leave before the dancing, or did you see me after that? The day was just so chaotic. I don't know.'

She stared at me. 'You don't remember what happened?'

'It's unclear.'

'Oh.'

Silence, and she took the meat out again and jabbed it.

'It wasn't what I thought it would be,' I said. 'The day, in the end.'

'You mentioned he's angry with you?' she asked, changing the subject deftly. 'He knew about your health stuff before. He's always known. I think . . .' She trailed off.

'What?'

'Nothing.' She turned away and busied herself drying her hands on a kitchen towel. 'Let's just try to enjoy tonight,' she said. 'We're having fun, aren't we?'

I knew what she was about to say. *He's always known about your health. It's what he likes about you, in a way.*

Harry appeared and grimaced at the drink Spencer had given him. He hid it, but we all saw.

We ate and drank and we even laughed. The meat was too bloody, but I managed enough so as not to appear rude.

Spencer was on a roll. He told us all about his job until Siobhan let out a sigh. Harry retaliated with gusto, trying to impress them with a story about *his* work. They listened politely and made the right sounds. Siobhan debated decorating the flat with herself for a while, a perky kind of monologue.

It was easy because they were well practised; the three of them took it in turns to speak until their plates were empty. Then there was a tired, spent feeling to the evening, and they turned their attention to me. The problem of me.

Siobhan sipped her wine and began on one of her favourite topics. 'I mean, no one our age ever actually feels well! Not really. So there's no point in even mentioning it. We're all battling on with the pain of things not being quite right. I have a killer tension headache, and look!' She thrust a finger in my direction to show where her nail bed was ragged. 'Painful, see!'

The two men laughed, not unkindly.

She had done it before, many times, and I'd let it go. But I couldn't forgive her that night, on top of everything else. It was clear which side Siobhan had chosen; she wasn't quite parroting Harry, but she'd chosen him anyway. It was three against one. She'd peeled herself away from the weakest of the group.

'You look like death,' Siobhan said to me.

'I think I just need to lie down,' I said, and I started to make my way to the sofa.

She stood and steered me away. 'Go take our room,' she said, as if she was doing me the biggest favour.

Their bedroom was stuffy. There was a door opening on to a balcony that stretched round the whole flat, and I went outside to breathe in the night air. It was laced with petrol. Leaving the door ajar, I wandered back inside and drew the curtains, so it was nice and dark. I crawled into their bed. Another bed was usually something that elicited a surge of fear, but Siobhan's smell was familiar, floral. The sheets were soft and unlaundered.

I pulled the duvet over my head. Even under the covers, I could hear the rest of them talking. Then, I was calmer. My breathing slowed.

When I woke, it was a lot later and I was on their balcony.

Harry was standing in front of me. He approached slowly. 'Betsy . . .'

The city was lit up, and the traffic was loud below us. My heart was racing so fast, and I shivered even though it was still warm outside, because of the cold in my bones with the spread of a fever. I'd bruised my feet somehow, the soles hurt, and I'd bitten my tongue – it felt sliced open, too much for a small cut, and the taste of blood like old coins. I looked down. I had a knife in my hand. I hadn't noticed it straight away because it had seemed so natural. The handle had warmed up to body temperature, and it fit well in my palm. I didn't recognize the knife, and I tried to think back to when I'd picked it up. Had I taken it from Siobhan's drawer? Was it the knife she'd used on the beef? I didn't remember.

The urge was to drop it, but I couldn't quite force my fingers to loosen.

'What's going on?' I tried to say, but it came out as an unintelligible moan.

'You must have had a bit of a funny turn.' He sounded as if I was hearing him through water. A funny turn made me think of wavy lines, a signal cut off. A wailing, desolate clown.

'What am I doing with this?' I barked at him like he'd done something. Despair ran through me at the failure of it. I had tried very hard to act normal, but still this had happened.

He came over and took the knife from my hand in a swift movement. He didn't break eye contact with me, but I looked past him to the glass, to the living room where Siobhan and Spencer watched us.

'Come on.' He reached out to touch my arm. He was so warm, and I was so cold. He led me inside and washed the knife carefully, though it had seemed clean. Then, he handed it to Siobhan; she took it, and she put it away.

A woman called Elise had made me an offer.

I chose to go to Carn.

And so I left Harry because I knew I had to be the one to go.

4.

The next morning, I left for Carn.

Harry was out at the gym. He was enacting his prized Saturday routine, and it meant he could avoid me. He was on a mission to improve himself with mail-ordered vitamins in glass bottles and complicated exercise routines. It was a whole world of optimizing bodily performance, and he cycled through it regularly. Harry's fads were always a little insulting because he was extremely healthy. They made me angry as well as envious, because I had tried it all.

How much I'd given up!

I'd limited my phone use to mere minutes a day. No caffeine most of the time and very little alcohol. A stripping of all known sleep disruptors. In any case, it wasn't just about the sleep. I needed the right kind of rest, something truly restorative. No sugar, no cheese – these things that impinged upon a normal night's sleep. I gave them up for short periods, but nothing ever stuck because nothing ever really worked. It was all very unfair.

I got out of bed. I dressed simply: a plain shirt, a long skirt. The waistband was uncomfortable, and the cut of the shirt was wrong. It looked like I was wearing clothes made for someone else.

Then, I laid his breakfast out – a bowl of unsweetened granola, a small jug of chilled almond milk, some berries. If there had been sharp knives in the flat, I would have chopped the berries for him, but he'd taken them all away and hidden them the night before, after we'd arrived home from Spencer and Siobhan's.

I left it all for Harry when he returned, but he might not have eaten it because he may not have trusted it.

What would he do when he got home?

Perhaps he'd assume I was there somewhere in the flat, being quiet, resting? He would stomp around for a while, stabbing at his phone in anger, calling out to me even if I didn't respond. Then, eventually, he would notice. At some point, he'd find my note.

I practically floated out of the flat. I felt almost high as I locked the door. I was planning on coming back, but in an action that was unplanned, I posted the key back through the door.

Carn

5.

Many people enjoy travelling. Siobhan, for example, was constantly babbling on about getting away. I noted her sandwiches wrapped in clingfilm, hoarding away cash each month with a distant plan to book a long holiday – *Not holidays, Bets! Trips.* Maybe if I had been well, I would have enjoyed it like Siobhan and the rest of them. Planning had been one of the first fatalities of my condition. But this journey to Carn did not make me weary, it excited me. Elise had told me how to get there. She said to take the train, like it was nothing to leave a life. She'd sent a paper ticket in the post; no note, just the destination, a flimsy thing. I'd pushed it deep into my underwear drawer. On the day I left, I had nothing else on me besides that ticket. It was a lot of trust to put in her.

There were a few stony stares when I got on the train. Perhaps people found it suspicious to see a woman with no possessions. I looked untethered from real life. But I didn't care, and, after a while, there was no one else in my carriage as the passengers disembarked one after another. The train ride seemed to go on forever, and we stopped at many places I didn't recognize as the route snaked through the countryside. Through the window, the scenery passed in a blur of green, and the carriage shook as we raced over viaducts. Finally, the train came to the end of the line and the conductor shooed me off.

The station name was the first thing I saw – *Portlethen* – on a cracked white sign.

I stepped on to the platform and there stood a girl who I hoped was waiting for me. She was about my age, and she wore an old-fashioned uniform. It wasn't so dissimilar to what I wore, a shirt with a crisp collar and a black skirt, but the effect was very different and far smarter. The girl beckoned for me to come to her.

'I'm here to get you,' she said quickly as I approached. 'I work at Carn as one of the helpers. I'm parked just over here.' She pointed to a car, and as we walked towards it, she kept talking. 'We're so looking forward to having you. Elise has been telling us all about you.' She reeled it off, as if from a script. Her tone didn't sound like she was looking forward to it at all. 'You know the basic rules. No phones.'

'That's fine. I don't have one with me.' I gestured to my lack of luggage.

The girl regarded me with narrowed eyes. 'Really?'

'Really.'

I could tell she didn't believe me, but there wasn't much she could do apart from pat me down, and she seemed unwilling to come too close.

'I'm Betsy, by the way, and you're . . .?'

She stared at me blankly. 'You won't need my name, any of our names. We're helpers.'

Helpers. What a strange term.

She reminded me of a prefect. Somehow, I felt I had committed a faux pas, though it was normal to ask someone's name, wasn't it? I didn't push her, and we fell into silence until we reached the car.

After I got in, she handed me a blindfold and told me to put it on. It sent fear coursing through me, the idea of travelling along blindly, letting her take me anywhere, but I did what she said, because I thought she might send me back on the train if I refused. So, we embarked on the drive to wherever Carn was. I tried to keep a track of the turns in the road, but it was too difficult.

'What do you do for work?' she asked, not seeming particularly interested. Perhaps it had been quiet in the car for too long. A breeze came in through the window – bracing, like being doused in cold water. I mulled over what to tell her.

6.

The girl didn't want my entire history, of course, but in the quiet of the car, with the blindfold oppressive, it was tempting to hand it over to her. Let it all out. Lay down what had happened for my own inspection. I did not tell the girl where it started. I did not tell her about my old job.

As I said, I quit my job while we were away on honeymoon. I had worked in marketing for a cosmetic company for a few years, but I was tired of it. I was tired of the freckle problem. It had been billed as anyone's dream project – *so creative and just so much fun to work on!* – the kind of job you're lucky to have. It was where I'd met Siobhan.

I hadn't known her too long, but we'd become inseparable quickly. She could look at me and see in an instant how I was doing – she would crinkle her forehead, *Are you okay?* Although I often found it maddening, I grew to think that maybe this was just what friendship was, or at least that was what ours was – a tiresome series of swift check-ins.

It frustrated me, but at the same time I grew greedy for her attention. To the outside world, it was hard to understand, and people seemed surprised that we were friends. They didn't hide that they saw me as an inferior version of her. Own-brand squash versus freshly squeezed juice. When colleagues asked me how I was, I tended to talk about my ongoing problems with tiredness, and Siobhan would sigh, admonish me if we were in a group. *Of course you're tired, we're all tired! We get up early, we work, we go out at night and then we do it all again. That's life, and why wouldn't it be tiring? What did you expect?*

I had been *that* girl around the office. A downer. I was sure people used that word about me. And *downers* weren't a good fit for the company.

Oh, the years spent on creating a particular smudge-resistant freckle pen. Then we had to make people buy the product. We went on the offensive to make it so they desperately didn't want to be without freckles. Conjure up pitying disdain against the deficiency with a drip of emails. I was not engaged by the freckle problem. I felt like a fraud when I compiled lists of unfreckled celebrities in unflattering shots, placed against lists of beaming, freckled celebrities. However, the job had impressed my parents – it was stable and the pay was okay.

They were unsure about me quitting; unlike Harry, who had been generally supportive if it meant I became less unhinged. He didn't say it outright, but we both understood it to be the case. So, in a short email from the sun lounger, I left the expenses and the HR portal and the many benefits. The freckle company didn't make me work my notice, and I'm sure they were glad to see the back of me.

It had turned out to be surprisingly easy to find casual employment. Days after we returned from our disastrous honeymoon, I heard back from an ad online with very few details. A part-time job in a second-hand bookshop. Something relaxed that I could do on little sleep.

I met a man called Patrick who was the owner and only other person in the shop. When I first came in to interview, he was smoking a cigarette and hovering on a small stepladder, stroking the outline of an ancient map. He got down and – seeing my expression – he stubbed the cigarette out in a coffee cup with a loud sigh.

My wedding ring was visible.

My mother: *If you keep it on, sometimes they think you're going to leave straight away and have a baby.*

Surely not, not now, not in this day and age, I said, but she just nodded.

I wore the ring anyway, mostly just because I forgot to take it off. I got the impression that Patrick couldn't have cared less about my marital status, but he was very interested in my appearance. He drank me in, examined the purple bags under my eyes and focused on my mouth where the skin was dry. Took it all in slowly, savouring it. Finally, he came in close and kind of jammed his face to mine, lifted his arm. I thought he might poke at me with his finger.

He didn't, but he spoke. 'You worked in make-up?' he asked with horror.

I nodded. 'Yes, I did. Make-up.'

He peered down at my CV and then back up to scan every inch of my face again. 'Hmm. You look very *ill*, dear,' he said brightly. Then he spoke a little more softly. 'No reason to worry, of course! Really, it's a sign of intelligence. The Brontë sisters all had TB, you know?'

Rising excitement in his voice.

'I don't have tuberculosis,' I said, and I was almost firm. I was used to letting most things slide, all *perhaps* and *maybe* and *it's fine*, but something about that dark room brought out steel. It was the right call to be assertive with him, to cut ideas off before they got out of hand.

'I wasn't suggesting you did,' he said. 'Don't be ridiculous . . .' He seemed to drift off into his own world. 'God knows what you were doing before here,' he mused to himself, ignoring the fact he'd just read out my work history. 'I don't like to think of it much.'

My past was off-putting.

Patrick said I could start the next day. He gave me a tour, and he even offered me a key to the front door.

The place was shaded and dusty. Just one long space lined with too many shelves, then the back steps down to a basement that Patrick went to often.

As soon as I saw it, I'd been transported back in time. This tiny old shop in Stockbridge had been in Patrick's family forever, and each time it was passed down, the wares aligned with a different hobby. It had once been a florist, and I often found screws of thick green wire brushed up against the skirting boards.

Patrick didn't care if I had a passion for books or not. 'If anything, I find it quite distracting,' he declared on that first day. 'No offence, my dear, but the books belong to me, and it really becomes . . . difficult if you think they're yours too, if you become too fond of them. A certain level of detachment will do us all well here, and you seem rather frail. Best not to overexert yourself.' That was the way he spoke.

So, there was no misunderstanding from the beginning. When Patrick touched the books, it was with reverence, as if they were an endangered species. He wasn't against selling one occasionally, as long as there wasn't too much *chatter*. The other thing about Patrick was that he was not . . . well. When he walked, he struggled with his hip, and it made him stop and gather himself before he moved on. But it was rude to stare, and I tried not to react if he seemed unstable. I knew, almost subconsciously, that he would not want me to discuss his ailment or acknowledge it. He did not show me the same courtesy, and he launched into his set piece on hysterical women, fraying nerves and sensitive dispositions in my first few days in the job.

Of course, I didn't say any of this to the helper as we drove in darkness. It's a bad habit of mine to craft these stories in such a way that Patrick sounds charming and eccentric, to transform him into this grandfather figure with loveable quirks. Actually, he was messy and mean and irritable, spending much of the day in his office down in the bookshop's basement. At least he was easy to avoid.

So, in my brief spell there, we developed a fraught but bearable relationship; I spent a lot of time getting things for him and he didn't speak to me often, outside of jarring remarks – a comment about the vein on my neck; a suspicion I might have a dental abscess because my jaw looked uneven. And he *liked* that. He liked all of it.

Patrick had questions he wanted to ask. On my second day, he was um-ing and ah-ing around the shop, and I just wanted him to spit it out.

Eventually, he sidled up to me. 'You're not a vegetarian, are you?' he asked in a way that made me know his thoughts on such preferences.

'No,' I said.

He grinned and pushed a sweaty container in my face. It contained meaty, samosa-type snacks. They were shrivelled and deeply unappealing, with a strong whiff of . . . old goat? I declined the packed lunch, and he put the box back in his desk out of sight.

Despite my dislike of Patrick, my rejection of his food and my general suspicion of him, the job itself was far more pleasurable than creating reports about the long-term popularity of freckles. I hoped it would help, in some roundabout way, with my sleep. That was the whole reason for the change in career – something less taxing. And though I did not feel well, there was an easy joy somewhere in higgledy-piggledy shelves with our stock stacked high. Dust everywhere with Patrick in the middle of it all, writing notes and letters with a beautiful old fountain pen, looking up shyly to watch me many times during my shifts.

I fainted in my first week at work. It happened in a flash; I was fine one minute, standing, arranging books, and the next I was on the floor with no idea how I got there. I knew instinctively that it was probably just tiredness, and I could have gone home; I would have been okay after a while if I'd sat up and had some water, but Patrick called an ambulance. Speeding towards the hospital, I protested a little. But, by the time we got there, I was resigned. Then I woke up on a trolley in a private room, and there was a woman leaning over me.

At first, I thought it was my mother – she would have come

if I'd called. And then the woman came into focus and I could see she was not like my mother, not like anyone I knew. Her face was a large pale moon hovering over mine and her breath was minty. I felt a surge of racing embarrassment at someone seeing me like this.

She smiled. 'You're awake!' she said, delighted. 'I'm Elise.' Elise.

She was an uninvited guest. Quite interesting to look at, with her long hair – greyer than I had initially thought – spilling down her back.

Bulbous rings on each of her fingers drew my attention to her hands. They were delicate, and they moved in a kind of dance as she spoke: the fingers of a musician. But that wasn't what was most noticeable about her. Many rich and eccentric people in Edinburgh have grey hair and wear piles of jewellery. What struck me was how at ease she was, how every movement was slow and relaxed.

She had my attention, so she sat down and leaned back in her chair, as if she was at home. There was no one to push her out of the way and say she wasn't family and she shouldn't be there. And it wasn't in my nature to kick up a fuss. Anyway, she was familiar. Trying to place her, I realized I'd seen her in the bookshop. She had gone straight to Patrick, and they had left me to go downstairs to his basement to speak in private. This was not unusual; Patrick had many people he escorted down into his lair.

I went to sit up, but she leaned forward and put her hand on mine, stopping me. 'I hope you don't mind my intrusion. Patrick told me you were here – he's an old friend of mine.'

'Why would he tell you?' I asked. It came out ruder than I'd intended.

'He was worried about you; he didn't know who to call, so I thought I'd come and see you to make sure you were okay. Patrick said you collapsed. Has that happened before?'

'A long time ago,' I said. 'I'll be fine. He really didn't need to call an ambulance.'

'He said you have problems with sleep.'

I nodded blearily. I had told Patrick a little about my struggles. I'd told him too much, and he'd clearly passed it on to her.

'What *exactly* is the problem?' she asked.

'Why do you want to know?'

She put her hands up. 'I mean no harm! I just want to help. Okay, let's frame it differently. What would you like from your sleep?'

That was easy. 'I want it to be normal,' I said. 'I want to not even think of it. I want to put my head down on the pillow and wake up the next morning. Just deep, blank sleep.'

Could I tell her so little and could she still help me? I'd say more eventually, but I didn't know her or trust her, not that first time I met her.

She considered it. 'I could help. Only if you'd like?'

'Help how?'

'You could come to Carn.'

'What's that?'

A wide grin. She was keen to explain. 'It's a place for people like you. Small, carefully chosen groups come to stay. We've had some fantastic groups in the past. Used some incredibly interesting techniques.'

She was standing now, hovering above me, looking down and rubbing at my hand in a way that should have been intrusive, but the combination of her words and her touch soothed me.

'You think it would work for me?' I asked.

'I think it could be very good for you.'

How could she know that?

'Can you tell me more about it?' I asked.

'Not now. Now's not the right time.'

She was still very relaxed, but I could feel that she was about to leave and that the burst of closeness we'd had was about to end.

'Are the others like me? Others who go there?'

'No,' she said. 'They will have their own problems, but I don't think any of them have such issues with sleep, not this time. That's yours, Betsy. Anyway, have a think about it, and when you're ready, let me know if it's something you're interested in.'

'How much is it?' I asked. 'To come?'

'Oh,' she said, surprised. 'It's free.'

That day, she spoke with a silky kindness. Just the two of us in that sterile hospital room, and even when she took her hand away, a trickling, warm sensation continued to run through my arm. It travelled upwards. My chest loosened somewhat.

I heard a noise – a tap on the glass.

A nurse peered in at us.

Elise left quickly, without saying goodbye. At first, I couldn't work out what was odd in her departure, but I realized it was that she wasn't carrying anything – no jacket, no bag, no phone, no jumble of shopping bags around her wrist. She was a woman without things to hold or look after. And she charmed me; she comforted me. Women are usually good. Some innate maternal instinct. *If you're in a gripe on the street, just speak to a mother, one with a buggy, ideally*, my mother had said to me. *It's men you need to watch out for*, she'd said. *Women will help you, surely.*

I kept thinking of Elise when I got home from the hospital. Her offer would sneak up on me: *You could come to Carn.*

When I'd met her, I hadn't known if it was bad enough, if I was broken enough. But as time went on, it became clear that Elise had happened for a reason.

I was meant to go.

Come to Carn, Elise had said, again and again. She'd promised one-on-one sessions, which were a great lure – the chance to spend more time in her presence. In fact, she'd wooed me for a week or so, coming to the bookshop regularly. Implored me airily, like going was the easiest thing in the world, and in the end, it was.

I had thought about it for some time. We had only just got married, but still I considered leaving Harry. I went back and forth on it. Could this be the missing piece? A place that could change everything?

34

Then, the dinner party with Siobhan and Spencer. The final straw was standing out there on the balcony; I knew I had to make a change and Carn could be the solution. Stepping on the train to go was a breeze in the end. No anxiety, nothing at all, just the feeling of being whisked away by some unknown force.

There I was, in the car, blindfolded, with a girl I didn't know and a powerful urge to tell the whole story. I thought it might spill out in the dark. But I wasn't a sharer – I'd been burned by Siobhan and Harry.

I kept it simple. 'I had a job. But I don't think I'll go back to it. Who knows what will happen after this.'

The girl did not seem surprised by my answer, though it was curt. Rude, even. I supposed it might have been a normal explanation from someone who was going to Carn. Someone who was not coping well with life.

There was a gear change and then a judder. The car slowed down.

'You can take it off now,' she said.

I almost didn't want to untie the blindfold. I wanted to prolong the unknown because I'd left my entire life behind, and Carn needed to be the cure, but perhaps when the covering came off and light hit, it wouldn't be enough.

7.

I pulled the blindfold off, and I saw a large body of water blocking the entrance. There wasn't a visible crossing. As we approached, I noticed something unusual on the ground, a raised lump like a smooth stone, studded almost randomly with little silver buttons.

My driver – Driver Helper as I'd labelled her in my head – jumped out and pressed in some unseen code. Seconds passed and then a coppery structure rose through the water.

A bridge.

'It's a bit . . . high tech,' Driver Helper said, climbing back into the car with an apologetic grimace.

'Does the water go round the whole house?' I asked. That would be a problem.

'Yes.'

The bridge was more of a platform, really. It sliced upwards through the mottled, reddish water, parting the floating masses of algae.

I had heard of algae making water green, but never red.

Chunks drifted.

As we drove over the crossing, I looked down. Now we were closer, the surface transformed, hit by shadows; it altered from meat red to candy pink.

There were fish and you could just about make them out through the algae. Koi carp. Undeterred by the metal bridge, they swam away easily. They were bright and striped with orange or black and white. To see them made me hungry, with their fat bodies snaking through the water below us, but I didn't dwell on any of it for long, because the house came into clear view.

Carn.

A faded illustration from an ancient book, worn at the seams and bleached by the light. It seemed the sun would always shine on this place. The house was a light blush colour all over. The heightened hue of a fever dream, an orgasm flush, and then a deeper pink for the front door like the wet flash of a gummy smile. A creamy fug of knotted clematis covered the front of the house, and I could smell it from the open car window – sugar in the air.

There was a *No Trespassing* sign swallowed by the crimped mouth of an old tree; a lustrous expanse of grass that circled the house and led to a forest; a croquet set laid out to form a loose triangle. A swinging bench too – I could just make it out to the back of the house, fresh plastic, the chains glinting in the sun. It appeared staged, but the artifice was beautiful.

I was just thinking that the whole place reminded me a little of my wedding cake when Elise emerged from the front door, a dark cut-out against the pink. Seeing Elise at Carn was a relief. She was in her element, the sun shining down on her inky, billowing smock, a scarf tied around her head in a bow the exact same shade as the door.

Driver Helper heaved an icebox out of the car and dumped it on the ground. 'Dinner,' she said to me in explanation. 'You can go in.' She gestured for me to get out of the car.

'Betsy!' Elise called out in joy. Then she stood to one side and beckoned me into Carn. 'Are you ready?' she asked, and there it was: that rising uncertainty, the knowledge that I could turn away.

That was when I could have left, before I was under the spell of Carn, of Elise. I could have returned to my job, to Harry, to Siobhan. Solved the problem of me on my own.

Jolted by the mechanical whirr of the bridge against the birdsong in the distance, I glanced back.

The bridge retracted. I was right at the beginning of whatever *this* was, and the whole place was a drug; a sweet, medicated syrup.

I nodded.

★

Inside was quiet. It was cool too. Elise passed me, walking through the entrance hall, which was lined with rooms on either side. I followed her. There were no bags or shoes or coats lying around – no evidence of any inhabitants.

I had expected an old manor house with dusty relics. My expectations included fussy antiques and wood panels, but it was not like that. Nor was it understated – the hall featured wallpaper covered with flamingos, and every part appeared brand new. Carn was a little like a chain hotel, albeit an expensive one. Slightly tacky perhaps, just unboxed, with the scent of something synthetic in the air.

'Welcome.' Elise was sombre, and she turned back to face me. I could tell she had said it right there for effect, in the centre of the hallway – though it was more than a hallway, it was the size of my flat. The entrance was light, with soaring ceilings and an impressive view of the curved staircase.

'Is it what you expected?' she asked.

'Not really.' I was truthful.

'But you approve?'

'I mean, it's beautiful.'

She seemed satisfied. 'I'm aware we didn't discuss details about the house much before you arrived,' she said as we hovered in the hall. 'That was on purpose. It will all become clear once you've been here for a while.'

'What's the history of Carn?' I asked, because I knew people liked to talk about the story behind these kinds of places. But she whipped around in visible irritation. I'd said the wrong thing.

'It doesn't matter about the *history*. Everything here, every facet of it, has been chosen on purpose. Dining room there – for all our meals while you're here – a library in there. Then the kitchen's down in the basement with a cellar. You don't need to go in there. My office is to the right, but that's private too. Our room for the sessions you'll have with me is to the back. Do explore the rooms that are open to you, but don't go any further. Use them as you wish, but for now, just take it easy. You must be exhausted, you should freshen up.'

Her words tumbled out, so eager. She was trying to entice me, but at the same time there was a steeliness below. She was firm when it came to the instructions, and so much was off-limits. Patrick's bookshop had been the same – a new place with forbidden areas. I'd found myself unable to keep to Patrick's rules back at the bookshop. Perhaps it was simple curiosity, but, in my first week, I'd walked down the stairs to his basement, feeling the temperature drop. My hand touched the doorknob. *Just going down to find a dustpan and brush to sweep up.* I hadn't been that surprised to find it locked with a flashing keypad. Then, Patrick was there behind me, breathing down my neck. 'No, my dear,' he'd said. 'No need to go there. Nothing for you in there.' He'd spoken like I was a child, with his thick goaty breath. I wondered if it would be the same at Carn, if I'd be able to settle for just the rooms I was permitted to enter.

'Okay,' I said to Elise.

'The owner is very supportive,' she continued. 'He understands it has the potential to be a space where we can help people who are in trouble.' Her entire expression changed into one of deep empathy. 'Oh, you were in *terrible* distress, Betsy. I could tell when I found you that you had a strong need for this place. It was wise of you to come.'

'So, who else is here?' I asked.

'Well, I have my lovely helpers. They assist. But you mean our guests, don't you? We accept those who are youngish, like you. Everyone is in their mid to late twenties. It's a good age, I think, for what we do here.'

I nodded.

She continued, 'For you, I'm interested in your relationship with sleep. And the other young women who are staying here at Carn have their own challenges.' She paused and frowned. 'Perhaps challenge is too strong a word. Anyway, you all have your own things to develop. But also, you are all quite exceptional.'

She said the word 'exceptional' with care, placing it in front of me, offering it up for comment with a rising intonation at the end, like I might question her, or maybe she was questioning me. But I had nothing to say.

We'd been edging towards the bottom of the staircase, and there was a small table with a box on it. I could see phones, their screens black and dead, bodies all packed together.

I followed Elise up the stairs.

'I'm sure you'll get on fine here,' she continued without looking back.

'How long do people usually stay?'

'Oh, don't worry about that. You're here for as long as you're here.'

We both looked out of the window towards the water and something passed between us. My stomach dropped as I registered a mutual understanding of the situation I was in, but when I caught her eye she looked at me blankly.

The room was sparse, with a small bathroom set off to the side. A neat single bed; a deep but firm mattress; thick white towels with neat, embroidered edges in navy.

There was a note, written on a small piece of heavy paper nestled in the quilts, and when I picked it up, it cut my finger, a clean cut that bled and bled. I sucked on it and waited for it to clot.

Breakfast – eight.

Lunch – twelve.

Dinner – seven.

Pointless as I had no way to know what the time was – there were no clocks, and watches were not allowed. We had been told not to bring anything with us, and I noted a filled clothes rail to the side of the room. I went closer to inspect and found an array of clothes, expensive and plain. Sleek, tapered trousers, loose shirts and cashmere jumpers. Without thinking about it too much, I chose items from the rack that looked to be the most comfortable. They were all loose, all a size too big, and so I looped a belt around my waist. Despite the fit, they suited me well, far better than what I'd been wearing when I'd arrived.

As I lay down on the bed, thin light came in through the curtains. I watched the rays scatter over the floorboards. Back at home, afternoons were usually the worst bit, when the fatigue hit me in the face like a brick, but that afternoon I could observe myself in a detached way. I contemplated the sleep I could have if I lay back and welcomed it. Thick sleep, waking with a coated tongue. Or perhaps a short nap and I'd still be conscious, floating above my body.

I fell into it, gave up entirely.

8.

Sounds from the rooms across the hall woke me. The other girls getting ready, changing, with the clack of heels against wood and the slam of doors.

An echoing gong. I left the bedroom in a rush, so I'd be the first to get to dinner.

What would they be like? Would they accept me? Those jumping thoughts turned my stomach into a mess of worms. At the beginning, I so wanted to impress. But also, I didn't know what Elise was looking for. So, I made a mental list of what I needed to do, tracking out the next few hours: *walk down the stairs, go to dinner, go to bed*. Focusing on the next immediate task instead of thinking too far ahead.

Down the grand stairs. Lights came on automatically as I passed. The house seemed clever, attuned to my movement. Then, I reached a door. With a deep breath, I stepped into the dining room, and I was hit by fresh paint, layered with wood and a hint of lilies. I reached out to the walls to steady myself.

It was still bright outside, but the curtains were drawn, and the sun leaked in only a little around the sides. Light came mainly from candles – tall white ones, stuck in silver candelabras, casting a glow on five place settings. The walls were decorated with contorted bodies and I peered at them: gilded nudes. Some danced with their arms above their heads. Others appeared incapacitated. They lay on stretchers with their skinny limbs bandaged, all of it finished with flecks of gold – in their hair and stuck in their teeth.

In the shadows, Elise and her 'helpers' waited for us. The helpers did not look alike, but they blended into one with their almost-uniforms – all in the same white shirts and dark skirts – and in the coming days they would move in a singular mass of peaceful surveillance, and I would try and label them, differentiate them where I could. Certainly, they were all nice to watch. Pretty, capable girls. Balletic in the way they floated around the room that night – laid out bottles of wine and carafes of something fizzy and purple. I counted eight of them, and finally they stood along the edge of the room, hands to their sides, their backs pressed against the wall. I spotted Driver Helper from earlier in the day.

They made eye contact with me and then averted their gazes to the floor. Elise moved away from the wall and sat at the head of the table, a striking vision in black silk.

'Betsy,' she said with exuberance, placing her napkin on her lap. 'First to arrive! Well done, you, and you look so charming.' She leaned in as if letting me in on a secret. 'If there's anything else you want to wear while you're here, then just let me know. You can have it all! A particular brand or style. Anything that helps you feel like *you*.'

'Thank you,' I said. 'The clothes are lovely.'

The door creaked open, and we both turned.

The first girl.

She peered round the door, meek and careful.

It was hard to tell how old she was. She could have been the same age as me, though she looked younger. I saw her clenched fists. As she came in, she unclenched them. Her thumb twitched. The girl had long blonde hair that was frazzled at the ends, but it was the only flaw I could see, as she was almost obnoxiously beautiful. I took a second to analyse it and I decided it was because her face was very symmetrical. But there had to be something wrong with her. She was here, after all. What were her problems?

She sat next to me. 'I'm Sally.' She beamed at me. She had a clipped, boarding-school accent that was detectable even in those two words.

'Betsy,' I offered back.

Elise watched us.

'Are you hungry?' Sally asked, and her voice was shaky. 'I'm so starving, I could eat a horse!' she said and laughed a little too loudly.

Elise was delighted at that.

I was distracted because another girl entered the room. As with Sally, I tried to not stare at this second girl, which was harder than it should have been because she wanted my attention, sticking her tongue out at me as she came in.

'Abigail,' Elise announced as she bestowed a smile that seemed warmer than it had with Sally and me.

This Abigail had brown hair, cropped very close to her head. She was unkempt in a way that suited her, with mascara flaking away under her eyes in dry shreds and eyebrows that were quite magnificent: dark, unplucked, crawling to meet each other as her expression changed. I liked her rangy arms, elbows and knuckles protruding, covered in a web of tattoos. Some looked like old-fashioned sailor's tattoos and others were drooping flowers, the petals falling down her wrists. On her jiggling ankle, I saw a blurred cluster of black stars.

I estimated us to be around the same age, late twenties, and she had a quickness to her, not unlike Elise in a way.

Abigail sat down, pulling the chair out with care. She nodded at me.

When she saw Sally, she seemed a little taken aback, but recovered and said hello.

The door creaked open for the last time.

One more girl entered.

'This is Caroline,' Elise said.

Caroline.

A crescendo to the final girl, the headliner, but to me she was a disappointment.

Dark coppery curls, springy and a little greasy. A smattering of dull freckles – I was conditioned to notice freckles in everyone. She was of average height, neither fat nor thin. Not memorable, which sounds like a cruel thing to say, but it was true. The way she moved struck me, though. The final girl creaked, like there were knots in her neck, in her back, like she was stiff and every part of her was painful. It was a relief to see her sit down and her pain seemed to ease; she finally smiled. It was a strained expression that did not reach her eyes, and there was such a chill to her. She was unwilling to engage, and that made me reticent when I smiled back.

That was us, the four of us, and we judged each other. I wanted to look at Abigail the most, telling myself it was her tattoos that drew me in.

'Betsy, Abigail, Sally, Caroline . . .' Elise said, listing our names. 'It's time for dinner, but first a few words. Let me explain the ethos of Carn. We are patient-led. We offer an environment to change your relationship with your illness. Most importantly, we are not a hospital. Nothing like that.

'So, what *are* we? I'm sure you're wondering what to expect. While you're here, the days and weeks will unfold and you will start to understand. We'll work together, leave some parts of any diagnoses you may have at the door. It will seem unnatural, that's to be expected with this kind of thing, but we'll explore what's happened to you in the past and what makes you different. We'll run therapeutic activities, and we will do whatever we can to make you feel relaxed.'

She beamed at us, and then she turned more sombre. 'I must ask that you abide by the few rules we have. First, that means no phones.'

We had known that before we'd come in, and presumably they'd given theirs up. Still, a gurgled, strangled cry from one of the others, though I didn't catch which one.

'No time for pickiness. You'll eat everything you are given.'
We all nodded.

'And finally . . . absolutely no contact at all with the outside world,' she continued. 'And limited discussion of it while you're here, please. It throws the schedule off-balance. I've found in the past that other groups have shared their lives before Carn. Sadly, this makes the treatment far, far less effective.'

She sighed as if this was truly sad. I wondered about the groups that had come before us. I knew if Harry was here, he would be asking about success rates because he was very keen on metrics.

'This will be a very special time,' Elise said.

Excitement crept upwards in that silly tickle of butterfly wings. It was something close to hope. Oh, I knew it so well, and still I fell for it. That familiar eagerness at the advent of a new set of rules, a new process and a new regimen! I had experienced it many times before, enough to recognize that none of it was certain, but the expectation that a cure might come was still so enticing. And she was our slick-speaking sales brochure:

'This is probably the first time in all your lives where everything will be about you. You are the centre of it all! However different you are from each other, there are some common threads. All your lives you've been ignored when things have gone wrong for you, when your body or mind fails you. Doctors have investigated. It doesn't matter, because regardless of what they do or do not find, they really can't help you. Can they?'

We watched her, and we were quiet. I was in awe at her performance.

'*Can they?*' she said again, irked by our silence, and we all shook our heads.

'The implication has always been that you're broken. Let me tell you, I don't believe that at all. I *know* you're not broken.'

I wasn't sure of that. It had been possible to hide it so far, but the fog of tiredness was there underneath like a lingering infection.

Elise continued, 'I'm going to help you. Do you trust me to do that?'

We'd just met her. Still, we said *yes*.

We said it more than once, and the helpers said it too, a low hiss that rose from the wall as they spoke as one.

'Right. Enough,' Elise said swiftly, and in an instant the helpers came and topped up our wine glasses, although I saw Caroline cover hers with her hand politely. Usually, I would have done the same, but that night I let them pour away.

I had stopped eating before Carn. I prepared meals for Harry, but I was rarely hungry, and I knew I was losing weight. At Carn, I was willing to be more open to food, but there were certain dishes that repulsed me: anything caked in icing, eggs in all their forms, smoked salmon. Food sitting in the warmth, all gloss and sponge. So there came the first unexpected change, because that night I was ravenous for it all.

A banquet, and it came out on platters, the helpers serving us, deciding for themselves what we'd like. They dished up huge portions for everyone: meat sliced thinly and drenched in a thick, peppery sauce; langoustines with gritty black eyes swimming in melted butter.

I dug in greedily; I wouldn't normally have eaten meat so rare, but that day it was fine, paired with the creamiest potato dauphinoise I'd ever tasted. It rested on my tongue, claggy and thick. And the more I ate, the more I wanted, because it was unbelievably good. At first, I tried to show restraint, to remember my table manners and wipe down my chin. At home, I would have been thinking of how it would affect me and how I would feel later. But at Carn it was different, and I did not think the meal would hurt me. I could barely cram the food into my mouth fast enough.

The room was quiet as we ate, just the sound of chewing and some euphoric expressions of joy at the tastes. I thought we were all enjoying it. Sally tore off a bit of the steak, and Caroline had no meat, but she was digging into a huge portion of fish, quite content, and then I looked to Abigail.

Abigail's expression was a twisted, moving grimace, like she was trying to smile nicely, but she couldn't. Then she looked at me searchingly, trying to tell me something. She had a few salad leaves on her plate, some kind of burger patty without a bun that a helper had given her, and she pushed it around unhappily with her fork. It seemed to me that she was in terrible pain, and I instinctively moved a fraction, raised off my seat to get up, to help.

My chair scraped against the floor, and Abigail winced. I was too late because, in a flash, Elise was there next to her. She was stroking Abigail's hand.

Abigail's eyes were closed, and it was as if she was processing the sensations. She checked in with Elise, and then, with only a slight hesitation, she picked up her fork and ate.

And as I watched her, it hit me in a bubbling sensation. I was smug.

You see, there was something palpably . . . 'off' about all of them. Though it was guesswork to establish what was wrong, still, these girls, their maladies sat so close to the surface, floated like oil on water, even if I couldn't figure out what they were yet. I wasn't able to stop the shameful relief that my own secrets, my problems, the things I'd done, were more concealed. I didn't look tired that day, and I believed I was hiding it all well.

Food consumed and our plates clean, we were escorted to bed by a helper who walked behind us. I trailed up alongside the others, full and bloated, my tongue fuzzy with wine and my head heavy.

9.

My bedroom smelled of summer. The window only opened a little, and it was so hot outside it barely cooled the room. Still, it was good to let the air in. The night was young, and it was too early to go to bed really, but for once I was relaxed about it. The lights in my room dimmed automatically. They must have been on a timer, and it felt like everything was responsive to what I was doing.

I lay down.

Would I go to sleep now? This early?

Was that what they wanted?

Being in a single bed made me think of being a child. My mother used to come into the room with a glass of water, trying to soothe me when I called out. She would drift in, all lightness, wispy hair and faded clothes like she'd disappear into the walls if she could. She didn't have to bother with my brothers: they were a noisy – snoring, farting, grunting – but ultimately restful species.

My mother would hover, tut, drift out, speak to my father outside the bedroom door, and I'd hear them: *Is she okay? Are you sure she's okay? Is she crying? The boys are fine (sigh). They all sleep so well! They sleep anywhere.*

But I was not like them, and that was no one's fault, it was just how it had worked out. I became petrified of sleep. I said no to sleepovers, to anything my parents suggested. They sighed, agreed and said maybe next month or next year. Maybe one day.

I cried a lot then because life didn't fit in the right way, and everything was always uncomfortable – clothes and feelings, all of it tight and airless; rooms too stuffy, days too windy, nothing ever easy. I wanted a different life, had a fantasy of going to boarding school, and I think that's a common desire amongst girls of a certain age – mini kilts, Latin lessons, wooden tuck boxes. A picture of boarding school that isn't rooted in reality. By the time I was a teenager, I'd decided I would stop crying, even if I felt it in my throat – that lump that turns into tears – and I didn't cry again, not for a long time.

Many years later I would feel that familiar lump when Harry asked me what I came to see as *his question*. His main demand: 'Where do you see yourself in five years?'

It seemed too prepared, too adult, but Harry *planned*. He was tentative and formal like a job interview. But I couldn't articulate a response that he'd understand. Just a good day was enough for me, and I'd told him that, but he didn't really get it. There were tears of frustration behind my eyes, because all I wanted was to be well.

I tried. 'I just want to feel good,' I said simply. 'Be happy.'

A naive goal, but by that, I meant be normal. A spell of time where I felt good was all I aimed for. Be well. That's what I really meant. A paltry goal, and in those early days there were some wonderful stretches when I *did* feel quite normal.

How to explain that to someone like Harry?

'We are happy,' he said firmly.

'I want to be normal,' I clarified.

'You are.' An incredulous laugh. 'Completely, adorably normal.'

I have always liked the sound of certain words. Others I have an aversion to. 'Adorable' made me think of a rabbit squashed into a ball of fur on a road. This was not the type of thing to bring up after he'd just pronounced me (slightly patronizingly) normal.

As I lay there, still in my clothes, I heard a knock. I didn't respond, but the door clicked open, and Elise peered round it. 'Can I come in?' she asked.

She walked in with a helper before I replied, but I said 'Sure' anyway. Then, in one fluid movement, a practised one, she produced a tourniquet, and she came over to the bed, gestured for me to sit up and then strapped it round my upper arm.

'Are you okay with this?' she asked quite seriously. 'We need to ask. I'll only take some if that's fine with you?'

I nodded, because I was used to having my blood taken.

'Just a sharp scratch,' she said, practically a purr, and she placed the needle to my skin. 'How did you find dinner?'

'It was nice,' I said. 'I'm . . . excited, I think.'

I couldn't string words together in the right way when I was with Elise, but it was honest enough.

She handed the blood to the helper, who rushed out of the room with it.

'Now, here you go,' Elise said as she opened her hand, and in the middle of her palm there was a single round pill the colour of earth. Every muscle in my body tightened at the *betrayal* of it! I edged away from her.

'I said no medication.' I was scrambling, clawing at the sheets, and her eyes widened with genuine concern. I'd rattled her – she showed it for a second, but she recovered. Her fingers closed round the pill one at a time, the gold of her rings forming a cage.

'Absolutely! This isn't medication in that way. It's natural, just some select herbs from the gardens. We make them here. Something to relax you. Valerian; a mere dash of liquorice.'

'I'm sensitive to medication.'

I had taken many pills in the past; the worst ones were legal, prescribed by a doctor.

My mother had suggested him. He said it would help with my issues, that it would smooth the world out for me, perhaps make me feel better, though there was also the possibility it could make it all worse. I'd taken the doctor's pill, lain back, and then I was being torn in two. When I ran my tongue over my teeth, there was a vile chalkiness where I'd ground them together, thrashing away in the night. I went back to the doctor to tell him, and he seemed surprised that I was upset. He'd sighed. *Every drug has some side effects, things we have to balance in treatment.* By that he meant: *What did you think was going to happen? How could you possibly expect me to give you something for it and make you better without making some kind of sacrifice?* He'd looked at the clock to show the appointment was over.

Had I been wrong to trust Elise? I had snapped, but she wasn't put off. She came close and knelt beside the bed, and she laid her hand on mine. There was warmth because that was her instinct, to light everything up for me, but then she drew back abruptly and when she spoke it was like she was lecturing me. 'I understand you're scared,' she said. 'But I really have no desire to harm you.'

'I have to be careful. I react badly.'

'Of course you do. So many do.' She paused for a moment, as if she was thinking, and then continued, 'If you take this pill tonight, what if I sit here? For as long as it takes – all night, if you like. I'll watch over you. I think tonight will be good for you. A proper night's sleep, I'm almost sure of it. I'll be here, and I'll look after you.'

It was just one night, and so far Elise had proved capable. Plus, it was why I was there. To get better.

I took the pill, and Elise was true to her word. She stayed watching over me, fiddling with her rings, and I twitched, reaching out to the side of my narrow bed with some muscle memory, and then remembered that Harry was back in Edinburgh.

Relief. It was nice to be away from him, away from my anger and the feeling that I could gouge out his eyes in rage. My brothers had said this was normal: *My wife wants to kill me too when I snore!*

These thoughts were leaping and confusing; they came in a loopy kind of barrage. Lying there, I thought of Elise's words and of her smooth announcer tone, the phrase on repeat until it made little sense:

reallyhavenodesiretoharmyouIreallyhavenodesiretoharmyouIreally havenodesiretoharmyouIrea

10.

It felt early when I heard the door open and a helper with a wide and very fake smile (Smiler Helper, I called her) told me it was time to get up in a tone that made it clear I was late. My throat was a tender length of sandpaper and my arm was a little sore. Then, the slow bash of blood against my skull. But . . . there was nothing new about the pain. Really, it was mundane – just the scratchy annoyance of a hangover.

I *had* slept.

The pill had worked and the reward was a deep and dreamless sleep. A rare breed, so thick that I had no recollection of Elise leaving my bedside. And it felt unmedicated; the grogginess wasn't there. So, despite the light hangover, I was energized, and I almost skipped down to breakfast.

In the corridor I saw a set of paintings, five large square canvases; they sat prominently. Only when I got closer did I see there were no brushstrokes. It struck me that they could be photographs, and I went nearer still. The colours were striking: rings of purple with green and yellow dotted through, like a constellation perhaps. They could be sunrises, but the green made me think of the aurora borealis. With no other hint of landscape to give any context, I suspected a close-up composition of the sky, but it was impossible to tell if it was night or day. They forced contemplation, and I would have stayed looking at them for longer, but the smell of bacon was too tempting.

I reached the dining room and went straight to the long buffet filled with cereals and jugs of milk and slices of mango fanned out on platters. A heaped bowl of strawberries lay in the middle of the table – hundreds of them – and each one was cut in half, as if we'd choke on full berries.

Elise and the helpers were noticeable in their absence, although one helper stood at the door, and Abigail sat alone. She had a huge plate of soggy crêpes in front of her, stuffed with meat and cheese, and some kind of garnish on the side.

'Morning,' she said without enthusiasm. She saw I was staring at her meal and her lips curled at the sight of it. '*They* bring it.' She gave the helpers a dismissive wave. That might have put me off her, but she was so jumpy, and it was clear to me that her spikiness came from nerves rather than rudeness.

A helper had emerged from nowhere, fussing with a pair of tongs around the mango station, and she brought me over a similar plate of food.

'Looks good,' I said.

I ate, and I started slowly, but ended up eating the stuffed crêpe fast. It was delicious; unusual too.

Abigail put a loaded fork to her mouth like there was nothing she wanted to do less, but she forced herself.

'I've been here for ages, thought I'd be able to eat before you all arrived,' she said. 'But it looks like the other two were here really early. Not obeying the rules!' She pushed her knife and fork together carefully, leaving lots of food on her plate, and then she kind of retched.

'Sorry,' I said.

'Oh, don't worry about it, it's just this condition I have.'

I wondered whether she might have an eating disorder. She raised her hands above her head and pushed her shoulders back, and I got a glimpse of her stomach, with a tree trunk inked all up the side. I was embarrassed by the way I was staring.

'So.' She gave me a huge smile. 'Are we doing it?'

'Doing what?'

'*Doing* it.' A laugh, dirty and thick. 'You've gone so red,' she said fondly, and she sat up and moved her chair back gently, so it didn't make a noise. 'I meant are we saying how absolutely fucked we are? Beyond repair? *Obviously*, we should.'

I stuttered a little.

'We should, we should,' she chanted; she was up, and she edged towards me.

'I don't know,' I said. I was unsure, trying to remember the exact wording of the rules. Elise had said something about it being less effective if we discussed things, that it might impact our treatments, but I felt like she had meant our backgrounds, she hadn't meant our ailments. We were fine to discuss those, surely, and we couldn't *not*.

'I'll start?' she asked. 'I mean, you may have guessed.'

'You seemed like you were in pain . . . last night?' I was cautious, didn't want to offend her.

'Oh, I was okay. It was the noise.'

'Noise?' I asked, trying to recall what had even happened.

'Noise,' she repeated, and then she was inching towards me again until she crouched close to my side like that was a normal thing to do. 'Not *all* noises. Just some. They hurt me. Physically hurt me – it's real pain.'

'How does it feel?' I asked before I could help myself. It was there again, that smugness and that hungriness for their sicknesses.

She licked her lips. 'It starts like an unbearable burning in my mouth. It's a thing, I promise. It's real.'

'That sounds tough,' I said. Tough and surprising, because she did not seem like a quiet person.

'It is, yes. Speaking's not so bad, most of the time anyway. It's just certain noises. It's hard to describe.'

'Try me,' I said, greedy to hear more.

'God, where to start! Chair scraping is awful, alarms, children screaming. I can sense it before it happens,' she said, 'the vibrations of it, and when it hits, it's like *bam*,' and here she gestured to her head. She placed one hand on her sternum and patted at it. 'Here too. Like a heart attack or something. It's not that it's annoying or I'm just being intolerant. But when you explain that to someone, they think you're overreacting.'

'I get that.'

'But *do* you?' she asked with a winning smile. 'Do you *really*? Now, what's your problem?'

She leaned in and I couldn't refuse her.

'Sleep,' I said. 'It's the same thing, when you tell people they just think that you're a poor sleeper.'

Her face lit up. 'Oh, totally, totally. People just don't understand at all, do they?' she said. 'They're all, *Oh yes, I can't stand loud noises – so overstimulating!* They try to say the right things, but they don't get it.'

I nodded and she was emboldened.

'I often think we are all far too quick to compare,' she said, kind of dreamily, 'to add our own experiences in, but we're all lonely, just soldiering on. It doesn't work. I know what I have is unique to me. Others may have something similar, but I know I'm alone in what I'm suffering.'

It rang true. The sensation that no one in the world could feel what I felt. I was kind of comforted that she believed the same.

'Where are the others?' I asked, not really because I cared where they were, but the moment between us was becoming so personal, so quickly. This kind of intimacy was addictive, but it scared me.

She sensed my discomfort and looked away. 'Oh, outside.' She flicked her hand to the window.

They were sitting on the grass on a big picnic blanket. Sally sat hunched over, her skirt around her, and Caroline was talking. We couldn't hear them.

'There's something about her,' I said, looking at Sally.

'I know.' Abigail pointed at Sally. 'You recognize her, right?' she said under her breath, all gossipy. The smell of her was good and mossy and deep. I obviously didn't want it to seem like I was smelling her, but by doing this I started breathing a bit funnily.

She raised an eyebrow.

'No. I've never seen her before; at least, I don't think so anyway,' I said.

'You *must* have. Right,' she said, standing, and she started to mime, but she was so chaotic that I couldn't make it out.

'Just tell me,' I said.

'Oh, you're no fun! Come on, you can work it out!' She put her hand to her hip. 'Have a go.'

I stood up. I was not careful. My chair legs scraped on the floor in a screech.

She winced and closed her eyes, and she breathed in and out, deeply.

'Sorry,' I said.

I saw how she reacted. I liked her so much on that first morning and I shouldn't have done it. When you are in pain, you think about your body all the time, but also you see it in others. I think you see where their weaknesses are, and it gives you the capacity to see where others really feel it. This was a power I didn't want to use.

I was so taken with Abigail, but I had meant to hurt her in that moment.

I wanted to see where she felt it.

II.

We went outside, Abigail and me walking in time together. I had adjusted my gait so I moved at the same speed as her, a slight skip to my step. It was all very natural, and she noticed, offered me a twitchy smile.

A pair, already.

We reached the other two; they sat on a blanket and there was very little else on the vast lawn. We all said 'hi' to each other awkwardly, and the charge between Abigail and me vanished.

'How did you sleep?' Sally asked. She had a babyish voice, sweet and grating, and she appeared to be amping it up to hide her accent. She was fidgety, too, with her nails at her arms.

She twitched.

What was her problem?

Perhaps she did not like the distinct lack of *objects* at Carn? An antique croquet mallet would not be stimulating enough. I sensed that hot and desperate itch to inhale feeds and pictures and opinions. The desire for a leaden refuge, to concentrate fully on nothing at all, losing yourself in it. She might be missing the flood of information. I understood, because I'd been the same, though I was more used to it now after swearing off my phone.

We all kind of nodded and Caroline shuffled a smidgen to let me sit down. Then, a stillness that was not comfortable. It was very hard to know what to say when so many topics seemed banned. Small talk made no sense.

Where are you from?

What are you doing at the weekend?

Have you got any holidays planned?

I didn't know what was permitted, and the questions wouldn't form.

Abigail was relaxed about the situation, lying out on the ground, occasionally looking up and yawning. She embraced the stilted silence between the four of us, but I couldn't bear it. It was all too much – I was aching to get away from them, and so I said something about getting water, and I rose. None of them were bothered by this, apart from Sally, who seemed a little stricken.

I walked away from the entire group. I was quick, and I set off before a helper approached. To the side of the path, I could just about make out a little walled garden, herbs perhaps. And there was the forest, shadowy and unwelcoming, a long, gravelled path that led to it snaking away into the distance until it became consumed by the trees overhanging.

My focus went to the house with its many windows.

Closer.

I froze.

I saw a man. He had a terrible skinniness to his face; he was insubstantial, like he could vanish in a second. He stood there, framed by a window on the second storey.

The window was full-length, and so I could see his body too; he was hunched, and he teetered, and he was too far away for me to make out his expression. All I could establish was that he was staring at me. I wanted to see him better. I edged towards him until I was halfway across the lawn and he became a little clearer. Even as I advanced towards him with purpose, he didn't look away. I was close enough that I could see his face, but it was still hard to make out his features. Then, I saw how he bent in and pressed his frame against the glass to get closer, which sent a wave of disgust through me. But I was complicit because I needed to get closer too.

In our twisted dance, the man stepped backwards into the corridor.

I watched in horror. He lurched forward. Then he fell back again in a kind of shaky desperation. He slid, slowly crumpling down, then tipped headlong and nearly smashed into the glass.

I wanted to shout out, and I started to run to him, but I only made it a few steps before a firm hand on my shoulder drew me back. Turning round, I saw Smiler Helper, and she wrenched at me further, pulling at my arm.

'No, no,' she said.

'Who was that?' I asked.

'Who was what?'

'There's someone –'

'No one's there,' she said in a monotone, pointing upwards, and she was right. The window was empty. Just a long corridor and a hint of white wall visible in my field of vision. The helper shook her head and tried to steer me back to the blanket. I had the urge to argue with her, because I wanted to stay and see if he'd come back. There was a sick kind of squeezing sensation deep inside me. Something about the man. I needed to see him again.

Perhaps I would have fought to stay and pushed the helper more, but then I heard a scream.

Back in the group, Sally's head was bobbing up and down like it might fly off. She was having some kind of outburst. 'I can't be here,' she said as she paced up and down the lawn.

Then she saw me. 'I need to leave,' she called out, and she scratched at her arms.

The helper backed away from me to confer with the others – there were three of them huddled around, and I jogged to the group.

'What happened?' I directed the question to Caroline and Abigail.

'Nothing at all!' Abigail was adamant. 'I pointed out she had a bit of a rash on her leg. I think it might be some kind of reaction to a plant or something. Poison ivy, maybe? No big deal. She just flipped.'

'Are you okay?' I asked Sally, and she shook her head. Her hair swung around her face, sticking to her lips.

Caroline had a go at calming her. 'What's the matter?' she said, and she extended a hand to touch her on the shoulder.

'Get off me,' Sally shrieked.

The helpers watched, and I wondered if one of them would take over, but they seemed unsure of what to do, like they didn't know who was in charge.

Caroline was not unsure. She smoothed down her hair, though the curls sprang back up straight away, and she went to Sally. There was no hesitation as she took Sally's wrist in her hand and turned it over gently, so the palm faced upwards like she was about to read her fortune.

'You're okay,' Caroline said. 'You're absolutely fine.'

I didn't expect it. Quick as a flash, she used the nail on her forefinger, and she dug down hard. The skin creased inwards as she pushed into Sally's wrist.

Sally did not seem shocked and she didn't pull away much, but she uttered a small, submissive yelp. Abigail and I watched, and we saw the red mark on Sally's wrist develop as Caroline took her finger away and pressed down the other way, across, just as hard.

'You're fine.' Caroline's words were barely audible as she drew her hand away. We could see the angry red cross on Sally's skin.

Sally looked down at her wrist and rubbed at it. She appeared kind of stunned, but it had calmed her down.

The helpers saw. They seemed relieved, and they retreated from us as I gawped at Caroline.

Crisis resolved.

'It's . . . grounding,' Caroline said reluctantly, and she muttered something I couldn't quite make out about the vagus nerve. 'Stop looking at me like that,' she snapped. 'It worked on me when I was younger, and so I thought I'd try it. The pain grounds you, the cross thing. It brings you into the present.'

'You meant it to be hard, to hurt her!' Abigail said, and her voice spiked with outrage, but she also seemed impressed.

Caroline ignored her. 'How do you feel now?' she asked Sally. 'Better?'

'Yes,' Sally said, dazed. 'I feel . . . I feel nothing.'

'And that's a good thing?' Abigail asked, sceptical.

'Oh yes,' Sally said. 'To feel nothing at all is perfect.' And the babyish voice was gone. She was almost absent in the way she spoke, and it was astonishing how she sounded like a different person, like a competent adult.

'The pain distracts and then there's a blankness?' Caroline asked.

'Yes,' Sally said distantly.

Caroline continued, 'You feel the rush and then it goes, and then it's even better. A stillness as the nervous system regulates and you're quite calm.'

Sally came round, like she was emerging from a coma, and she looked at Caroline tenderly. 'You're amazing,' she said shakily.

Caroline squinted in discomfort at the compliment. 'I'm not. Not at all. I just have a few . . . tricks. You'll feel better if you have something to eat. Why don't we have a snack?'

Sally trotted to the house, behind Caroline, and Abigail and I followed.

12.

The next morning, I stood in the bathroom for a while, just taking it in. I'd slept very well again, even better than the first night, and I could hardly believe it.

The recollection of the pill was lovely; I thought of how it had melted against my tongue for a second before I'd swallowed it down. It had been a warm, thick kind of rest. I'd struggled to wake up, and even though I'd heard the gong, I'd drifted back into a restless half-sleep and missed breakfast. It would be the only time I'd be permitted to adjust the schedule in such a way.

As I stood, I could feel the blood pumping around my body. A quick glance in the window's reflection, and I saw someone I didn't recognize. I wore creamy cashmere, and the fabric draped over my body like it was made for me. Skin so unblemished and glowing. My hair had a shine to it, something I'd only ever seen in others because I was not the kind of person who had shiny hair.

My eyes! It was astonishing to see my eyes so clear, no longer bloodshot; the pupils were a little off-putting, though – big and black. Could it be the effects of the pill? If Carn healed, perhaps it worked that quickly. Certainly, something had shifted, and I could see that this would be addictive.

But it wasn't . . . comfortable.

I crackled. Such intensity flowed through it all. It was the nails on the wrist and Sally's yelp. It was the whole place, filled with a new kind of pain. Our bodies stopped us in our tracks, and I sensed it was a crucial part of Carn.

To be clear, there were no serious injuries, just plenty of prickles and stings. These sensations were always so fleeting: Abigail biting her tongue and swearing, my paper cut that was clean and deep and just didn't seem to heal properly, and my stomach – it clenched up with the food, not in a spasm that hurt particularly but like the organ was reshaping and expanding. I could almost feel the meal from the night before giving me energy.

I'll admit it wasn't comfortable, but it felt right. Light bouncing off a needle, delicious when it pressed down through skin, and the blood draining as the first step in an old-fashioned 'cure'. There was a moreish sharpness to it all; I was plagued by my body, nerve endings on fire. And then, after those brief moments of pain, a cool emptiness that I suppose felt like a welcome calm, just as Caroline had said.

I splashed at myself with cold water, and I could feel that I was moving stiffly, self-consciously. After my brief interaction with the mystery man in the window, the bristling sensation of being watched persisted, even though there was nowhere to watch from. I sensed the presence of an onlooker taking in my every move. I imagined they would see my glorious transformation, and I wasn't scared.

I didn't bother to beg for the breakfast I'd missed, lunch would be fine, and I went straight outside to see Caroline, who was alone. She had spread out a picnic blanket and lay there in silence, but it didn't bother me after the day before; she'd warm up in time. She pulled her legs up and massaged roughly at her right calf, and I knew better than to ask her about it.

There was all the time in the world on that second full day at Carn. After Caroline had placated Sally so masterfully, it had pierced something, loosened any kind of awkwardness. Everything had changed, and though tension often crackled between us, at least I would never feel the overall woodenness of the previous day. I enjoyed the new, easier atmosphere between us.

'You seem happy,' Caroline said.

I shrugged. I wanted to ask her more about the thing she'd

done with her nails, but then Abigail appeared and my heart kind of skipped a beat to see her. I didn't show it, because I didn't want anyone to see this unexpected fixation I had developed so quickly, but they probably knew. I was sure I saw Caroline roll her eyes.

Abigail flounced over, collapsing in front of us in a heap of white linen. She'd worn white on the first day too, and it made her tattoos seem packed and brilliant. The writhing pile of her rearranged itself and she stretched, reached into the pocket of her dress without hesitation and pulled out a vape pen, puffing away in a cloud of synthetic strawberry and spearmint.

'How did you get that in?' I blurted out.

She just smiled, which made me wonder if some kind of orifice might have been involved.

Abigail was only stationary for a minute, and then she was up and down, jiggling away. Cartwheels on the grass, openly challenging the helpers to confiscate the pen, but they ignored her and stayed pinned to the sides of the lawn, our silent guards.

Caroline turned up her nose at the smell of the vape but didn't comment. She ignored me studiously. Then Sally appeared, wandering over to us. 'Hey, gang,' she said with an American twang. When she wasn't doing her babyish voice, she did this faintly embarrassing yet endearing thing where she put on random accents.

We said 'hi'.

There was no need for anything else. It was fine to just be, to just lie on the grass. I had a fleeting urge to tell them about the man in the window, to see if anyone else had seen him, but I held back. It had been such an odd sight that I wasn't sure how to explain it without scaring them.

Caroline started some games. She barked out instructions: cities that began with D, I-Spy, something that required counting backwards and prime numbers. So many games, and Sally was good at all of them. Sally even dropped the silly voice and sounded colder and more competent as she raced through the tasks.

We didn't do questions. There were no genuine conversations when we were in our group, although Abigail and I would speak far more freely in the coming days when the other two weren't around. So, when the games petered out, we talked about Carn itself.

Sally was awestruck. 'Imagine if we hadn't come here,' she said. 'I'm not sure what would have happened to me in the outside world.'

'All those people out there that don't get to experience this,' Abigail said, nodding. She gestured around at *this*.

'We are fortunate,' Caroline conceded stiffly.

We were so lucky, and it was a physical sensation that day as I heard them talk, a sparkling rush through me.

Then Sally got up and walked over to the moat. 'Oh my God, the fish!' she squeaked in delight.

Abigail let out a snide laugh.

Sally didn't seem to notice, and I was glad because I was overcome by her sweetness.

'The fish are amazing,' Sally gushed loudly as she floated back over to us. 'The food is divine, isn't it? And the house! This house might be the best house in the world.'

She finished in a joyous pirouette. So earnest, and it was just who she was. In the first week, I would find her cooing over a dying butterfly on the lawn and moving her fingers in the air to trace a cloud – a single dreamy motion, her palms cupping the sky. But in between these moments of delight, there was tension. She would press her hands to her stomach like she was checking for something, or she would scratch at her arms in a way that made me want to grab at them and tell her to stop. That was all to come.

As we talked about how lucky we were, I caught any fears, any questions, before they bubbled up. I folded them away and we played our little games and we sat in the sun together. Things arrived later: thick sandwiches with the crusts cut off and an enormous glass bottle of sparkling water.

Abigail and I were bonding more and more, reaching for food.

'Did you miss a lot of school?' she asked me abruptly, ignoring the other two.

'Some,' I said, surprised. It seemed out of the blue.

She nodded. 'It's hard,' she said. 'You're out of sync with the rest of the world.'

That opened up more conversation for us and we talked in the vaguest terms in those early days.

I admitted how I felt when sleep was impossible, how it was like my eyes were burning and I could barely get through the day, and my skin was all stretched. Abigail did not offer words of sympathy, but she listened and that was enough. We shared our ailments, but the other two did not join in.

Abigail and I had tiny little pots of French yoghurt with honey. There were long bloody sausages too, flavoured with paprika, covered in mustard. She ate one messily, the yellow mustard all around her mouth. 'Have more,' she said to me, grimacing, even though it was delicious.

An eating disorder, that was what I thought, again.

And I was sure she retched a little, but still she kept on cramming the sausage into her mouth, as if she couldn't get enough, and I was slightly repulsed, but I didn't stop watching her, even seeing it churn in her mouth, the shudder as she swallowed. I just could not look away.

13.

Breakfast – eight. Lunch – twelve. Dinner – seven.

The first week of Carn passed swiftly.

I'd never been without access to a clock before, but the helpers kept us right. They chivvied us along and gave us all the extras: everything we could have wanted, every day, like we were staying at the fanciest hotel. They handed out stubs of pencils and slips of paper, and we asked for a pancake bar, donuts, and it all appeared. Maple syrup running down my chin, swigging orange juice and asking for more.

More, more, more. Even when I was fit to burst, when eating was uncomfortable. All the dietary restrictions I had carefully read and assessed for sleep improvements, they were all abandoned heartily. A meat-rich diet. *Good for iron*, Elise said. All the vegetables seemed freshly picked and everything tasted delicious.

After a few days came the treatments and they were predictable. Massages and facials and a bespoke ritual with hot stones, all performed by the helpers. Then we had a long yoga session, led half-heartedly by Yoga Helper out on the grass.

Oh, to see us! We bumbled through the downward dog and cobra poses. Sally was quiet; Abigail was ridiculously bendy. The helpers ran it all with a clinical competency, good at everything but not enthusiastic about any of it.

I'd known that there would be treatments. When Elise had come into the bookshop to woo me, after she'd initially posited the idea of Carn, she had spoken with me about things that didn't seem so unusual; she'd chatted breezily about acupuncture, yoga, massage, reiki, and she'd been telling the truth. There was a whole menu of options on offer in the rooms that peeled off from that imposing entrance hall at Carn, and it was up to us to choose our own set of cures. They were mostly things I'd tried before. I did a lot of acupuncture back in Edinburgh. Many hours spent lying on a bed listening to panpipes.

With the activities, we developed our alliances. I found Abigail to be unenthusiastic about the other two, but with me, she was almost too close, and I loved it. She clung to me as we strutted out from breakfast together, and I didn't really know why. On the outside I was the downer, the one who bored everyone with her complaints, my life *was* my ailments, but at Carn perhaps I was the person you'd want to be friends with.

Though we spoke about our experiences of being unwell, Abigail also focused on pleasure. She seemed to have mastered the art of moulding our time for optimal enjoyment. 'Let's ask for Pilates?' she would say. 'Then mimosas, but with grapefruit juice?' And these were good ideas, especially the booze. We requested and drank it all, drained our glasses every day: daiquiris with wedges of lime, squat green bottles of beer and cold white-wine spritzers.

Sally padded behind Abigail and me, easy to go along with whatever, permanently a little oily, trotting back for an Indian head massage daily. Caroline was monitoring her, and I tried to watch what I talked about with Sally, but she seemed okay, and there had been no more outbursts.

As the days passed, we settled into a routine. I'd expected something more like magic or some kind of science that would astound me. That interaction between Caroline and Sally at the beginning had promised something completely different, and that was what I craved. I couldn't deny that I was a little disappointed (when sober) about the relative mundanity of our days. I tried to stay enthusiastic because my hair was still shiny, my head felt clear and my sleep was much better. It wasn't perfect but there had been vast improvements.

Surely our full cures were coming in a way that would dazzle me, perhaps through our sessions with Elise?

*

The sessions began towards the end of that week.

The first time, Elise came out alone, and she gestured for me to come inside. After that, they became a daily occurrence, taking place at random times.

Whenever she led me through, the helpers appeared, following as if I might run away. Which, of course, I wouldn't. We went, not to Elise's office, but to a sunroom to the back of the house, and we sat facing each other on two chairs made of steel with leather padding. The room was hot, the leather chair almost burning my thighs. It worked as a setting, and it felt quite professional, with Elise taking the therapist role, saying some things I didn't focus on much about transference and boundaries.

In our initial session, she sat curling her body up in her chair, leaning in towards me, pen in hand, poised to write. She stared at me intently, like ours was the most important conversation in the world, but deep down I knew it was an act and she'd be the same with all four of us. Right from the outset, the sessions with Elise felt somewhat manufactured, and that was my fault too. She didn't delve into what was wrong with me, but at the same time I'd hardly told her anything. I knew we'd get there eventually and I was just waiting to see how it panned out.

There were parts of me she was interested in, but she was calculated, and I never felt I was giving her what she wanted at the beginning. I thought our sessions were just a means to give some kind of structure to Carn, and that worked for me. They were a distraction.

We'll start with him and go from there. How did you meet your husband?

That was fine. To go back further to the time before him was harder, but certain bits of our history were perfectly palatable. Meeting him and the move from ill, difficult child to ill, marginally less difficult adult. All easy, just words, and with Elise, I raced to the end, cringing a little at myself as I rattled through it all and exaggerated parts, underplayed other bits – a dramatic habit I'd stolen from Harry.

14.

It was a chilly night in September – a weekend because we weren't students any more and so we only went out on weekends. We were dancing at some club night. I recognized him from around; not in a good or bad way, but he wasn't a stranger.

He was part of a group – the centre of it, actually. He impressed people. *A go-getter*, that's what my parents would comment when they met him for the first time. They were right. There was an air of pure efficiency about him, and I was sure I wasn't the only one who saw it. He accepted that, when he spoke, everyone listened.

It sounds so boring to say our eyes met, but they really did. His friends were a bit grotty-looking, but Harry wasn't at all. He had light, straight hair, with an almost feminine wave of fringe that fell over one eye and a prim delicateness to his features. But his expression was resolute in a way that his friends' weren't. They were flushed with drink; he was sober and serious.

He strutted over to me. Most people couldn't have walked like that without seeming over the top, but he just came across as self-assured. Then he introduced himself and asked me what I'd like to drink.

I asked for a vodka and coke with no ice. The bartender handed over the vodka and coke (with ice) and I saw Harry covertly fish the cubes out before brandishing the glass at me with a brilliant smile, flicking his fringe so he could see better.

'Here you go,' he said.

'Thanks.' I sipped and cocked my head. 'I saw that!'

'I just wanted you to have the right drink,' he said stiffly. It was sweet and it was who Harry was. He changed the world so it suited him better.

Harry barely left my side for the next hour, but when he went to the bar I was alone with my wretched body, and it hummed, waiting for him to return. I went outside later, and the cold air hit my arms, and it hurt my teeth when I breathed in. The tingling sensation of a cold sore forming. Everything was exaggerated a million times, and I wondered if that was what falling in love was. If it was always so horribly . . . raw? Needles forced against the arch of my foot or flames on skin. All grating and electric.

I was glad that it was dark as I was sure I must have looked pained, and then he pressed another drink into my hands and told me I *wasn't like the other girls*. The worst kind of cliché.

'What do you mean?' I asked.

'You're less giggly,' he said seriously, and I realized he was a little drunk.

He reached a hand to my waist and then pulled it back, like he knew it was too much and he didn't want to come on too strong. His attention shifted and he shook his head at the other girls sitting in the smoking area. He laughed at how they seemed petrified to leave each other even for a second, hovering in clusters and trooping to the toilet together, and I ended up laughing along with him even though I wanted to be as carefree as those girls. He wasn't so mean about people back then at the beginning; it felt gentle.

'You're different,' he said to me.

I knew it wouldn't be just the one night. Perhaps because his attention never left me, unlike his friends, who moved from one girl to the next. Harry always had the ability to stay focused. Already, he was home to me – it was that fast between us.

Then, it was closing time and the lights came up, those surrounding us either recoiling from or smashing their faces into each other, all drunken kisses and gropes. But Harry was prim.

We moved outside. This time his arm crept around me tentatively and I leaned into him a fraction.

'Do you want me to walk you home?' he asked.

'You don't need to do that.'

It was a game. I wanted him to insist.

The timing was right. I was in a period of respite where I didn't feel too bad, and in those brief phases it was much easier to do things, to meet people and open up to something. There was the potential that this could work.

'I could buy you some chips?' he said. He'd already bought me too many drinks, but Harry liked to serve, that was clear.

'Chips?' I asked.

'You seem like you might like some,' he said.

'Really?' I smiled. I think I was trying to flirt.

'Sure,' he said, and he looked so fresh considering it was three a.m. 'The night's young. I want to keep talking to you, so let's go get chips.'

I nodded.

We went to the bus stop because it was somewhere to sit and eat the chips. We didn't tell the friends we'd arrived with. Traffic sped past and night buses stopped for us as we sat perched on the plastic bench. Eventually, we got up and walked through the city.

The magic of that conversation that stopped and started through the night is hard to bring to life. I can only just remember what we discussed, and there was a clumsiness to it all, but it also felt right. I didn't tell Elise that – too soppy.

I disclosed a little to Harry, right when we first met. 'I have some problems with sleep,' I said to him later, as we got close to my flat.

He was nonplussed. The next morning, he called, early. 'Well, you said you didn't sleep so much. I figured I'd catch you straight away. I'm an early bird myself,' he said with pride.

I imagined him gobbling me up in a single slurp like I was a long, pink worm.

We'd finished our studies and the opportunities felt endless. I'd graduated in English, he did Business Studies, both at Edinburgh.

The first office jobs we had were not important because Harry and I lived in a blessed bubble. I didn't even dream of him. He was there so vividly in my days, but at night he was absent.

We'd only been together for a few months before Christmas crept up on us with a single carol trickling from the radio at the end of a segment in early November. Then it was everywhere: couples entwined for balance on the ice-skating rink; mulled wine in plastic cups. When the shops put out tinsel, two-for-one offers and gift-wrapping services, Harry seemed jolly, singing along, suggesting we watch old films. He was one of those people who really, really likes Christmas. For me, it was something to get through as opposed to something enjoyable.

'What are you doing for Christmas Day?' he asked as we sat on the sofa in front of the TV, my legs slung across him, his phone in his hand.

He knew I didn't want to spend it with family. I found them all too much: my brothers were too loud and my parents were always so worried about me. I usually left the celebrations worried for myself.

'Why?' I asked.

'I was thinking, let's do it just the two of us. What do you say?'

His train of thought was clear. He'd just seen a particularly tear-inducing advert that had played on repeat over the last few months, involving a life-sized snow globe. He'd sung along to the theme tune; he was sometimes unexpectedly sentimental.

Then he fixed me with an intense stare. His phone was down. He shook at my knees with both hands. 'Come on, Bets! Say yes, don't leave me hanging!'

'Won't your family be angry?' I asked. 'Won't they want you to go home?'

Because they would be annoyed. His family lived outside of Glasgow and he went regularly. I had expected him to go back there because Harry got on well enough with them. I'd gathered snippets of information that didn't add up to full characters. I knew that his mother had lots of handbags that she stored in big dust bags. She'd petitioned Harry's father for them to have their own room. There was a sister who liked horses. His father drank Scotch, an abiding memory from Harry's childhood, and had a chair in the living room only for him.

I was so distant from my own at that point that Harry's family represented a new start. I had thought, right at the beginning, that he might want to share them with me. I had hoped I would bond with his mother, but it hadn't worked out like that. There was no immediate sense that she wanted to take me under her wing, and she let it slip to me early on that they didn't believe in people being *sickly*. When we'd first met and she had asked what I did, I'd clocked the wide, vacant smile on her face as she listened to me describing my job. Babies. That's what she was thinking. She didn't know that when Harry brought up the idea of children, sometimes it hurt because I didn't feel I could do that, and I couldn't commit to them, but I didn't *not* want them either. We were so young, but it was still something I thought about, and I knew Harry was planning and plotting away – he couldn't not, that was who he was. Anyway, I could feel his mother's interest: *babiesbabiesbabies*. I hid in the kitchen to avoid her. Harry kept us separate after that initial meeting.

Thoughts of Harry's family and how they'd react to him abandoning them over Christmas were largely irrelevant, because one thing I loved about him from the beginning was that he wouldn't suggest a plan that he wasn't a hundred per cent set on. In a way, even before he asked, he'd decided, and it was just a case of waiting for me to agree.

Even though our relationship was so fresh, he was all in. 'I mean, it's only one year,' he said. 'It's not a big deal. They won't care. But look at you, so thoughtful!'

'Let's do it,' I said.

He clapped his hands together. 'Success! It's going to be so good. Just you wait.'

And that Christmas showed me that Harry did indeed have the ability to make life good. We spent days in festive bliss. We sacked off work for the week with dashed-off out-of-offices – our jobs weren't stressful at that point, and I don't remember us talking about them much. I wasn't even sure what Harry did all day.

We decorated the parched cheese plant in my flat with fairy lights and lurched around the ice-skating rink.

'Turkey?' I asked him a few days before, on the phone from the supermarket.

'You're cooking? I can cook?' he said.

'I want to,' I said. 'What would you have on Christmas Day if you did it your way? If you could have your favourite meal?' I picked up part of a goose, all packaged up, the flesh mottled against plastic.

He hummed on the other end of the phone, taking the question seriously. He threw out many potential menu ideas, piping up with something and then saying *no, not that, something else, something better, something more us.*

But what was *us*?

I didn't sleep at all on Christmas Eve, but that was normal. No one sleeps well the night before Christmas. We spent so much time at each other's flats, but we slept apart that night. It meant a joyous reunion, and he turned up in the morning in a red scarf, ironed trousers, with an icy bottle of champagne. When he pressed it into my hand, the glass was so cold that I flinched. He pulled the bottle away from me and opened it with a flourish in the middle of the flat. It spilled all over the floor.

We made our own traditions.

So unique; so original. Ditched the Christmas dinner that required timings and consideration of oven space. We ate swollen green olives stuffed with anchovies, followed by a burnt lasagne. After lunch, he brought out presents, but they weren't extravagant gifts, they were nice little bits wrapped up in tissue paper – a necklace, a book about art that I'd mentioned in passing. They were thoughtful choices. I'd bought him presents too, just socks and aftershave. He put the socks on straight away, delighted.

Later, full of food, we lay out on the floor wearing paper crowns. We had tumblers of red wine and tried a game of Monopoly. But we gave up almost immediately and fiddled with the pieces. Harry stacked up the hotels at the side of the board, like he was creating an empire, rifling through the money.

'I didn't know Christmas could be like this,' I said, tired and happy and spinning. 'It's been so . . . easy.'

'A good one,' he agreed.

'The perfect day,' I announced. I was drunk.

'The perfect day,' he said in an impression of me, his voice high and kind of dozy. He always did impressions of me and they were sometimes nice.

He reached out to tickle me. 'I'm glad you enjoyed today.'

'This is all I want,' I said. 'This.' And I looked around at the plates waiting to be washed up, the Christmas lights, the wrapping paper and the fire that we played on the TV to add some atmosphere.

He laughed. 'This is all you want? It's a little home-made . . .'

'Yes,' I said, quite honestly. 'More days like this, where I feel like this.'

'It's one day, Bets – a good day, but just a day.' He stretched and arched his back, picked up a cracker with cheese and crammed the whole thing into his mouth.

I didn't push any further, because for me, it never really changed. All I wanted were those home-made days. But for him it was . . . fine. Enjoyable but one out of a series of many, many other good days where things just went right. And his expectations changed. With time, none of it was enough, and he sought out a towering tree, professionally wrapped presents and lavish Christmas parties. The clues were there but we didn't want to see them. We didn't appreciate how differently we imagined a life.

★

I shared the highlights with Elise.

'Those early days are the best,' she said, and it seemed that she understood. 'But it went wrong, between the two of you?'

Rage spiked within me.

Skip to the end.

I had always thought I would tell her what had happened that day, but I wasn't sure how we'd got to it so quickly. I was stalling. I didn't really want to talk about my sleep, because it felt kind of shameful.

Skip to the wedding.

In sickness and in health. The words, as soon as they were uttered, contained a distinct lack of balance. The scales tipped. Sickness is longer, a hiss of green, liquid and dripping. Health is lighter, a neat word. Rectangular and solid. In my mind, it is fresh as an ironed lab coat, or maybe something sterilized and sealed in plastic.

After that, *Do you take her?*

And he said yes, looked deep into my eyes. He said yes loudly, in front of our guests as they watched us and thought how perfect we were, how good it would feel to be us.

After the meal, the cake-cutting. Everything became sticky. Handprints on glasses, sugar, the taste of it throughout. Two of my brothers hung on to the DJ booth. Even though it was still early, they pleaded for their favourite songs, slinking away and booing loudly when the DJ shook his head. Harry and I had cut the cake, and then he was gone, and I went to search for him outside, where burnt-orange festoon lights lit up the grounds and there was a small makeshift cocktail bar. I moved away and then to the side, by the rhododendron bush, I saw them.

They were standing close together. Harry with Siobhan.

She was in the shadows, and she reached out and fingered the lapel of his jacket, gripping it in her hand and then pulling him in to speak in his ear like they were in a film. The green of his jacket against the tangerine of her dress. She let him go only because he pushed her away. It was that gesture. Not the way she pulled him in, or how she whispered in his ear, so her lips almost touched him. It was the way he navigated her. There was a familiarity between them.

He turned as he did it. And he was unlucky because, when he turned, he saw me.

Just the three of us. She saw me too. The curse of being the bride – I was unmissable.

Without thinking much, I walked back into the marquee and, minutes later, Harry was there at my side.

'Where's Siobhan?' I said, then louder, 'Where is she?'

Our guests were curious, why were we fighting? I think that was when he decided. The humiliation would have been unbearable to him. It was his only option. And so, he took me into the hotel and up the stairs.

There were many other ways the night could have gone. I could have escaped from the room after he locked it. The next morning, I could have confronted him, demanded to know how long it had been going on. But I didn't, and he didn't say anything to me. In the days that followed, I took what had happened and blurred it all in my mind. If I worked hard to focus, then I barely thought of what I'd seen and done.

After the wedding, I tried to make changes: the job at the bookshop and a new start. I was set on getting better, and I thought I could make things right between Harry and me. But the knife on the balcony made me see that I was unable to trust myself, and I needed to leave him.

I told Elise a cut-back version and I felt that she truly understood. She looked at me for a long time with such compassion; I knew I'd done the right thing in sharing what had happened on that horrible night when I lost them both.

15.

On a normal afternoon, two weeks into our time at Carn, the others drifted to different parts of the house after lunch. I did a speedy appraisal of their location. Abigail had possibly drunk too much; she'd downed beer after beer, and I thought she might have gone to throw up after we'd eaten. Sally could have been in a session, and I had no idea about Caroline.

I sat on a big, squashy chair in the dining room for a while, alone with my thoughts. I was fine to rest and think of nothing at all. They'd all emerge soon. But then I realized that I was . . . truly alone, and this was very rare.

I sat upright with a start and peered out of the window. The helpers were nowhere to be seen. As soon as I noted their absence, I was hit by a desire to explore without being watched.

I walked out of the dining room. There was a giddiness in the freedom as I continued around the perimeter of the lawns. A set of sprinklers sprayed in a soothing hiss, creating a constant wet sheen over the grass and some small pools. I padded through, letting the water cool my feet a little. Then I went towards the forest, neat to the side of the grounds with lanky saplings that thickened after a few metres into a spread of mature trees, stretching into the distance.

I had little desire to explore the forest, though I was interested to see where it ended and if the water circled the entire estate. I didn't really know what I was doing, but when I reached the edge of the trees, I ducked down. A rich and earthy smell came from the reddish compost, which appeared freshly laid. I kicked at it with my foot. There was something white poking out.

Bending down, I pushed the soil away to make a small hole,

and there it was: what looked like a tiny bone. I'd only noticed it because the soil was so uniform, there was nothing else in it.

The bone had no flesh stuck to the surface. I turned it between two fingers and rubbed. A human bone? I pushed the thought away and figured it must have come from a rabbit or a vole because it was so small. The only thing that jarred was the cleanness of it. It looked as if someone had buried it here recently, very shallow and on purpose.

It didn't bother me so much, and I didn't think to dig for more bones immediately, I simply held it in my hand. Soon, I was able to just enjoy it for what it was. The bone was appealing to me in its colour (greyish white and kind of glowy) and the form was unusual: organic but lumpy, resembling a grossly misshapen pearl. I was about to have more of a root around in the earth for the rest of a skeleton, but then I heard voices.

Elise.

She was quite far away, and she strode into the walled garden with a huge straw basket on her arm and a matching hat that flopped over her eyes. Abigail stood close to her.

They went to the beds and Elise stopped, bent over and sniffed at some herbs. Abigail did the same. She picked a bunch, handed them over for feedback, and Elise nodded. Abigail laughed, and I didn't hear it, but I saw her throw back her head, her mouth open.

A thud of jealousy at the sight of them together, alone outside the confines of the therapy room. It was silly and I tried to ignore it. So childish.

Still, I wanted to get up and join them, or just see how they interacted from a closer vantage point, perhaps hear their conversation. But there was no way of doing it without them seeing me, and it would be an obvious interruption.

'Betsy!'

I turned and saw Sally. She raced towards me, and as she came closer, she staggered, then slid on the grass.

'What are you up to?' she asked, her voice slurred.

'Not much. I was going to see what they were doing.' I gestured to Elise and Abigail.

The two of them had heard Sally shout too, and they waved at us.

'Oh,' Sally said vacantly.

'Are you all right?' I asked.

She made herself stand taller and beamed. 'Ohmygod, I mean, I'm brilliant! I feel fantastic. I've no pain anywhere, not a bit! Do you feel the same? Oh, tell me you do?' She clutched at my hand.

I nodded. I still had the bone and I didn't want to show her, not really. Rubbing it between my hands, I wanted to keep it for myself. I tried to transfer it to my pocket, but she saw, and she reached out to snatch it from me.

She held it up and peered at it. 'That could be the incus,' she said. She'd sobered up. Her baby voice had gone and there was no put-on accent either.

'What's the incus?'

'A bone from the ear.' She turned it round and inspected it.

'An *ear*?' I said. 'Like, a human ear? How do you know that?'

'The human ear, yes. Well, maybe.' She shuddered and handed it to me.

'Is there any more you can tell from it?' I asked, offering it back to her to examine. I didn't believe for a second it was a human bone, but I was curious.

She shook her head. 'No,' she said. 'Don't want it.'

'Fine.' I put the bone into my pocket.

She turned in the direction of Elise and Abigail.

'Will we go over there? To see them?' she asked.

'It looks like a private conversation.'

She stared past them, looking at the herb garden. 'Sage, rosemary, thyme, basil, oregano,' she said. 'Then lemon verbena, horseradish and fennel,' she recited mechanically. Her baby voice was back.

I was confused.

'That's the order they're planted in,' she said. 'Elise talks about herbs a lot, and she once said it was very important to flavour things correctly.'

That sounded true. The flavours at Carn were quite odd. Like nothing I'd ever experienced before. I couldn't align them with a particular cuisine.

'How can you remember?' I asked. We'd only been in there as a group once at the beginning and there had been no identification in the herb beds, unless she'd been in again with Elise. And why would you *bother* to memorize it?

'I have a good memory,' she said.

I considered this, considered her. I was increasingly interested in Sally. She claimed she could identify the bone, which I didn't believe, but it was unexpected, and now this revelation.

'Oh, really?' I said, inviting her to expand, but she wasn't listening, she was watching Abigail and Elise as they walked out of the walled garden.

Elise offered another half-wave. Abigail stuck her tongue out at me. I waved back at them and Sally did too.

Then I put my hand in my pocket to touch my bone. I enjoyed the solidity, and I pressed at the curves. My tiny animal bone would tether me to real life when things felt like a dream. I went up to my room and put it down on the wooden floor, then pushed it far under my bed until I could only reach with the tips of my nails. My bone lived against the skirting board and you could barely see it. This did not seem wrong, and in fact I believed that it belonged at Carn, and that I had been destined to find it. That was what Carn was, all sharp pains and little bones.

16.

Another breakfast buffet of fruit piled up in glass bowls, and quickly warming yoghurt, and a vast assortment of unidentifiable cured meat.

The helpers blocked our paths to outside. They were stickier than usual, if that was possible, barricading us in.

'I wonder what we're doing?' Sally asked. She lifted a hand and curled one finger around the strands of hair that fell about her shoulders. Slowly, she pulled and then twisted more and more until it started to knot. She winced but didn't stop. Then she smiled, and I smiled back because I always smiled at Sally.

'I don't know,' I said.

'I bet it'll be something literally amazing,' Sally practically gasped.

Abigail let out a small chuckle and met my eye. I think she was trying to impress me when she mocked Sally, but Sally was just saying what we were all thinking, acknowledging that today would be different.

You see, not much had really *happened* at that point. I was a lot better, but if there was some magic experience meant for us, we were all waiting for it. There was a feeling in the air that day that something was going to happen that would change us.

Abigail felt it too, I'm sure, but she couldn't help herself. 'Literally amazing,' she said nasally, in a surprisingly accurate impression of Sally.

'Focus on yourself,' Caroline barked at Abigail.

Caroline didn't say that much, but when she did, her words had bite. I wondered whether she'd picked up on the closeness between Elise and Abigail. Was she jealous like I was?

Abigail laughed. 'Fuck *off*, I'm just teasing.'

'Girls!' Elise said, entering the room and greeting us with joy. She beamed at Abigail and then sat; a coffee landed in front of her within a minute and she nodded her thanks to the helper.

'We're doing pictures today,' Elise continued, stirring her drink with a long spoon. She flicked it up and out, and laid it on the table, as exacting as a surgeon. A weighted silence, until Smiler Helper scuttled up and removed the spoon, wiping the splash of coffee away.

'Why?' I asked Elise.

Elise looked as if she was working out exactly how to phrase it. 'It's necessary,' she said, and then pursed her lips together.

'What kind of photos?' I pressed.

'Professional ones.'

'But why?'

'*Because.*' She had snapped. A double snap with the second syllable hitting hard and mean, and then she sighed. 'This isn't what I want from you. To *interrogate* things, to lose the trust.'

I knew everyone could see the reddening of my cheeks.

She was right. I'd been well behaved since I'd arrived. We all had. I was happy to live in ignorance, and I had made a lot of guesses about the girls without knowing much for sure. I assumed they had pensions to pay into and jobs and cars. Bills and laundry and mid-week meal prepping, and I assumed we all fucked, drank, occasionally did a line, had a smoke, made mistakes. We were adults, but you wouldn't have thought it to see us that day, preparing for what sounded suspiciously like school photographs. White-collared shirts and eyes squinting at the flash.

'What if I don't want to do it?' I didn't say it aggressively. I just wanted to understand my options.

'Then you'll need to leave,' Elise said. 'Straight away.'

I thought of the bridge rising through the pink waters, pictured Driver Helper taking me back to the station in silence, and the reality of leaving Carn.

It was out of the question; I would stay because she would cure me.

I shook my head.

Then Abigail piped up. 'If someone wants to take a photo of me, I'm game.'

An admission of trust; she didn't need to know what was going on; she was willing to walk into whatever they threw at us.

Elise nodded.

The helper who applied my make-up did it like a professional – Make-up Helper. She didn't say a word, just slapped on primer, choosing from many different palettes and creams. I didn't wear a lot of make-up in general, only when I was trying to cover my tiredness, and even then, it was never fully successful.

This all took place in my room. There was no mirror so I was unaware of what she was doing. Make-up Helper applied a tacky kind of gel to my eyelids, and I tried to talk to her – complimented her technique, asked her if she was a make-up artist – but she wouldn't engage.

'Stay still, please.' She patted at my face roughly.

So, I let Make-up Helper do her thing, and finally I was allowed to leave. I went down the stairs and outside, led by the helper, and she took me to the back of the house.

We walked all the way to the side of the grounds and passed an outbuilding that was in disrepair, the glass all splintered, but I could make out a little of my reflection. I peered at myself. The colours were not what I had expected; my face was fragmented by the broken window, a gaudy and distorted reflection, with what looked like blue under the eyes. I squinted to try to see more, but the helper was urging me to follow her.

And as we approached and moved into the woods through the trees, I noticed another building, far back on a path, on the outskirts of Carn. It was partially hidden, but it appeared to be some kind of renovated barn.

As I got closer, I saw what they'd done to the others.

17.

I had expectations of what I would look like. Assumed it would be straightforward, and that they'd do a better job than I could do myself at home. I thought we'd become beautified versions of ourselves, but I was wrong.

Sally, first. She stood in the doorway, framed like a portrait. They had made her appear incredibly gaunt, drained of colour, with dark shadows under her eyes.

It was art. Meticulous in the way they'd added puffed-up bags of papery skin using cosmetic wizardry or perhaps some kind of prosthetics. The helpers had fashioned an angry fake scar near her hairline – lumpy and raised. I glimpsed Caroline behind her, and she had pale, dead lips, and a sheen of sweat covered her entire face.

Then there was Abigail, and her lips were pale too. They'd done something to make them appear cracked, and they'd somehow forced a vein to stand out on her forehead. It was costume make-up. I must have looked the same as them. I could imagine it: skin flaky, grease-slicked hair.

Abigail didn't seem too concerned. Ambling over, she linked her arm with mine. 'How do I look?' she asked me in fake jollity, hand on hip.

'It's unusual,' I said.

'Are you two all right?' Sally asked, still kind of out of it. She hadn't registered our make-up.

'We're fine,' I said. 'Let's do this.'

And so we walked inside. The helpers followed.

The barn had been set up with care. There was a white screen pulled down against a wall and the set of studio lights blinded me when I walked in. I tried not to show it, but I was surprised by this professional-looking space.

A man sidled up to us. 'I'm going to take some pictures,' he said.

There was no introduction or gentleness to him, but he seemed like a real photographer.

Abigail went first, which was no surprise. She sauntered into the frame with a tilted neck and offered up some long, somewhat vacant stares.

'Headshots mainly,' the man called out to no one in particular as he clicked away.

Elise appeared, skulking by the door. I had expected some involvement from her, but she had very little input, and she watched with the rest of us.

'Will we see the pictures?' I asked her.

'I don't think so,' she said.

'I just thought if they're for the brochure or something . . .'

Although I had never seen a brochure.

'This is what we do,' she said. 'There's no need to talk about it, no need to question it.' She dismissed me with a shake of the wrist. She was ever so restless that day.

When I think back on this exchange, I wonder why she didn't lie and tell me the pictures had a therapeutic benefit. I would have believed her, I'm sure of it.

'They'll come out well,' she said and there was something in her tone that I couldn't read – sadness or perhaps fear. 'They always do.'

For my turn, I stood there not knowing what to do with my arms or my legs, while the photographer took shot after shot. The lights shone, boiling hot on my face, and my skin was all oily and uncomfortable. Every forced expression I made, I could only imagine how I looked.

The photographer asked me to show a few different emotions, some more unusual than others. We did shock, horror . . .

acceptance. I didn't know how to show acceptance and a grim stare was all I could summon. It was unexpected. But still, I felt relieved this was all that was being asked of me. My shoulders loosened and my body was less tense.

I identified what it was when I spoke to Abigail. 'I think I thought it was going to be . . . nudes,' I whispered when I went back to join her at the side of the barn, my face finally cooling, away from the lights.

'Nudes!' she croaked in delight. 'Seriously?'

I shushed her, feeling stupid.

'I don't know why I thought that,' I said. 'It was just the atmosphere this morning . . .'

Abigail laughed.

Caroline's shoot was not eventful; she stood there stoically. Her charisma was draining by the day and there hadn't been much to begin with.

Sally was last. She continued to ignore our appearance. She walked up, sedate, and she fiddled a little with her dress and then stood there, more relaxed than the rest of us. A Dutch portrait with the dark circles even more obvious under the lights; her eyes were deep pools of blue. She was devastatingly lovely, even with the make-up, and she did not smile, though she looked very relaxed. But then I saw her face change, crumple into despair, and I thought she was going to scream, but she didn't. Instead, she ran. Before anyone could stop her, she was stumbling out through the barn, crying. She wiped away her tears and her hair was everywhere, all over her face.

Caroline raced behind her.

I eyed Abigail, who shrugged at me.

The photographer put down his camera and tutted. I was sure I heard him mutter *girls* under his breath.

'Do you want to go get her?' he called to Elise.

Elise shook her head and left the barn, but not to find Sally. I could see her from the window as she walked across the lawn and back into the house. It struck me. I knew what had freaked

Sally out. I looked past the photographer to the wall of the barn: a dirty mirror.

Abigail and I followed the sound of weeping, and we found Sally lying on the ground. She might have started in the foetal position and then unfurled a little, her legs out at an angle and blades of grass pressed into her shins. Hair fanned out, make-up smeared.

Caroline was beside her on the ground. She had her hand on Sally's shoulder, rubbing it in a confident yet soothing gesture. I thought she'd shoo us away, but she let Abigail and me join the two of them.

We sat.

'What's the matter?' Abigail asked Sally.

'My face,' said Sally, gasping. 'Why have they made me look like this? Like I – I'm . . . dying.' The word led to a fresh eruption – a wail so loud that I could see Abigail flinch.

'It's not that bad.' Abigail tipped her head to one side and examined Sally's face.

Sally was slightly comforted; she stopped howling so loudly.

'I'm sorry. I wasn't always like this,' she said, sniffing. She was so apologetic that it hurt me. I wanted to tell her she didn't need to say sorry and that we understood.

'Things didn't use to get to me,' Sally said.

We'd been told not to share right from the very start, and we'd kept that rule, but I had always suspected that our stories couldn't be contained, and they would spill out eventually in the long days with so little to do.

Sally spoke.

18.

She was a doctor. I probably should have guessed that; I'd seen a flash of her training when she'd attempted to identify the bone.

More than your average GP.

She had been on TV, on some morning show, answering embarrassing medical questions from the public through stilted on-air phone calls. It was an ideal level of fame that allowed her to fly under the radar – although Abigail had recognized her on the first day, I saw that now.

Sally considered herself to be very normal. She had a flat and she had lots of friends. Her family was wealthy and there were many siblings – eight, can you believe it! Half and step included. They were mostly doctors, a medical family. And she fitted in just fine, which was good because it was the kind of family where you had to fit in, and if you didn't, people tended not to speak to you much or bother with you. But she was someone a bit unusual – on TV! – a bit glamorous. People at parties loved to hear about it, and she liked to talk about her work.

She knew how lucky she was, but she wasn't perfect, she had her flaws. Her friends said she spent too much time on her phone, but everyone she knew spent too much time on their phones.

There were parts of the internet that she found almost impossible to ignore because people online talked about her endlessly, and it was hard not to read those comments. 'That's what happens when you become a bit of a celebrity. It's something you have to accept,' Sally said with a sad sigh.

The people behind the screen were varied. There were those who wanted to fuck her, to kill her, to marry her, to save her from the people who wanted to kill her.

She said all this quite matter-of-factly.

Some just enjoyed watching her talk and dissected it when she advised about high blood pressure in her morning slot. They discussed it endlessly in their chatrooms. But she could deal with it. It was all bearable and came with the territory. She talked with her friends about going down the rabbit hole, how she took strict pains to avoid it when she could, but she had to peek – that was only natural.

An ache in her stomach one day progressed to a knife-like sensation moving downwards and then a relentless, twisting throb in the lower gut. The pain was startling in its intensity at first and it took her breath away, but when the sensation faded, she thought that was it. Most people she knew seemed to have reoccurring digestive problems.

The pain came back a week later, worse. She knew what it could be, of course. She knew too much, had a broad training that made her want to push for answers from other experts. She decided she should go see her GP, but they weren't too concerned.

She wasn't deterred, though, and at first she did more research. Sally dived into the detail with journal articles and studies. Then it was impossible to stop researching, and she sought out more and more information to plug the gaps. She went for all the tests, but they revealed nothing. The stomach pain faded after a while. Her friends, also medics, suspected it might be stress, and she believed them.

One day in the shower there was an *abnormality* on her skin, just a patch of scaly redness that started to flake. So, she went back to the doctor. They were a little less patient with her, but the patch got worse, started to spread, and the stomach pain came back.

The next time, at the GP's surgery, she made sure to see a different one and they were even less concerned about the whole thing. She worried about what they'd written in her notes.

She stopped going to the doctor – *she* was a doctor; she should be able to sort this herself! – but her body didn't change. It was everything: every twitch, every niggle, amplified in her mind, her hand to her phone as she researched. She knew what she was doing, she'd seen patients behave in this exact way and tried to coach them through it. It was destructive, but she couldn't stop, and she certainly couldn't tell anyone.

As I listened, I thought about myself. I did not suffer in the same way as her, not at the beginning. While Sally dreaded the doctor, I often took solace in the appointments, even if sometimes the experiences were bad. When I went to the doctor's, there was always an expectation that this time would be different and whatever pill they handed out would cure me. Every time I turned up in the waiting room, I expected a new condition. I'd hold out my arm, enjoy the quick stab from the needle, watch the blood flow into the syringe and delight in it. I would think of the contents with pleasure, how they could reveal what was wrong with some marker or an elevated level of something. But, like Sally, there was never anything concrete, not really. The two of us were different in many ways, but I understood her. I understood the way a pesky body can take over everything. The awareness of discomfort, of pain, it becomes all you can focus on.

Abigail looked concerned. 'What happened in the end?' she asked. I knew where the question had come from. We were primed to root out the final event that had pushed someone over the edge. We wanted to see if it mirrored our own.

'There were posters everywhere this summer,' Sally said. 'Maybe it would have been fine if I hadn't seen all those posters. *Go to the doctor, explore this and that.* Every time you picked something up, *Ask your doctor.* So many patients. I couldn't do it. One day, I ripped one down in the street and tore it up, and then I went home and didn't get out of bed for a week.'

'What do you know about sound sensitivity?' Abigail was trying to get a professional opinion, but Sally shook her head, and she wouldn't talk to either of us any more, not after she'd told her story.

'Relax with the questions,' Caroline said.

'Sorry,' Abigail replied, with no hint of apology.

Caroline seemed to have reached the end of her tether. 'Just leave her, leave us,' she said.

'Why do you keep speaking for her? What's your deal?' I asked.

Caroline did not flinch, even though I had shouted.

'You're not helping, actually, neither of you are,' she said.

Sally was back on the ground, crying quietly – the story seemed to have caused more distress.

We saw someone coming over from the studio barn. There he was, the photographer looking down on us as we sat, and he took a photo of Sally right there on the lawn. He grinned at us. 'Just something . . . for my own records,' he said, which made my stomach turn. I think he'd have taken more, but Caroline was shooing him away.

She was up in his face, solid and powerful.

'Get away from us, you leech,' she shouted, batting at him with both hands, but he didn't seem scared of her. He walked back to the barn with his camera swinging by his side, and I noticed that he clutched at one shoulder as if he was hurt.

19.

Abigail and I left the other two and headed towards her favourite place – a swinging bench which looked on to the back of the house. After what we'd just heard, some of Sally's behaviour made sense. Abigail and I talked about our health, even though we probably weren't supposed to. *Medical sharing* – that was what we called it.

It had started early on. Abigail didn't talk about her personal life outside of Carn, not at all, not ever. That seemed to be her interpretation of the rules we'd been given. The only time she verged upon discussing her life on the outside was when she talked about her experiences with doctors poking at her, ignoring her. She kept it nebulous, but these kinds of discussions were her absolute favourite. I participated occasionally and selectively.

Caroline had shown a loose kind of annoyance at these conversations, but Sally always had a disproportionate reaction. Every time we discussed doctors or hospitals, Sally had made a swift exit. Her reactions were abrupt, and I had just written it off as part of her overall strangeness. Now I could see those topics were unbearable for her; she was at Carn to escape all that. But, even if we knew Sally didn't like it, that hardly meant we were going to stop.

'Health anxiety,' Abigail said as we walked away from the other two. 'There are loads of people with it. Hypochondria. It's so common now, isn't it?'

'I hope she's okay,' I said.

'She seems very upset, doesn't she? Also, I can't believe you didn't recognize her!'

'I don't watch TV much.'

Abigail mulled that over. 'It's so weird, isn't it?' she said.

'It is,' I agreed. 'But she'll calm down.'

Abigail nodded. She was done with the topic. 'Did they tell you that you had to learn to manage your pain?' she asked. 'On the outside? The doctors?' She gripped my hand, focused on me like I was the only person in the world.

I wanted to please her with my response.

'Of course!' I said. I could feel myself trying to match her exuberance and I hated myself for that. 'Not pain so much, but manage my energy, then they sent me on my way.'

She cackled. 'I *hate* it when they say that, manage it.'

We reached the swing and climbed on.

I smiled. 'Reduce stress.'

'Stress! I forgot that one. As if you can magic away your stress. Did you *manage* to do that?'

I thought of Harry – it was possible that he had become the main source of my stress by the end. She didn't know much about Harry, of course, though she knew I was married.

'Sometimes. Not all the time,' I said.

'Of course you didn't. You were stressed because you weren't sleeping. It's hard on the outside,' she said.

'Yes,' I said.

'To make friends, I mean.'

'Yes,' I repeated.

We weren't supposed to talk about the outside.

'I . . . struggle with it.' She offered a quivering, apologetic smile that made me terribly sad.

'Me too,' I said.

'On the outside,' she said, 'people find me weird. They don't get it. But here, it fades away, and I'm just a different person.'

I didn't say anything, because I didn't know how to be comforting, to show her I knew what she meant, without being patronizing.

'It's okay for you,' Abigail snapped. The easy tone had gone, and her voice sounded sharp.

'What do you mean?'

'Ugh, nothing.'

'Come on, say it!'

'Well . . . you just seem really together.'

I was delighted. On the outside, I was the one who was never well, reducing my world incrementally over the years, all in the pursuit of a good night's sleep. Someone who was entirely focused on the body, on what was wrong with it, and now I seemed *so together*. But then, I did see it, when I looked at myself in the mirror – I burned with something, my sleep was good, and Abigail saw this too. It made her want to be around me.

'I know you have things going on,' she continued. 'I didn't mean it like that, but it feels as if you're getting better.'

'Well, thanks.'

We couldn't talk any more, because Driver Helper was summoning Abigail, calling her name. Abigail gave my arm a last squeeze and then she jumped off the swing. The sudden absence of her weight made it jolt and I had to steady myself. She rushed inside. It was clear in the way she sped up that she wasn't expecting me to follow. Wherever she was going, this was a private thing, but I sensed an opportunity. The day was altered; the photoshoot had disrupted the flow of things. I thought the other helpers must have been back in the studio, and Elise was nowhere to be seen. I waited for a minute, and then, when Abigail was inside, the front door closed, I approached the house.

I didn't think I'd get away with it. I suspected a helper would be watching, and they'd stop me, lead me away as they were prone to do. But they were nowhere to be seen. So, I opened the front door and went inside.

I saw Abigail shuffling around at the top of the stairs. She was in her own world. Quietly, I followed, staying out of sight. I was hidden at the bottom of the stairs, looking up at her as she moved to the end of the corridor. She was standing at the wall and then she pushed against it once and then a second time.

A switch flicked; the world changed and the wall opened. She stepped through and it closed behind her.

A secret place.

The quick thrill of it. I forced myself to take a deep breath and wait for at least a minute – I wanted to leave a good distance between us. Then, I went up the stairs to where she had stood. It was well camouflaged, painted the same as the walls and panelled. When you went very close, you could see the light behind. I pressed against the wall. It opened smoothly. I went through.

20.

I was hit by the memory of our flat back in Edinburgh, which was a hostile place. Harry was always thinking bigger and better, and so we bought (or *he* bought) a flat.

It was a glass cage on the Quartermile. This area of Edinburgh was developed, expensive but somewhat sterile. It was silent at night, because money could buy peace, and there was even a doorman – uncommon in Edinburgh – and Harry liked that. When we'd gone to view it, the estate agent told us that a friend had once seen a woman with a thin whip standing at the window, leather and chains; bodies pressed against the glass. The estate agent recalled the story with delight, and we both imagined the scene.

Harry was certainly amused by the tale. 'Exhibitionists!' he'd crowed. I'm sure that anecdote swayed him, and I could see he was gratified that the estate agent would think that we were young enough, edgy enough, to find that story invigorating, and that it would push us to put an offer in.

After we moved, I worked to condition myself to a minimalist lifestyle (his preference). This turned out to be expensive (his money) and involved lots of white boxy things. Everything was concealed in drawers, and he became very preoccupied with the complicated art of hiding cables.

So, we hid the cables. We listened to what the flat wanted, and it was needy from the start; it bleated for attention, beginning with the crunch of broken cabinets and floors buckling with water damage. Showy and fragile and vast, with very few doors.

Through the hidden door and walking down the corridor at Carn, the colours took me back to the flat in Edinburgh. The walls were white like a gallery. Not a bright, cheap colour, but the kind of white that has pricey nuance. At home, Harry and I had deliberated over whites for hours, flicking through books of swatches, intending to bring softness to the walls.

Lashings of double cream. Fat clouds.

Imagine a long, bare corridor, more institutional than I'd seen before at Carn, but not entirely bleak. I moved down the hall, unsure of exactly where I was, and I found an entire wing that I'd never been in before. I tried to work out where I was, in the context of the house. It might have been the same corridor from that first day, where I'd looked up from the lawns and seen the haggard man, watched him fall.

I couldn't see Abigail, so I kept moving. The smell of paint was strong. The place felt new, all of it felt new. On and on I went. I sensed that I was snaking around the house many times, circling the inner rooms. There were windows so I could look outside, but no one was down there on the lawns.

Finally, I reached the end. A door. There was nowhere else she could have gone. I pushed it open and went into a room like nothing I'd seen before. It was very small, made smaller by chunky foam spikes on the walls. Nothing else, no furniture and no windows. The room was only slightly disorientating at first. It was silent and, to begin with, I thought it might be relaxing. It felt like a test.

Stay and wait for Abigail to appear?

For a few minutes it was not too bad. Perhaps ten minutes passed. I didn't leave and slowly the feel of the room changed, and it started to push in on me. Flight. That was my immediate instinct – get out – and I had to override that, to focus and release the tension in my hands.

I didn't want to run, but breathing was hard. A vigorous patter of my heartbeat. Air coming in through my nostrils noisily. Combined, it all hurt, though I couldn't pinpoint the exact location of the pain. It made me want to stop breathing entirely just to stop the sounds of my body, and I found I was holding my breath, which made me feel quite dizzy. There was a hiss, and I was panicky as I couldn't even locate what part of me it was coming from. My body was turning against me, taking over like a nightmare, and it was all so much louder than I wanted it to be.

Wait.

Abigail would return to this room, surely?

I stayed for a few seconds more. I wanted to test myself, to know I could do it and it wouldn't kill me. This was a conscious effort, and I clutched at my stomach. I prised my hands away from myself.

I couldn't do it. Across the room, I went to feel for an escape. There it was: a join that was barely visible in the wall, and a door. I pushed and it opened. I raced through and the relief was immediate as I slumped, my shoulders relaxed. More white corridor and Abigail was there at the end. She sat on the floor cross-legged, looking content.

'Hello! You followed me,' she said cheerfully. 'I like that you followed me.'

My heart leaped a little. 'What was that room?'

'Shut the door,' she said with a smile.

I did as she said. The thought of going back in made me shudder.

'It's what they've done for me.' Her voice sounded distant and echoing; my ears were ringing. 'They made a room for me.'

'But what *is* it?'

'It's an anechoic chamber. There's no noise. That's how it was designed.'

'And you go in there often?'

She nodded vigorously. 'All the time,' she said. 'Every day if I want. And then I've started coming on my own without her even telling me I can. She built it for me, you see. She wants me to use it.'

It was such a bizarre boast. So, Elise had made a room for Abigail to protect her from the sounds that bothered her so much. And it kind of tracked that Elise would do that for Abigail – there was such tenderness there between them. But how healthy was it? The room had been terrible for me.

'How can you stand it?' I asked.

'Oh, did you not like it?'

'No! It was . . . horrible. I couldn't wait to get out.'

'Well, it's helping me so much,' Abigail said. 'This is what I've always wanted.'

'I can't believe she made it for you.'

'I know, right,' she said brightly, misinterpreting me. 'I'm very lucky. Anyway, you should go.' She pointed to the way back, through the room.

My throat tightened up at the thought of going back into the room, but I did it. I went out to the first corridor, my head spinning from the submersion in her chamber.

How far would Elise go to build a world for us?

I didn't like it, felt a compulsion to go back in there and drag Abigail out. I had never been the one who cared for people. I was the one who was cared for. But there was such a pull with Abigail, and I had to fight the urge to go and take her back with me.

Down I went, along the corridor. As I walked, I recovered, step by step, and it was quite blissful as the sounds of my own body – all those unpleasant gurgles and creaks and things I didn't want to notice – faded away and merged with the noises of the world.

I welcomed it as I drifted, freed from the heaviness of that room. Out of the windows that lined the corridor, the sun shone, and Sally and Caroline were on the lawns. I planned to go back down to them. But then, just before I reached where the hidden door met the landing, I spotted another door to the side. I don't know how I'd missed it as it was slightly ajar.

I pushed it open further and peered in. There was nothing inherently sinister in the room, though it wasn't curated like so many of the other spaces in Carn. A hospital bed and lights positioned overhead. Laid out, equipment glittered to the side on that flimsy disposable blue paper you see in medical settings, but apart from that it was a drab little space.

A memory of Elise crackled through my mind. Elise flicking the spoon and placing it down like a scalpel.

This was an operating table.

An operating theatre.

And I felt . . . nothing. No curiosity, no great desire to explore. Logically, I knew I should go in, and I teetered at the door, but I couldn't make myself do it. The room repelled me. It did not seem right; it did not fit. The room was hidden, and it wasn't for me. They hadn't intended for me to find it, and I wasn't set on exploring Carn fully, not at that point.

All I can say to explain my reaction is that, after the anechoic chamber, I was dazed to the extreme, and a dullness had taken over all my senses. I pushed it from my mind, and I walked back out on to the lawns. We did not speak of Abigail's soundless room again that day. She emerged later and winked at me, pulling her hand across her mouth to mime a neat zip.

21.

The next morning, as I shovelled breakfast into my mouth, ravenous, I observed Sally from across the table. She did not seem hungry; she ate only a little, and the helper encouraged her to take more. Sally did as she was told because that was who she was. She was quite happy sitting there, but I felt that she had become reserved after she'd disclosed so much in that one episode.

It had surprised me. A doctor, who would have thought it! It was intriguing, but every time I tried to ask her more over breakfast, she did a funny accent or went into her baby voice. Plus, Caroline was hanging around, clearing her throat, signalling it was time to be quiet, so there really wasn't an opportunity to dig deeper.

I looked to Abigail and she grinned at me. Elise's favourite, always the best seat at dinner, furthest from the helpers, but always served first; a hand on her arm as Elise herself glided over to take her to their sessions together. Just that extra bit of attention a few times a day that must have meant something. It was motherly, and jealousy ate at me that morning, especially after seeing the room Elise had made for her. I hated myself for caring. I tried to focus instead on Abigail and our own strange entanglement.

I sipped my tea.

Time to plot.

As I drank, I considered the events of the day before.

I had changed my mind about the operating theatre, and I was annoyed at myself for being so reticent. I should have gone in while I'd had the chance, and I started to think how I might go back. It was exciting, this ability. I had the capacity to actually form a plan, which was new, and I possessed a level of conniving that was so unlike the old me – but I was not a hamster any more, and I possessed a new appreciation for night-time. I didn't dread it, and I was enjoying my pill so much. Even in the morning, with so many hours still to go, filled with sessions and pointless activities, I looked forward to going to my room.

I could sense my body regenerating with dinner and then the pill and then welcome rest. Perhaps I wouldn't even have to go into the details of my sleep problems with Elise? We could just talk about Harry for my whole time at Carn, and that would be enough to keep me on this road of healing.

That evening, I walked up to my room, and my eyelids were pleasantly heavy as usual. I was counting down the minutes until I could drift off.

I noticed when I reached the top of the stairs that Caroline was too close behind me. She was breathing heavily, but I didn't turn to confront her. I let her follow.

When I reached my room, as I was about to go in, she stopped. She waited until the helper escorting Sally down the corridor had gone into the bedroom.

'Watch yourself,' she said to me, her voice low.

'What do you mean?'

'Abigail.'

It was no secret I was spending a lot of time with Abigail.

'Why?' I asked.

'Just don't get too . . . attached.'

'I'm not attached!' I was flustered, thinking of how complicated it was, my jealousy paired with my absurd desire to be around her.

'Don't think that it's something real, something you can continue on the outside. There's more to it than you know with her,' she said.

'What?'

She rubbed at her eyes. 'I shouldn't have said anything. This isn't my priority. I don't know, hold back.'

'*Why?*' I pressed. 'Is this to do with Elise? Because Elise . . . likes her best?'

Caroline grunted something under her breath. 'I told you, just watch yourself, okay?'

'Okay, will do. What's going on with Sally? How is she?' I asked. I hadn't spoken to her much since her breakdown over the photographs the day before, though she'd seemed to have recovered enough to participate again. I'd overheard her ask a helper about the possibility of horse-riding and the helper had stifled a laugh.

Caroline shrugged; she was a little jittery.

'I've got something I need to do,' she said, and she wasn't directing her words at me; instead, she looked around; she twitched.

'What do you mean?' I asked.

'Just . . . I need to sort something out.'

She didn't want to tell me. Her presence was holding me back from my sleep and I was ready to leave her, but then a helper came down the corridor and looked at Caroline.

Caroline offered a quick head dip back, barely perceptible if you weren't watching the two of them.

I caught it – the way the helper nodded her head to the door. This was simply not the way we interacted with the helpers.

Caroline was always irritated and, from the beginning, she had annoyed me for that reason. I had never focused on her as she snapped away at us about anything, but now it was like a screen had been lifted. The irritation had hidden a familiarity with Carn.

It hit me with a thud.

Caroline was part of this place.

Now, it was obvious: the way she moved up the staircase, moved through Carn in general – there was no hesitation. I felt an annoying pang of self-reproach for not seeing it before.

I think she recognized that it had clicked for me. All talk of Abigail was forgotten. I could tell she was about to make some kind of excuse, but I jumped in first. 'What was *that*?'

'What do you mean?' she asked.

'I saw that! The way you nodded. You . . . you know them,' I said. 'You're not here as a patient?'

We had never been called patients by Elise. The word made her wince, and I grabbed her wrist.

'Get off me!' she said. But she wasn't scared and she shook me away easily.

'What's going on?'

She rubbed at her arm. 'Why involve yourself?' she asked. 'Why involve yourself at all?' She looked at me searchingly, didn't deny it. Caroline didn't seem angry, she just seemed very tired. 'You don't need to be involved.' Her words were a little shaky, and she walked away from me, down the corridor, without looking back.

I didn't follow her. There would be more time to unravel it all and I craved peace; I wanted my pill.

In my room, I waited. There was some kerfuffle from downstairs and I pulled the duvet over my head to drown it out, then I pushed Caroline, her searching expression, gently to one side of my mind. I folded her away and waited for the helper.

It came: my trusty pill dished out on time. I didn't question the helper about what I'd seen. There I lay, expecting sleep, as the evening light came in through the window.

The helper left. No Elise that night, and after I took the pill I was a bit more buzzy than usual, and that was irritating. The pill had been the same, but I think I was on edge after my interaction with Caroline. It was unexpected, but that night I had a dream, and it was a familiar and unwanted one.

I dreamed of girls a lot back at home, the dead ones, and even though they were dead, they were actually some of my less distressing dreams. The living girls sat on the sidelines, forgettable, always – they were never the stars of the trashy crime programmes we watched, the variety that have series after series and run to a strict, comforting formula. Harry and I used to argue about it when we sat on the sofa. Bickered over the way I saw his eyes widen in delight and horror, his face cast yellow in the light from the screen, his expression one of guilty delight when he spotted a dead girl. I told him off for it when I dared, but I was intrigued too. A body flat on an autopsy table, the white sheet peeled back to reveal the jut of a hip.

She is young. She is quite beautiful, more so because she is pleasingly inoffensive in her behaviour. A new purity, regardless of her shady past. She cannot make any further mistakes – after all, she is dead. It's important that her looks don't eclipse the living characters who gather around in bland sympathy, wondering if they're next. The dead girl is blonde, or her hair is darkened by blood, so it is more black than yellow. Sometimes you only get a glimpse of her hair – it is ancillary to the plot – but you usually notice her eyes, one a different colour to the other, or that she wears a stiff uniform as opposed to lying in a state of undress, or the camera frame lingers a little too long on a tattoo that you know will be important later to the storyline. Maybe she is . . . scantily clad? Torn clothing that suggests the worst to the viewer. To hint is enough when there are only forty or so minutes to tell the whole sordid story. Beauty, death and sex. A lazy and salacious beginning.

I dreamed.

That night, at Carn, the dead girl moved from the autopsy table to the water, floating there, and then I was swimming in a lake, on my back, staring upwards at the sky. It started pleasant and then the scream entered my dream, changing the story, tearing me out.

And just as in a dream people can merge and change, it became Abigail's body, tattooed and lifeless, and I was reaching to touch it, but she came back to life and she was shrieking in my face, a grim rip of a sound with no defined edges to it. As the pitch rose, I realized it was real.

A shriek.

It was real.

I sat up.

Was it Abigail?

Then my thoughts went to the man I'd seen collapse in the window. Was it him?

The sound faded, but then it rose once more. I didn't think it was coming from the other girls' rooms because it felt low, living in the bowels of the house. I got out of bed and followed the sound to a gap in the floorboards, where I put my ear to the small crack so I could hear better. It continued, and then came a moan that was unfamiliar, fading away to nothing.

I waited until I was sure that the screams wouldn't start up again, and it was silly to stay on the floor. I got up and returned to bed.

After, I noted Carn was not as quiet as before. The house stirred as if the scream had torn through a film of something to let the noise trickle in. Then, the gentle gurgle of water flowing through pipes – a comfort really – and the birds sang, and it was so, so hot again and a new day was about to begin.

22.

I'd rationalized what was happening because so much of it was working. My sleep was transformed; I was eating well, and I felt the energy surge through my body. The soundproofed room, the surgical theatre, I could just about neutralize my reactions to them. When I considered the surreal picture session and the make-up, it was bordering on bearable. However, the sound was something else. I couldn't ignore it.

There had been a desperation in it, like someone was being hurt, the sharp pains of Carn that had been there from the beginning becoming louder, more insistent. So, there I was, working up the courage at breakfast to bring up the scream, careful not to scrape my chair against the floor; I had become adept at being quiet – we all had.

Each of the others emerged.

First came Sally, rubbing her eyes with wide smiles for us all, and she touched my shoulder lightly as she passed.

I waited. Spooned up long rashers of streaky bacon that tasted funny. It was a strange colour with oil dripping. Then I added browning half-moons of avocado. A gesture – to fill my plate was enough to show I was willing to cooperate.

'Finish it all,' Elise said. 'No fussiness.'

Abigail arrived, tiptoeing. Usually, she tried to avoid the others at breakfast, as she preferred to eat alone, or only with me.

Just Caroline left to arrive.

The gang, together apart from one.

We ate; no one spoke. Her seat remained empty, and I thought of the night before. Caroline was involved in some way, certainly, and she hadn't denied it when I'd questioned her, so where was she?

Was it because of my discovery?

'Something happened last night,' I said to Elise.

'Oh yes?'

'There was a sound that woke me up.'

'What kind of sound?' Elise was rattled, her expression drawn.

'It was a scream, I think.'

I was annoyed at myself. Such a tentative, *I think*. I knew what I'd heard, but it was so ingrained. That habit of spending years slotting *if it's not too much trouble* at the end of emails.

'A scream.' She actually lifted one eyebrow. 'So, you mean you think it was a person?'

'Yes.'

'How odd. Maybe you were dreaming?' she asked. There was a touch of hostility in her suggestion. It was a questioning of my sanity, and my cheeks went hot.

Perhaps she was right and it had all just been an extension of my dream. It wouldn't be the first time. I tried to claw back the feeling of my feet on the floor and then my ear against wood; the specific light in the room. Had there been anything to prove it had been a dream?

'Did you two hear this scream?' Elise said to Abigail and Sally.

Sally dithered. 'I don't think so,' she said, her attention darting between Elise and me like she didn't know who to trust.

'I slept like a log last night,' Abigail said sweetly.

Elise rewarded her with a huge smile.

Something was out of sorts. Why were we not addressing the disappearance? I looked around and the helpers sidled in slightly from the wall, as if they were ready to pounce on me.

'Where's Caroline?' I asked. A hard knot had formed in my stomach.

'Caroline had to leave,' Elise said.

'Where did she go?' I asked.

'Back home.'

'But why would she leave now? Did something happen?'

'It doesn't concern you,' Elise said.

And I wanted to shout back at her, because it was obviously too much of a coincidence. A scream in the night and then Caroline suddenly disappears into thin air? It could have been her, though I'd never heard her scream before.

I looked to Sally for support, but she averted her eyes.

'Don't you think it's strange?' I addressed both Sally and Abigail in one last try.

There was a long pause.

'Nothing happened last night,' Elise said. 'You heard a fox outside; you jumped to conclusions. We all do it, but that's the end. That's the story. Forget about it.'

To be told off by her was unbearable. The way she was lecturing me was too frustrating, and I walked out of the room. I just wanted to get away. No one stopped me leaving, so I went into the main entrance hall, sweating, unsure of where to go. I knew I needed to be far from them all, so I jogged out through the front door.

Outside, the sprinkler hissed at me, and I ran to distance myself further from the house. I reached the water, and there I saw them. It was all wrong; they were floating on the surface, their bodies like dull confetti.

The koi.

As I went closer, I expected to see them writhe in the water, but they didn't move. Dead eyes staring at me as they lay on their sides with their lips pursed in final kisses. They were horrible, their faces expressionless, and I wanted to be sick, but also I felt immensely hungry in that moment. I could have ripped open a fish and crammed it down my throat. I tried to quieten the urge, to push it away deep down and focus on what they were.

Dead fish. Was it real? Were the fish really dead?

'Betsy!'

It was Elise. She came to me, and we stood over the water.

She placed her hand low on the small of my back, presumably to comfort me. 'Tell me,' she said.

It just came out like vomit, with shame hot in my cheeks as I spoke. 'They make me feel hungry.'

Disgusting.

Elise didn't care. She pressed her hands together and squealed, and then she recovered and went back to comforting me. 'It's fine,' she said. 'These things happen. It's the heat, the algae. You're very special, Betsy. You show it to me every day. Every single day here.'

I thought of our sessions. She started most of them with this insistence that I had such admirable qualities. I squirmed under her attention. I had noticed that Elise told me I was special so often. Repetition, this was what Harry did too, repeating his questioning: *Where do you see yourself in five years*, he would say, bludgeoning me with the demand until I came up with a response.

'You're thinking about Caroline?' Elise said.

I nodded.

'Forget about the others,' she said. 'Concentrate on you. We're away from the world in a place for recovery. Someone like you needs this place because you're not like other people. Some people move through the world with ease, don't they? Nothing touches them. You know those kinds of people? Normal people.'

I agreed. Easy for the normal people. Siobhan was one. Harry was one.

There was such empathy in her expression. Even if I didn't trust Elise, I couldn't resist letting her coddle me, because she offered that deep understanding and a kindness that I could barely believe.

You're lovely, you're special.

That was what she said in our sessions. It might have been overkill for some people . . . but not for me. My mother would never have called me lovely or special. I don't think I'd encountered empathy that also seemed tinged with adoration. I just loved the way she was with me, and that made me weak.

We stayed there a little longer. When I returned to the house, the others weren't around. I watched from the window and saw the helpers stride out to the water. They cleared up the fish from the moat with a long net and I saw Make-up Helper and Driver Helper argue for a few minutes as they negotiated the angle to scoop them out.

An hour later, it was like nothing had happened; the pink waters rippled with a slight current and the fish were all gone.

When I dream someone is dead, I desperately want to touch them as soon as I wake up. This happened all the time with Harry. After my nights were filled with unpleasant images, I'd grasp for his arm when morning came, sweating and chaotic, and he'd look at me, confused. *You're fine*, he would say, *just your imagination*.

When I'd dreamed of Abigail, I experienced that same impulse later – the necessity of touching skin when you're losing the plot.

We sat on the swing together that morning. I reached out for her hand. She didn't pull away; she didn't seem to think it was a strange gesture. We held hands without comment.

'Caroline's missing,' I said. 'I don't understand why no one else finds that worrying.'

There was more I could say. How I was quite preoccupied by it. How every time the house stirred, I thought it was Caroline. When a door opened or I heard someone approaching, I kept expecting her to come in. This hadn't happened, and I'd come to understand rationally that I'd probably never see her again and to ignore this instinct. Everyone else seemed resigned to the fact that she was gone.

Abigail and I swung away, and the sunlight warmed our skin.

'She left.' Abigail pointed her toes, and she focused on stretching her legs. She wouldn't meet my eye.

Like grit in the shoe, the thought was there annoying me. The last thing Caroline had done was warn me to stay away from Abigail.

'Do you really think she left?' I probed.

'Oh, I don't know,' she said. We came down and she pressed her feet against the ground and pushed us off with so much strength, we went higher than before.

Was Abigail a good person?

Did she care at all for others, or for me?

She didn't show it in the ways I would expect.

We went so high.

I clung to her instinctively, and she clasped on to me as if we were drowning and I could keep her afloat. Sweaty little arm on mine, nails digging in.

23.

'Will we go to the library tonight?' Abigail asked me after dinner a few days later.

Usually, the evenings formed an unremarkable slice of time compared to our sessions with Elise, where she massaged our egos and we told her our stories.

It was still light after we ate, but we often just went to our separate bedrooms. I didn't mind the quiet so much, and there was the sense that evenings were purely for relaxation. About one in three evenings, though, we ended up in the library for an hour or so. We went there willingly as soon as the plates were cleared, and I couldn't have told you who led the decision, but it just seemed to happen – a second burst of energy after dinner.

'They say they're opening a bottle of port,' Abigail said. 'Expensive stuff too.'

She meant the helpers. They were outside the room, far enough away from us that I couldn't hear anything, but Abigail picked up on it all.

Port sounded good, and then the best part of the day would arrive – when I went to my room to get my pill. The itch of anticipation was already there. A dash of port could only help.

They brought in canapés once we'd arrived in the library, buttery parcels filled with meat. An odd dessert.

Dig in, they said. *Dig in*. I still felt hungry, so I took one, and a glass of port. Without enthusiasm, Abigail picked up a canapé too, and we sat down.

I was surprised Abigail didn't want to come here every night. The soft furnishings ate up noise, so it was like putting your head underwater in the bath. The room was very pleasant with little mushroom-shaped lamps dotted around and a set of plump sofas opposite each other for full conversational effect – no TV, of course. Everything you'd see in a traditional library apart from real books. The tall shelves that lined the walls had fake ones bound in leather. If you opened them, every single page was blank.

We weren't alone; the helpers trundled along as usual. They sat away from us, by the door, and they watched as Abigail knocked back shots of port. Sally was peaceful from the off, spaced out by that point in the evening. I thought she was playing a game of chess against herself (something I'd only ever seen done in films), but I realized she was just pushing the pieces round the board in a sluggish rotation.

'Would you like to play?' she said to me, eager and a little desperate.

She had seemed a bit out of sorts since Caroline had disappeared, and I was aware we were probably leaving her out. I should have said yes, but the idea made me weary.

'No, not now,' I called from upside down because Abigail and I were doing legs against the wall, pushing up until the base of our spines touched near the skirting board. I'd heard it was good for the nervous system. Abigail said it made her *super horny*, and that was *very good*.

Sally continued to push her pieces around, looking a bit miserable. Then the helpers approached her with a large tray.

Sally looked up and nodded, like she understood what they wanted without them having to say anything.

On the tray were some items I didn't recognize, though I was watching the whole thing from upside down so my vantage point was distorted. It was an eclectic assortment: a tuft of crusty old fabric, something that resembled the battered skull of a small mammal, some tubing that could have been medical, but so many other things too. They gave her hardly any time, under half a minute, and then Smiler Helper did a thumbs-up and they covered the tray with a sheet.

126

Sally took a deep breath, and then she recited the items. 'Catheter, ribbon, needle, scissors, ace of spades, fishing hook . . .'

The way the helpers nodded made it clear she was getting it right.

I wasn't too surprised. She had told me about her excellent memory, and they were testing it, though I had no idea why.

The helpers cooed and applauded her.

Abigail watched next to me, and her skirt came down further as she fidgeted. Her legs were hairy, dry and marked in the spaces between where they'd been inked.

'What are those bruises?' I asked.

She had been fine the other day, but there they were, marks no bigger than coins. I saw they were peeking out from the backs of her knees too.

'Oh, yeah, I don't know how I got them. Sometimes things just happen here,' she said, not overly concerned. 'Could have been before we came here, like a delay. That's a thing.'

'You'd remember how you got so many, surely?'

'I dunno,' she said breezily. 'That felt amazing in my hamstrings.'

'How can you not know?'

'Oh, there are . . . chunks of time here that I can't recall. It's all a bit of a daze, isn't it?'

I nodded.

Abigail slid down the wall and stood. She shook her shoulders. I didn't know what she was doing. There was no music, but she stood in the centre of the room and danced. It was disjointed, all elbows and rough, pointed movements, as she swayed to a song playing in her head, and the dance should have been terribly awkward, but it wasn't at all. It was a beautiful thing. She moved clumsily, but remained herself, taking up space and showing no embarrassment.

I was so smitten with her. The confidence. It was for me, I was sure of it, because she looked at me occasionally from beneath lowered eyelids. Only Abigail could do it, perform in this way, and she edged closer and closer to me. I realized I was holding my breath, and it was just the two of us. She gasped, fast, almost like she was choking, like it was paining her, an exquisite show. We were building to something. All I could do was watch until the spell was broken by a helper who cleared her throat and filled up my glass of port.

Abigail jumped and came to. She moved over to lie on one of the sofas, her dance abandoned. Soon, her eyes were closed, and her lids flickered. The faint taps continued as Sally moved her chess pieces around the board, set against the low whispers of the helpers.

I heard something.

A cough?

I thought Abigail must have heard it too, but I looked over and she was snoring lightly.

It was a distinctly human noise, something that came from the throat and not from anyone who was in the room.

The hairs on my neck rose and my skin tingled. I scanned the rest of them. Sally continued to move her pieces. The helpers were not focused on me; they had gathered in the far corner.

I was unobserved. I didn't care to draw attention to myself, but I wanted to see what was going on. Slowly, I walked over to the bookshelves where the noise might have come from, and I heard it again.

It was more distinct the second time. A hacking cough.

The cough was coming . . . from the wall.

I reached for a book, flicked through the empty pages.

Silence again.

I loitered around the bookshelf. For a while, nothing happened. Edging in, I moved a book to one side, and then I saw it – though it was certainly supposed to be hidden – a perfectly circular hole in the wall, with books positioned to disguise it.

There was a split second where I had to decide what to do. Everyone else seemed deeply relaxed and no one was paying attention to me. So, I bent down as if I was returning the book to its place.

I looked through the hole. Whoever was on the other side, I could only see the shine of their eye. They did not turn away from me. The eyelid came down as they blinked. There was nothing about it that I could make a judgement on, because there was no way to see an expression, but then I heard the muffled clearing of a throat, connecting the eye to the very real person looking in.

The sound threw everything back into reality, and I had to stop myself from screaming out. Then a louder cough, which no one else seemed to hear. A slam as blackness came down over the peephole on the other side, shutting me out.

I turned away. It wasn't fear I felt in that moment, it was revulsion.

People living in the walls at Carn.

Watching us all the time? Who were they?

I moved away from the bookshelf. Everything was back to normal. I'd managed to do it all without any of them noticing, and so I walked to a sofa. As I sat, a helper looked up from her conversation, but didn't say anything. She didn't know what I'd seen.

Elise entered the room, and she came over to me and Abigail. She held out her hand.

'Do you want to go up to bed now?' she asked. 'It's getting late.'

I nodded.

In my bedroom, I lay down, and I heard a smooth click. I'd heard it many times and hadn't connected it to anything, but that night I rose and went to the door, pulled hard on the handle. It moved a fraction, but then I could feel the metal of a bolt holding it in place. I tried again. It wouldn't budge.

Locked.

It was so obvious. The door had probably been locked each night, and I'd never thought to even try to open it. I had lain there, always. Received my pill so many times and waited for sleep.

24.

The next morning, I considered my options.

I couldn't bear to go to Elise with what I'd discovered in the library. I knew she'd deny it, and her voice would change, become cold, strung with disappointment. The solution was there: I could just ask to leave, demand it even. Walk away from everything. Put a stop to it all and never delve further. Pack up my things. Forget Carn. As I lay there in bed, waiting for the click as the door unlocked – I had adjusted to being locked in with remarkable ease – I pushed the idea away.

The thing was, I was so much better. Sleep was better, and I was ravenous most days, waking up desperate for breakfast. My growing appetite was a positive sign. The clothes they'd provided had been a little loose at the beginning but now they fitted well.

If I left, I would have to believe that Carn's effects would be long-lasting, that I would stay like this: alive and well. I just didn't *want* to leave. Plus, there wasn't any imminent danger, and I didn't believe Elise would let any harm come to me, or to any of us.

I understood that they weren't going to listen to me, and so I needed to piece it together and work out what was on the other side of the library myself. Work out why they were looking at us. That was where to begin. But I also wanted to know why Caroline had warned me off Abigail. So, I edged closer to Abigail, which was no hardship.

She wanted to walk laps in the mornings, the same route always around the lawns until our feet marked a path on the grass; it must have been hundreds of times.

'The sky here is different,' Abigail said, and she linked her arm in mine.

'Bluer?' I asked. 'Yes, I see it too.'

'It seems so wide.'

'It does,' I agreed.

We could talk about Carn all day, but I wanted more. I wanted to go into her head, wrench out more from her.

'Tell me about back home?' I asked.

Speaking of her adulthood was off-limits, as per Elise's rules, and Abigail had given me so little. I didn't blame her, as I hadn't shared much either.

She considered my request seriously. 'You want to know about outside of Carn?' she asked, letting our steps fall into time with each other, and I noted the bruises up her legs again. She seemed well, though. Bold and less anxious about noise. The frenetic energy that had fizzed through her initially had lessened. She stopped staring at the sky and loosened her arm from mine. We walked and walked, just in circles, and in the end she spoke.

Abigail grew up near a seaside town, but it wasn't somewhere that anyone came to for holidays. There were boarded-up arcades and fish-and-chip shops that made the air smell of grease all year round. The beach was always windy; the sea, thick with grit, sloshed in white-fringed waves.

She wished she had a topsy-turvy house, an old one with creaky stairs and wooden floors, but her family lived in a modern cul-de-sac. There was a moment when she'd first heard the term cul-de-sac, and it had sounded so exotic that she couldn't tally it with the actual street they lived on, one with houses that all looked the same.

They'd often go into the other houses on the street, and she always enjoyed it when she found a difference. A wall that wasn't quite the same; a room that was slightly bigger; or in some cases even an *extra room*.

She got on fine with her sister and her parents – she brushed my questions about them away. She was an easy teenager; she thought so anyway. Yes, she spoke back, and she was loud, and teachers called her overconfident like it was bad, like she was a bad person, but she wasn't.

Something always felt off, but it wasn't even something she could really identify. She didn't think she fitted in with her family, and she asked if she was adopted once. Her parents didn't understand why she would ask something like that. Perhaps that was a normal teenage feeling and, looking back, she had thought at the time that she'd grow out of it, but she didn't grow out of the persistent state of unease, and it developed further into a creeping belief that she was unwelcome, and that things were not right, that she was living the wrong life.

An intruder – that's how she described herself. When she came home from school and opened the door, the house tightened up and braced for her entry.

Her father had a habit of eating a tuna sandwich every day. She smelled it as soon as she came in – here, Abigail stopped her story and mimicked a retch.

'Abby, tell me about your day?' her father would call as he heard the door slam.

So, one day he asked, and it was a normal question; she hovered with her bag over one shoulder, feeling the urge to get away, but that was normal too. Then, he took a big bite of his sandwich, just as he did each afternoon. She could see the ratio of mayonnaise to tuna – far too high.

The sound of his eating was insufferable, which made no sense. She heard it often when she walked through the living room to get to the kitchen after school. The same routine for years, and then one day something happened and the noise had a violence that was malevolent – a nail in her brain.

Each bite forced more saliva around his mouth, and it almost squeaked. Time slowed down as he chewed. He was oblivious to her discomfort at first, until he asked her, 'What on earth's wrong?'

It was a legitimate question, and she had no idea. She was stunned by how quickly the sensation had left.

'Are you okay?' he pushed.

She was. It was because he'd stopped eating the sandwich. The feeling had subsided.

That was the first time it happened, and she'd thought it was just a one-off, but reluctantly she added more sounds to the list: coughing and sneezing; the screech of cutlery on plates; chairs scraping against tiles. All sounds she encountered many times during the day.

When she explained it to her family, they were initially sympathetic, if a little confused by the whole thing – it seemed like it was all in her head. The doctors couldn't really explain why she was struggling, and they said it was a case of *keeping an eye on it and taking it day by day*.

Her parents were also unwilling to let their fourteen-year-old daughter dictate the noise output of the house. They thought pandering to her might make it worse, and so she ended up retreating to her room, skipping school.

That was how it started with Abigail. It wasn't constant. She would be fine for a while, and then she would be unwell again, and it became impossible to predict. It was what life was, with ups and downs.

She wouldn't go any further, and her story ended.

I wanted more. Did she have a job? A partner? What was her life like on the outside? Thoughts kept popping into my head. I circled back to that first night for clues. The way she'd struggled to eat and Elise had kind of coaxed her. There was something going on with Abigail and food. I wondered if it traced back to this story of a tuna sandwich that seemed to have started it all, but it seemed like the most personal thing, and it didn't feel right to push.

'Elise knows all this?' I asked.

'She knows,' Abigail said.

I nodded and bit into an apple I'd picked up from breakfast, but it was too tart to finish. Abigail only flinched slightly at the crunch of my teeth on the skin.

'How are you getting on with the room?' I asked.

'Good, most of the time,' she said breezily. Then she lowered her voice. 'This place . . . there's more to it than you think.'

I regarded her. A sense of déjà vu from Caroline's warning.

'What do you mean?' I asked gently, not wanting to scare her.

'You just need to trust it.'

What did she know? I wanted to involve her; maybe we could share intel. I took a second and considered what part of Carn I could talk about.

'Abigail . . . they lock us in at night. The rooms, they all lock.' I spoke calmly and turned to look straight at her, so I could gauge her reaction.

'Really?' she asked.

'Well, mine does. I tried to get out. I'm pretty sure yours will be the same.'

'Weird,' she said.

I kept pushing. 'The question is, *why* would they do that? They don't want us out wandering around at night. What do you think we'd find?'

Silence.

'Do you not even care?' I asked.

She was peaceful, but I saw a flicker of indecision too.

We were far from the house. Her face became shadowed by the trees and she came close to me; she didn't stop. She leaned right in and kissed me.

The smell of her was everything Harry wasn't. She was cheap floral body spray, heavy, but she still smelled of herself, of sun cream, of something real and grassy underneath. She was made of a different substance to Harry, something more fluid, but she was not softer. Abigail was a quick current, lips jammed into mine, and my head spun with it all. It made me want to eat her up, but still I pulled away from her to see her expression.

She was so beautiful to me. A white linen shirt flowed around her body, her short hair so dark against her pale clothes.

She laughed. 'I'm not concerned about the doors locking,' she said. 'I wanted to do that. To see how it felt.'

A kiss that wasn't leading to anything else; our bodies only just touched. It was something, though. Abigail went in again for another kiss, and then there was pain as she bit down. I let out a squeal. She licked her lips and walked away.

25.

In our sessions, Elise was probing into my sleep. I didn't want to tell her how the nights had started to impact the days back in Edinburgh. I didn't tell her about how it disintegrated with Harry.

A few years into our relationship, I woke up and I was convinced Harry was a lizard, specifically a leopard gecko. A human-sized one.

The leopard gecko walked upright like a human, with tiny scales all over his face and a lank tail behind him. He had a fringe.

Harry as the gecko approached the kitchen island and picked up the cafetière. I stared at him with what must have been horror plastered on my face. It only lasted for a few seconds and then the scales faded and I snapped right out of it. He became a man in an expensive suit. You see, I was not going mad, it was just that the nights were dripping into the days again.

Harry knew something was up, even more than usual. Things were getting worse and worse, and he'd seen the way my face went grey for weeks on end as sleep became my obsession.

Once I'd recovered, I tried to smile at him.

'What's wrong?' he asked, but he didn't really want to know.

'Nothing.'

I needed to wait for the right moment.

'Hmmm. You were looking at me weirdly.' He sat down at the kitchen counter, and I knew what he was going to say.

'Bets . . .' he started.

My heart sank. I knew what was coming. He had his phone out as if he was going to take notes. 'We need to get serious about this, about long-term plans,' he said gently. 'Where do you see yourself in five years in terms of your job?' he asked.

Always Harry's question.

I did not like my job. It was the one before the freckle job – a bit of admin and a bit of marketing. I went every day, but it was impossible to see five years into the future.

That day when he asked me, I gawped at him. He leaned across the expanse of white kitchen island, making direct eye contact. I shrugged and edged around the question by offering to cook him breakfast.

I had ignored his question, but he was unperturbed. He'd ask again. With time I was more forgiving to these questions. I think he was broaching the subject of children without outright asking. I couldn't explain to him that I did not trust myself to have a baby when I was unwell. We never quite managed the conversation.

And so he talked about his work. Harry had become markedly more senior, and I could see why. He pounced upon thorny problems and scrambled to untie them; he could make difficult decisions with ease. Through the ranks he rose and earned more and more, which meant he wanted more and more. And part of that was this obsession with organizing our lives.

He told me some complicated story with lots of office politics.

'– with Carrie it's laziness,' he sighed. 'I see it all the time. They expect the world, these newbies, but you need to pay your dues.'

'Which one's Carrie again?' I asked.

He was annoyed that I'd forgotten who she was, but he proceeded to describe her in unflattering terms.

'I wanted to talk to you about my sleep,' I jumped in.

He was surprised that I'd interrupted, but he adjusted quickly. 'Really?' he said with a yawn. 'Again? It doesn't help so much to dwell on it. Lots of people struggle with sleep.' He closed down the conversation.

Harry had decided a long time ago that it was insomnia. He

regarded me as a tired and placid creature, a hamster, and he liked that, until I had tried to explain it properly. I saw straight through him. He didn't want me to be chaotic, but mild insomnia he was fine with. After all, it's a normal and treatable state, like a headache or back pain. It could be seen as a positive thing, associated with the stress of hard work. People claimed it as an ailment with a sense of pride, *Oh I can never switch off, I'm an insomniac*, and I think when Harry first heard it, he considered it to be an almost pleasant quirk.

He moved away from the island. I saw a cloud of confusion in his face as he started to make a protein shake, shooting the occasional glance at me.

Why was my path always so full of obstacles, when his was always clear?

The thing is, while things were not good with us, he just pushed through, as if we could get to the next part and then all would be better. Harry collected milestones, and so, many months later, when we were in a restaurant, his behaviour was predictable.

A chocolate egg that I hadn't ordered came out of the kitchen, accompanied by two waiters. People watched because it was a marbled affair; creamy white and milk chocolate mixed together and wrapped up in a nest of threaded sugar. Clearly for me, because there was a swirling 'B' etched on top. The waiter laid it down.

I knew what *this* was, and I was aware that after I responded things would change. With a hard smash of a spoon, I cracked it open. The ring sat there nestled in a scabby pile of chocolate shavings. I was pretty clueless when it came to jewellery, but it was still impressive: a large diamond with a lemony hue to it. Harry to a T. He had taste, everyone said so. The other tables had twigged, and they took pictures.

'So, what do you think?' he asked with an almost cruel smile. Not the right question, but he did get down on one knee. He didn't seem nervous, and I could feel him enjoying everyone looking at us.

I said yes.

Yes, yes, a thousand times yes. Because what else was there to say?

The people around us were clapping loudly, drinking it all in and adding it to their personal list of experiences. One woman was crying, and when I looked at her, she wiped the tears away quickly, like she was stealing emotions that didn't belong to her.

Later, I found out that he hadn't asked my parents. That was fine; it would have been old-fashioned, and it wasn't as if we were close. I imagined my brothers clapping and cheering when I told them in a group text. They were all married and would be pleased. Once people get married and have children, they seem keen that others follow suit.

His family congratulated us, through him. Everyone *loved* the engagement story; they pawed at the ring and wanted to hear every tiny part of the tale.

I told myself I said yes because we were in love, but it was more than that. By that point only Harry could protect me, even if he didn't quite like who I was. Just me and him, and there was no one else. However messy and terrible it was, we were tied together. Surely no one else would have me?

In our sessions, Elise wanted to go deeper and deeper. I think I knew where she was going, but I didn't give her what she wanted. I didn't tell her what happened later, or about the long, long stretch of time where I kept myself awake, teetering on the edge of madness. I didn't tell her about how, before the wedding, I had tried to hold it together, but this had not been completely successful.

26.

At Carn, the small pains that I'd noticed at the outset continued with a predictable frequency over the next week. At dinner, the knives were serrated. A random piece of stainless steel appeared at the door with a sharpness, set against the frothiness of this pink dream house for effect. It jutted out and I nearly sliced open my arm.

The helpers knew, expected it even. They were there to bandage us up; on hand with tweezers to extract splinters when required. Abigail held out her hand promptly to be fixed like it was the most natural thing in the world. These minor ailments were sobering, and they didn't deter me. I wasn't going to leave; I wasn't the tired little creature who couldn't cope.

I felt confident that I could stay and work out what was going on. The kiss hadn't scared me; it had spurred me on to explore further. Like there was something she was telling me, but I just didn't know what. And so I had a new plan: gather up as much information as possible. And the long days lent themselves well to this scheme.

First, I thought to go back to the soundproofed room and the operating theatre, but I also wanted to find new parts of the house. There was more to discover, and that belief expanded over time. We'd been living and interacting with a fraction of the footprint of the place. The house was vast, and I needed to understand what else made up Carn.

I thought the helpers could be the key to unlocking it. They went everywhere, darting from room to room, and they had become lax in their surveillance of us. So, one morning, when no one was around – it was a dead part of the day when we all dispersed after breakfast – I went to the other side of the house. I was set on finding the helpers, but there was no more of a plan than that. I was winging it, but their voices led me with a sing-song chatter, and I followed the sound along a corridor directly off the main entrance. I had thought it led to a boiler room or something when I first arrived but, over time, I'd seen helpers go in and out. From the outside, if I mapped the house, it was clear there was a whole wing with curtains drawn, so from outside on the lawns it was impossible to see inside.

I walked down the corridor, and the walls turned to bare brick. I examined each side for peepholes as I went, but there were none. The corridor seemed to stretch on and on, but it wasn't like the hidden hallway I'd been in before; it was tatty with ripped wallpaper.

At the end, I found what appeared to be an office, the door slightly open. I could hear voices. I looked in, but stayed pressed against the wall in the corridor, quiet as anything so they didn't see me. There, I saw a space unlike any other at Carn, and I found the room very jarring, because it reminded me of the disorder of the outside world. The furniture was temporary and mismatched, which worked in my favour as there was a stack of cardboard boxes obscuring me.

The helpers sat in the middle of the room at wide computer screens. I saw papers all over the desks alongside other things, including one of those flasks that forces you to drink too much water with little motivational quotes spilling down the side: *Nearly there, hydration queen!*

They were jolly in their office. Some were in jeans, chatting away, their voices loud – giggling even. To listen to them was to let the outside in, because they were talking about normal things. One was telling a story about probiotics. Another nodded in agreement, then changed the conversation and asked about a spreadsheet formula.

Big flasks did not belong at Carn.

Spreadsheets did not belong at Carn.

I heard one say Abigail's name and another let out a groan, but I didn't hear why, it was all muffled.

'Need to get cooking soon,' one said. She typed into a scientific calculator.

A helper grunted something I couldn't make out. I thought it could be Driver Helper.

'Her daughter,' she said and then lowered her voice. Gossipy. 'We're not supposed to talk about her!'

'Seriously . . .' one jumped in. 'We're not supposed to.'

A gasp and then silence.

I edged back down the corridor.

A daughter.

They must have been talking about Elise, and there had been no mention of a daughter before, but why should there have been? It wasn't like I had much of an insight into who Elise was. She knew lots about me, but what I understood about her was limited. I'd quizzed Patrick about her before I'd left, and I'd asked him about her family, about her background, trying to pin down as much as I could, but he'd closed up and shuffled away down into his basement.

Mothers and daughters were a frequent source of interest. My mother and I hadn't spoken for a while. Not that we'd had some huge falling-out – in some ways that would have been easier – but we spoke less and less, and eventually news of the family seemed to come from other sources, like my brothers' wives.

After the wedding, I went over to see my mother, and I told her I wasn't sure that it was working out between Harry and me. She didn't give me advice, though she did hand me a gift voucher for a massage. I was so disappointed, and my eldest brother called me afterwards. *She was just being nice! Treat yourself, Betsy, you'll feel so much better.* But I couldn't feel better. I had tried hard for a long time, but I couldn't change who I was, and everything she said was wrong. She wanted me to be different; she didn't understand why I wasn't like my brothers. To not be understood at all was the loneliest place to live.

I had looked to Elise as a kind of mother figure from the moment I'd seen her at the hospital. I'd experienced a physical reaction to her comfort, and as soon as I'd cast her in this part, it created a certain idea of who I wanted her to be. I had never imagined a daughter. I had always, always pictured Elise unencumbered: bagless and childless.

For some reason, it changed everything, and when I had my opportunity for questions in my sessions with Elise, I didn't ask about the things I should have. When it came down to it, the peephole should have been my priority, but in the sunroom where the air was heavy and hot, I asked Elise about her daughter.

27.

Elise blinked rapidly in a confused state when I asked, but she recovered. 'You remind me of her,' she said. 'You both have that same urge to get to the truth, a questioning kind of nature.'

I think I must have looked confused.

'It's not unnatural,' she said with a sad smile. 'A sign of intelligence, probably. Anyway, she died. Five years ago, now. She was only twenty.'

I hadn't expected it. I was unsure how to react.

'I'm sorry,' I said. I meant I was sorry for even bringing it up.

'You want to know more?' Elise asked.

Of course I did. I didn't need to say yes, Elise kept speaking.

'She was an addict,' she said flatly. 'A drug addict. We were living in the US at the time. We lived all over before we came to Scotland. It didn't start that way, though. She injured her knee, you see, playing hockey, and they prescribed painkillers. The doctors didn't really seem to know any better. Now, they know better. Things are different now.

'The painkillers were so addictive. I could see when she first got them. But then, as far as I knew, she stopped taking them. She was fine for a few months and she seemed well. We didn't know anything was wrong.'

'Then what happened?'

'Well, we found out she hadn't been able to get off them.'

Who was *we*? A partner, perhaps?

Now, she spat out her words. 'Whenever she tried to come off them, she had awful side effects that she couldn't tolerate; she was ashamed. She hid how sick she was. And this is why I hate the story, Betsy, because it's so like all the others!

'She'd been stealing, she lied about that from the start. She was *extremely* ill. There were so many fabrications in the end, but it was impossible to see them at first because she seemed okay. She had good grades, you see. Athletic too, musical, set for Ivy League if she chose to stay in America, although we didn't push her, she pushed herself! She hid it all from us,' she continued. 'We thought she was moving out to stay with some friends because she never asked for any help, not once.'

'Asking for help is hard,' I said.

'It is, isn't it?' she pounced, agreeing with me. 'We moved quickly, though, when we found out.'

'What happened?'

'Well, we sent her away to a facility that offered a programme. I knew the success rate of those places. They weren't great but you grasp at anything when you're in that situation. Everyone said that was the right thing to do, scrape the money together. It's all you can do, and you're doing your best, trusting the experts because they know what works.'

'Yes,' I said. 'You trust the experts.'

She looked at me sharply. I had meant nothing by it, but she bristled, nonetheless.

'You think it's like here, don't you?' she said. 'That place was *not* like here. She was in and then out and then we tried another one, but it was no different. And we thought she'd be fine in the end, that we just needed to find the right place, but it's all the same techniques, for opioids. They have such a limited toolkit, but also their ideas about it all are . . . so limited too. She died. Died in some crack house.'

'Crack house' was not a term I'd expected to hear at Carn. This was not the type of conversation I wanted. I must have looked horrified because Elise's face softened.

'That was a lot. I shouldn't have said so much. It wasn't my intention to upset you.'

'I'm glad you told me.'

She sighed. 'I bring her up now, because she is the reason I do this work. Carn is the opposite of those kinds of places, and

146

you girls are special. Perhaps she wasn't as special as the three of you are.'

That statement shocked me, but she was breezy.

'It's why I understand about your aversion to pharmaceuticals,' she said with finality.

It was enough talking about the daughter, and we were straight back to me.

As usual, I gave her a happier, more functional version of me, a story about university, but it wasn't enough. She seemed frustrated with what I was saying; she wanted more, but I didn't know what to give. All this chat of Harry, constantly raking over our past, over our engagement and the chocolate egg; she glazed over slightly, looked out of the window, and it was time to be upfront.

'What do you want?' I asked, tired of dancing around it all. 'Just tell me what you think we should be talking about.'

Elise pursed her lips. 'Your dreams, Betsy,' she said, like it was obvious. 'Explain them to me.'

My stomach dropped. But I was not necessarily surprised. I had expected it, deep down. I kicked myself, because it had been crazy to think she would be able to solve my problems without me telling her about my dreams. I had thought I could just turn up and she'd help me sleep without me having to go there and tell her everything.

I saw that I needed to give her more and I would. I'd trusted the process and it felt good, like a weight off my shoulders. I had to open up. She'd help me.

'They are . . . a big part of the problem,' I said.

'Go on.' She was quite pleasant.

So where to begin? Still, the question stood: how did she know about my dreams? I had mentioned them to Patrick, but only in passing. I had never given any detail to him. My medical records, perhaps? This made me feel quite sick.

I didn't want to tell her the exact nature of my dreams; by talking about them I thought they'd return, and so I told her about a nice one instead.

It was about Abigail because, though my dreams were far reduced at Carn, I'd dreamed of her a little since I'd arrived, and then the kiss had led to more.

In this particular one, Abigail and I walked away from the house and we saw the lake. It was a jewel set in the gaps between pine trees. She tore her shoes off. She ripped away her dress and tossed it to the side without a care. I was jealous of how easy she was with her body; even in the dream those emotions persisted. Her skin was white; greying underwear with the elastic worn. There was the beginning of a thatch of black hair coming out of her knickers and tattoos dancing. And she charged straight in without a pause as the water consumed her body. Then she came out and pulled me in too, and she was sleek and almost scaled, reptilian like my leopard gecko Harry, with her short hair plastered to her head. I went in and, miraculously, I swam like a fish. No tiredness scrabbling at me. Abigail lay back in the water and it supported her entirely. I did the same. We were protected as the trees enveloped this perfect little lake. I reached out and took her hand in mine, and then it ended, and I woke up.

I told Elise about my dream in fits and starts.

This was what she had wanted.

'Fascinating,' she said. 'Sometimes we practise in our dreams, we go through the motions of things we need to do in the day. It makes us better able to cope with life.'

'Well, that was a good one. Usually, I don't enjoy them,' I said firmly. 'Still, it felt *so* real.'

She made a few notes and nodded, and then she put her pen and paper down.

'You know it's not, though, don't you?' she said. 'With this particular one you've just described, well, it couldn't be real.'

The scene had been so detailed, but she was right. I knew it wasn't real, because as a child I had screamed and cried at the mere suggestion of submersion. The water was too much, and my body shook each time my mother even mentioned it.

She knew about the dreams and she was probing more and

more at them. I had thought that she wanted to help me get rid of them. I had thought that was the whole point – to enable a deep and dreamless sleep – but I was starting to think this might not be the case.

That was not the most concerning thing, though, about the conversation.

It couldn't be real.
She clearly knew I could not swim.

28.

Picture me at six years old, heavy fringe rubbing against the top of my eyelashes. My mother commented one day that I had an intense stare, and she'd cut in a fringe (with love) to help soften me. But the fringe did not change who I was. I was still a serious child, shy around other children and hostile to adults.

I remember the harsh smell of chlorine and my bag over my shoulder so heavy, but most of all, I recall the stiffness that sat in every limb as I willed it all to be over. You see, we'd been bribed – promised snacks from the vending machine afterwards.

It's not your fault if you're not as fast as them. Boys are just better at swimming, my mother said in the car on the way, and then tried to backtrack. I waited for her to counteract with something girls were better at, but she did not.

I would not be as fast as them. My brothers had been learning for ages, and they headed to their advanced lessons. I could not swim; I'd been waiting for some time to start, but they hadn't been able to get me into a class. I was the youngest and my mother figured it was fine for me to learn late. She thought I'd pick it up easily, like my brothers had. It wasn't a big deal.

So, I stood at the side of the pool, shivering away. There were four of us in a line, two boys, me and another girl.

'Stay there,' the instructor said. 'Don't move.' And she faffed around with a clipboard. A big chunk of being a child revolves around the lethargy of waiting, of trusting some process you don't understand. We did as she said to begin with, though we fidgeted.

There was a combination of factors, all usual events that wouldn't lead to anything in isolation. The teenage lifeguard had skipped off to flirt near the changing rooms right on the other side of the pool, where he could only just about see what was going on. An administrative error meant too many lessons had been scheduled and there were too many children that day. An older boy in my brother's class ran along the poolside and crashed to the floor with a terrifying screech. Our teacher hurried over to help. Others crowded too, and the four of us were alone.

The two boys had moved off to the side; they were fighting. The girl didn't say a word to me, just surveyed the pool. She pulled at the gusset of her striped swimming costume, her chubby knees turning slightly inwards. She was too old to blame a lack of comprehension. We'd been told to stay there.

Wait, I thought. Although I didn't like adults, I was good at obeying them. I should have said it out loud but I didn't. We did not have any kind of interaction, and she didn't acknowledge me before she walked over to the steps and climbed in.

She was face down.

Did I stand there and watch?

I must have but I don't remember it looking like drowning. Surely I saw her flail in the water, but there is no recollection of any movement. There was no fear or urgency. I did nothing, and I should have shouted out straight away, but I was too young, my mother said when we talked about it. Far too young.

Twenty seconds they say, that's how long it can take to drown.

The sound of the teacher echoed around the pool, the scream as she saw, and she dived in, pulling the girl from the water. I remember wet hair covered her face, and her body looked far too heavy for the teacher to lift out.

Of course, they were careful with me afterwards. There was some attempt at counselling.

'She's fine,' my mother said, pushing me towards my brothers, back into the pack. 'She didn't see much; she didn't understand.'

Incorrect. I thought of the drowned girl all the time as I got older; instead of fading, she became more real. I imagined my lungs filling with water and at first my mother said, you should go back and learn to swim, and that might be the cure. Maybe it would have been, but I refused.

In controlled circumstances I craved water, and I went in the bath every day. At thirteen, I would run the bath and lie in it, the warm water around me all snug. Once, I added bubbles and then submerged my entire self, closed my eyes, felt everything and nothing, like I was about to burst, and my mother rushed in shouting.

After that they didn't send me back to learn. *Open up more,* that's what they said. *Open up to people and tell them how you feel.*

So, I tried. I talked about how I felt, and my brothers made faces. They breezed through the rest of childhood with a catalogue of normal problems. They had fleeting colds and sinus infections. Nothing serious. As a family, we didn't do serious. I was not the same, and I struggled with sleep after it happened, but it's not even called insomnia when you're a child. It was just being a bad sleeper.

My brothers kept their distance, because I had already infected my mother.

You're only as happy as your unhappiest child.

So, my mother was unhappy, and she was frequently more protective with me; she didn't want to expose me to anything that might be upsetting. I found I got on better with those who struggled with their health: the elderly relatives in particular. We visited them in their overheated houses and the conversation was a relaxing litany of health concerns; they spoke about their hips and their backs and their blood pressure, and I enjoyed that.

When I got older, I was able to find out who the drowned girl was with a quick search online. It was all I could think of. By the time I left to go to university, I was spending more and more time alone, struggling in the long nights.

I remember the T-shirt my mother wore in that final summer before I left. *Boy Mama* on the front, above an illustration of a woman flexing her bicep. I don't know if she bought it for herself or if someone else bought it for her. I'm not sure which would have been worse.

In my sessions with Elise, we'd never discussed this part of my childhood, so how did she know? I thought back to when Elise had seen me look over the water on that first day – there had been a shared understanding of my deficiencies that I had pushed away at the time.

I hadn't told her what had happened in the pool, because it wasn't something I ever talked about. Harry didn't know much about it either, though he was aware that I couldn't swim, and he had offered to teach me a few times.

So, like my dreams, this information must have come from Patrick. I kicked myself at the memory of our conversation. He'd been off on one: *Water is good for healing. Always has been. Good for the body. Good for the soul too. Do you happen to go to the pool?* I'd started to tell him that I couldn't swim, and it just came out even though it wasn't something I admitted very often. He'd slithered over to me, his interest ignited.

Leaving Carn would take more than just walking away; they'd need to let me go. This was why the helpers were fading in their presence. There was no reason to keep watch over me all the time, they knew I couldn't leave because I couldn't cross the water alone. I'd always have to make the request. Then it would be up to them to decide whether they'd allow it.

Elise was waiting for me to ask, I was sure of it, sat there waiting for me to tell her I wanted to go back to Edinburgh, but I wouldn't do it. I wasn't ready.

29.

When the men came, they were unannounced.

I walked down the stairs for breakfast and saw three helpers bent over, peering at an insect infestation. Ants worked their way out from deep in the walls and ran across the hall.

This kind of thing was not an uncommon task for the helpers. The house was part of their remit, and it seemed more and more adversarial as time passed. One day, pipes burst outside the door, and we watched from inside as the water sank into the front lawn. Carn was noisy at night too, unstable. A few times I stirred to that choking, warbling kind of scream that Elise had been so keen to write off as a fox, and the clang of metal from downstairs. These were unsettling changes, but I did not focus on them as my routine stayed the same: the dry gulp of the pill; the click locking me in.

I went over to look at the ants, and I passed the photographs. Light fell on them, changing the composition, and I realized what they were. The purple, you could see it so clearly now and, like some optical illusion, I couldn't unsee it. I had assumed they were landscapes, but they were bruises. Striking bruises; a rich kaleidoscope of purples and blacks framed with thick white borders and a greenish yellow. There was fat that puckered slightly, and it made me shiver. They reminded me of Abigail's bruises dotted up and down her legs.

I stared.

Had Elise taken these photographs?

A helper finished up her insect inspection and sidled over to me. 'Beautiful, aren't they?' she said, like we were friends.

'They're bruises,' I stated.

'Bruises, yes.'

We both looked at them together. We did not speak, and that felt respectful to the skin.

The other two helpers were chatting away, bent down over the skirting boards, sweeping up ants. They were growing more careless by the day, speaking like I wasn't in earshot.

Their voices rose and fell.

'It's so hot! I didn't think it ever got this hot in Scotland,' one said in the easy tone they used amongst themselves. But then Driver Helper sounded annoyed and said something I couldn't make out.

The helpers had so much information, and I willed them silently to continue.

'What do you mean?' the other asked as she aimed a spray can at the ants.

'It's not what I signed up for. It's so fucked up, and you know it.'

The helper who stood next to me was still staring dreamily at the photographs, oblivious to what I could hear.

I picked up more fragments.

'. . . doctor. I can't believe she'd take a doctor in.'

'. . . I can't bear mealtimes. I thought I could hack it but it's grim, and I can't bear seeing her.'

Their voices went low. The helper next to me clocked what I was hearing and came to; she'd remembered she had a job to do and she tore her gaze away from the bruises, peering at me to see what I'd heard. I ignored her and kept looking at the photos like I hadn't heard a thing.

Bruise Helper. That was her new name.

'Actually, I was looking for you,' Bruise Helper said as if it had just occurred to her. 'Elise is running something; come through to the drawing room now.'

I mulled over the other helpers' words.

Who couldn't they bear seeing?

What was the issue with mealtimes?

Then, Bruise Helper deposited me in the drawing room. It was reconfigured with chairs laid out in rows and music playing. I was struck by it because they never played music at Carn, but that day a concerto of violins came from somewhere.

Elise strode in and took my hand. Then she led me up to the front of the room and left me there, so I was looking out on to the rows of empty chairs. My stomach heaved because it was like my wedding, with the same sense of occasion and the understanding that I would be the focus.

There was no time to panic or prepare. It wasn't long before men started to filter in, and I just stood there. They all avoided making eye contact with me as they took their seats. Then, some looked up. Some seemed lascivious. Some seemed purely clinical in their scrutiny, and those were the ones who scared me. Many were much older than I was. I noticed when they were coming in that one hobbled a little and another winced as he sat.

The men settled in and some treated it like a business seminar. One got a laptop out, but the person next to him shook his head silently. The laptop owner slid it away into a bag without making a fuss.

I wanted to leave. I had a rushing desire to just run from the room, but that was not an option as there was a helper guarding me. She'd slunk over to position herself at my elbow.

'Welcome, everyone,' Elise said, and there was a chorus response, a subdued greeting back at her.

'Thank you all for coming.' She opened her arms to the crowd, a confident presenter.

'Now, do take notes,' she said to them. Some had notepads and charcoal pencils. She turned to me. 'You just need to stand here. Relax. Nothing more is required.'

A few minutes passed. I followed the instructions, and I stood there. The people in the crowd looked at me, and they whispered to each other every so often. Some jotted notes.

There was someone in the crowd that I recognized from the

outside world; the face was familiar in a way I couldn't place at first, and then it clicked. I didn't know him, but I'd seen him on TV. He ran a media company, though I couldn't remember his name. And there, right at the back, was the man from the window who'd toppled over on that first day. I could tell it was him because he was so terribly gaunt. He seemed delighted, though, and he smiled at me widely. I stared back.

Elise was speaking again. 'Think about how you . . . feel,' she said to the crowd, and they all nodded. Some had their eyes closed in something like ecstasy.

It was like I'd been there for hours, and I was desperate to leave. But time is a funny thing, and it was probably only five or ten minutes that passed as the crowd took their notes as directed. My skin was burning up, and I was breathing faster than usual. All I could do was look past them outside to the forest, imagine I was there, just at the place where I'd found the little bone, feel myself float out of the window.

Elise walked over and gestured for me to sit – there was a chair behind me – and then she tapped my knee with a small silver hammer. My knee jerked up. She was completely in control, and I couldn't stop looking at her. '*Relax*,' she said to me.

I was going; my eyelids were heavy, and then I was standing up without processing what I was doing. I followed Elise. I was her pet, walking behind her. My mind was blank. I followed her as she moved along to the men. When Elise walked up to them, they were attentive.

'This is Betsy,' she said.

Some scribbled on their pads; I was close enough to peer, but their writing made little sense to me – that was the kind of state she'd put me in. Everything was fuzzy, but it was all far less unpleasant now I'd given in. I could tell she was controlling it all; not that I knew how, but she was telling them how to feel about me and telling me how to move. I was floating above myself in a state of nothingness, but right at the back of my mind I could observe the electric snatch of fear, just out of reach.

A man rose. He was old and he staggered up, gasping as each foot touched the floor, taking his time, until finally he reached me. The man was unwell, with a downturn of the mouth and droopy eyelids. He came close, and he looked at me. He straightened up, seemed invigorated. Colour went through his face. He became alive, that's the best way I can describe it.

I turned to Elise, and her expression was a faint apology, though only for a second. I wanted to look away from him, couldn't bear his gaze, and then he reached out and touched my cheek. He twisted it between his two fingers.

It loosened – her clench on my mind.

His nails cut me. The sharp bodily pain of Carn, part of everything, always. I almost expected it, but still I screamed.

He seemed delighted. 'I feel it,' he chirped back to Elise. 'The connection.'

The connection.

I did not know what he meant. I didn't feel anything apart from disgust, like I was dirty, and I wanted to rip off all of my skin. Elise looked a little shaken, but she recovered quickly. The men who watched were surprised and seemed intrigued by my scream. And the end came – if you could call it the end – though it wasn't announced properly, but Elise stood up and gave a small bow, which I understood to mean we were done and I could relax. The crowd began to pack up their belongings. As they moved around, they spoke quietly to each other. If I strained, I could hear some of what they were saying, although they all ignored me. I'd become irrelevant.

'Just excellent! Really excellent.'

'Far less – what's the word – symptomatic? Far less symptomatic than the last bunch, though.'

'– desperate to see them . . .'

'The photographs are super, really give a good feeling . . .'

Then their chatter became inaudible as they began heading out of the room.

Elise came over. 'You liked it. You're fine,' she said.

Did I?

My cheek was raw where the man had touched me.

I thought Elise was going to tell me a bit more about what had just happened, but she didn't. She left me and moved through the crowd, enjoying her role. They were desperate to talk to her, but she just waved them along and they continued to filter out.

Soon, the room was empty. I realized there was no one monitoring me, which was surely an accident, and so I walked out behind the group.

I stumbled, because the return to myself was so overwhelming and I thought I might pass out. The only thing to do was to find somewhere to regroup – somewhere that was cool.

I knew there was a toilet, a store cupboard really, on the lower floor all the way down near the cellars. We weren't supposed to use it, but I went there. I raced down and ran into the toilet, closing the door shut.

Pull it together.

I thought I might throw up, so I sat down on the toilet with my head in my hands to block out the world. The room didn't have a lock, so I just hoped no one would come in, pressing my feet to the door. Then, there was a pressure against my feet as the door opened a little, and I shouted out, 'Someone's in here,' but they didn't listen. There was nothing I could do because he came at me without hesitation. All I saw was his hands as they landed firmly on my mouth, his fingers practically jabbing inside my lips, and my tongue pressed against the skin of his hand. The taste of old salt; the desire to bite down and draw blood.

30.

'Shut up, you *silly* girl,' he said as I pulled back. He let me go, though, because I recognized him, and I was quiet again. When he took his hands away, I could still feel where they had been on my face.

Patrick.

I hadn't seen him in the room, but he must have been there, at the back, skulking. Despite the confined space we were in, I wasn't actually scared of Patrick; it was almost comical him being there, like the caricature of a villain, scowling at me.

'What the *hell*?' I said. I stood up and turned away to spit in the toilet and get the taste of him out of my mouth. Then I hovered, unsure whether I should just push past him and leave.

He secured the door by leaning against it, and then he appraised me, seeming a little injured.

'Language!' A shaky murmur.

'What are you doing here in the *toilet*? I could have been . . .' I struggled to finish the sentence.

He laughed. 'Oh, my dear, let's not bother with all that. You're fine, aren't you? You're fully clothed. No *boundaries* have been crossed. Interesting . . .'

'What?'

'You've filled out a bit,' he said with a smirk.

'Why are you here?' I asked.

'So ungrateful.' He affected a sluggish drawl as he propped his upper body against the cistern as if we were hanging out for happy hour. 'Now I must insist that you *whisper* before I say another word.'

'Fine,' I lowered my voice. 'Now why are you here? What do you want?'

'What do I want? I don't *want* anything. I wish I hadn't both-ered now. I'm quickly going off the idea, and you were always so easy at work.' He had a soulful expression, remembering me at the shop when I did exactly what he asked. 'One-time offer, m'dear,' he said, yawning, hand running across the metal flush of the toilet with a tender caress. 'I'll get you out of here.' He offered me a twitchy smile and he reminded me of someone, but when I tried to grasp at the comparison it was gone, and he wasn't smiling any more. 'I had a delivery to make, and I was here to see someone, but they don't appear to be around.'

'What was that in there? That whole . . . show?'

Then he looked at me and it was with kindness, I think. 'No need to worry about that. So, do you want to hitch a ride with me?' He sounded almost coy.

My skin crawled. 'I don't get it. You let me come here!'

Patrick appraised me. 'Perhaps I shouldn't have.' He had stopped stroking the flush, and it seemed he was about to leave.

'Can you tell me exactly what this place is?' I asked with more confidence than I felt.

He chuckled. 'Oh, I can't do that! Look. I can't stay in here with you all day, but I can assure you there are many moving parts at play here.'

'You're just giving me random bits of information. You don't want to help me at all.' My whisper was faltering.

'I could get you out through a back exit,' he said. 'There's enough of those here. Whisk you to Edinburgh by car if you want me to. I could do it easily enough if we went now.' He seemed proud of this skill, and he waited for a response. When I didn't acquiesce, he sighed. 'You don't seem keen,' he said.

'You're not giving me anything concrete. You're treating me like a *child*.'

He tutted and then he lowered his voice even more. 'How are you finding it?' he asked.

I wasn't sure how much to tell him. I presumed he knew much of what was going on.

'Odd,' I said. 'This whole place has been . . . quieter than I thought it would be. I think we're being watched. Well, I'm sure we are.'

'Oh, really?' he said. 'What else?'

It just spilled out. 'We're locked in at night, and I don't know if that's right. We had photographs with this . . . make-up which was more like stage make-up. There are sessions, and then what happened today – I didn't understand what that was about. It's all . . . strange, creepy even, but it's working in the sense that I'm *sleeping*.' I stretched away from him, as far away as I could manage, but although I did not want to be in such proximity to Patrick, it was good to talk to someone quite openly.

He offered me a knowing smile. 'You are, are you? Of course you are. Well, then you *should* stay.' He gestured to the door. 'Shall we?'

'Tell me who they were. The men, just now.'

He shook his head. 'It seems you don't quite understand what I'm offering up. I was struck in that room by the desire to help you. I could get you out of here. No one would ever know it was me who helped you, they'd think something else happened, I'd make sure that was how it all looked. But please do not inter-pret this as some kind of protracted negotiation. Because this does not mean that I'm on your side. Be *quite* assured, I am not.'

I didn't want to be in the room with him, but at the same time I was aware if he left that was my chance gone.

My dislike of Patrick conquered all. I would stay.

I needed to see it through.

I told him so. He shrugged. 'Suit yourself. As I said, I have a delivery to make.' He gestured to a small black bag at his feet. 'If you don't want to come, then . . . adieu. Wait for five min-utes before you come out,' he said, thinking I'd do as he asked because I always had.

In the end, I waited for longer than five minutes, just to be safe. I sat there for at least fifteen, and when I came out and walked upstairs, the men who had looked at me with remark-able curiosity had all gone, and the grand hallway was dead.

31.

Outside, I found Sally. She must have left the house earlier as I'd last seen her in the corridor. Usually placid Sally, practically pinning Smiler Helper up against the wall, crushing the clematis in the struggle with her face pressed in close. Sally looked odder by the day; she was wearing layers and layers of clothes even though it was boiling hot.

'Who were they?' she wailed.

I rushed over and pulled her away from the helper. 'Come on,' I said. 'Calm down.'

She let me lead her and she relaxed a little into my arms.

The helper was rattled, and she fled inside. I wondered if Sally would get into trouble.

'Are you hurt?' I asked.

'I'm fine,' she said, but she didn't sound fine at all. 'Are *you* okay?' she asked, brows furrowed. She really meant it, and it struck me afterwards just how much Sally did care about us.

'I'm okay,' I said.

'What was that in there?' she asked.

'I don't know,' I said.

It sounded like Sally had been in a room with the men too; I wondered if it had happened earlier in the day, with different men?

'This is all getting way too much,' she said, tears catching in her throat.

I didn't have time to answer as Abigail emerged. 'What's going on?'

She was breezy with us, but I felt sure she had experienced the same thing.

'They took you into the room as well? With the men?' I asked.

She nodded, but it didn't seem to have affected her. 'A few days ago,' she said, shielding her eyes from the sun with her hand. 'It's a lot. Pretty overwhelming. You feel well, though, don't you?' she asked.

'I do,' I admitted. 'But that was . . . that was not right.' I lifted my hand to my cheek; it still stung.

'The symptoms are going,' Sally said.

'My room . . . my special chamber,' Abigail said, no longer talking to us, staring into the distance. 'You know, the room isn't *quite* right. It's started to feel a little heavy on me.'

'Heavy?' I asked.

She nodded. 'I don't know . . . maybe I'm imagining it.'

I edged over to Abigail and the memory of kissing her made me blush. 'Even if I feel better, this place, there's something not right about any of it, something rotten. You know that. So what if we left?' I said. 'What if this was the right time to say fuck it, this is all too much?'

The thing was, I was unsure if I wanted to or not, but I needed to know what Abigail thought about the idea.

Abigail came closer, to meet me, and she laid her head down on my shoulder. 'We can't just leave,' she said, a whisper in my ear.

I tried to work out what to do. I had so much ammunition. It would have been the perfect time to share about the peephole in the library. I had the power to shock them, but I held back because of the way they looked at me.

With Sally, it was a drugged kind of adulation. I knew she saw me as a leader, and she was waiting for me to decide what to do; it was a position I'd never held before. Then, with Abigail, it was something searing, a laugh about to erupt in every smile she shot at me; the whole place was a joke we were in on together.

They'd shared far more with me than I had with them. I'd needled away at them for their stories, extracted them with a ruthlessness I didn't think I had. And I half knew why. I needed to be unlike I was on the outside, be the one to be looked up to, the strong one.

Was it terrible of me that I wanted to be the least unwell and at the top of the pile in whatever hierarchy existed at Carn?

Abigail regarded me kindly. 'It's because we're different,' she said. 'That's why they want to watch us. You know that. They see something in us that others don't. Skills.'

Skills.

It made sense.

Elise had never really kept it a secret from us. She believed we were skilled.

Special.

Parts of the puzzle were there for me to put together, and I worked through it out loud.

What were the skills?

'She thinks you have some kind of extraordinary hearing, doesn't she?' I said to Abigail.

'Of course she does. I do,' Abigail said serenely.

I turned to Sally. 'What about you?'

She just looked at me.

'Come on,' I said.

'My memory?' She offered a confused kind of smile. 'They like that I can remember things.'

The library. The board of objects placed in front of her to test her. They thought she had a good memory, and she did, but she was here for her hypochondria.

'Okay, so we have something she wants or likes. But we've come here for her to cure us, and we feel better, but not . . . normal,' I said. 'I haven't felt normal. I don't really think she's trying to cure us exactly.'

Abigail seemed quite bored by the conversation. 'And what about you?' she asked me, hands on hips.

'My dreams,' I said.

Your dreams, your dreams.

The two girls were an echo, saying my words back to me,

but they weren't speaking and their mouths were closed. And I turned round, and it was Elise speaking. She had heard it all, and she smiled so wide that the skin looked stretched back, and her face became a skull.

32.

Elise was delighted in that moment outside; it was like she'd been waiting for it to click, and I think she enjoyed the theatre of seeing the parts of Carn come together as I worked it out for myself. I saw that for her, it all merged into one – the insomnia and then the dreams. Such things did not need distinguishing from each other as bad versus good, helpful or harmful. They were all equally deserving of examination.

I'd arrived and taken her pills, and spoken of Harry, and told her my problems. I'd watched as the dreams seemed to slip away within the first days, and that was all I wanted – a deep and dreamless sleep. But Elise did not necessarily want the dreams to stop. She had taken them away for a while, but our conversations were changing, and she certainly wanted to hear about them more and more. My dreams had started to return, though they weren't as bad as before.

Still, I had held back in our sessions. I had not told her how terrible they were, my violent dreams. I suppose you'd describe them as nightmares, but violent dreams as a term sits far better. It conveys the brutal nature of them and the colours too – red faces, corn-yellow hair, blue waters. Vivid and flimsy, ripped and floating circus silks swimming in my peripheral vision. I often woke up soaked with sweat, not understanding what I might have done.

They had begun properly a few years after the drowned girl, solidified as a problem by the time I was a teenager. The sleep problems morphed into something else, and it was hardly insomnia. I had experienced a trauma, and I dreamed of drowned girls more and more.

My parents thought it would get better, but it got far worse.

The nightmares were terrible, and I was advised to focus on the art of lucid dreaming. Some counsellor suggested it; one thing on a long list that they threw at me to try and help. My mother did not want to discuss it, and my father pretty much ignored me. They thought I'd learn to lucid dream and it would be a cure.

I was hopeful, because it came naturally to me. I was an attentive student, and I followed all the suggested ways to tap into lucidity. When it came to my dream journal, I was dutiful. At first, I enjoyed it, because it's nice to be talented. I entered my dreams, and then I took control of them for longer and longer stretches. But then came the sleep paralysis. Lying there, not able to move a muscle, feeling like I might die as a beast with curved talons climbed on me, its face blurred. Many people who lucid dream learn to overcome the paralysis, but I couldn't. I didn't like myself. Even when I knew it wasn't real, I was still trapped.

My days and nights started to change. It wasn't necessarily that I couldn't sleep, it was that I wouldn't let myself. I feared what I saw when I closed my eyes. I could take control, but that wasn't always a welcome thing, because I was not myself at night. I was very bad in those dream states, and I had a tendency to hurt people. I enjoyed it.

That was how it was – I did things I never would have done in real life, but in my dreams, I welcomed it. In the end, I stopped myself from sleeping, not because I wanted to, but because sleep was too frightening.

No sleep, then too much sleep. I made choices that I didn't understand with dreams of fish, and they came cooked, served up on a platter, their brilliant eyes bulging, and I ate them with my fingers. Their scales were too brightly coloured for food, but I ignored the colours and dug in, ripping the flesh away, and the fish squirmed in my hands, moving as I ate them.

I did things to Harry too. And when it was all very bad, I tried to stay awake. In fact, I hardly let myself sleep at all. This was all more complicated than insomnia.

★

It hadn't panned out well when I told those on the outside. Siobhan was startled, and then she looked at me with cheery concern.

'You can control your dreams? How odd!' she exclaimed. Not really something you could categorize. Not a hobby, or a side hustle, or a pleasing anecdote.

But I couldn't control how I was in them.

It didn't show me in a good light, and I saw her turning it round in her mind. Interesting, sure, but too abnormal for casual chitchat, and it wasn't an illness, not exactly. Perhaps a party trick? It was weird, and she didn't know what to do with weird.

'Well, it sounds fun!' she said with finality.

A party trick, then.

She propped herself up on one arm. 'Will you tell Harry?'

She was desperate for an insight into our relationship.

'It isn't an option *not* to tell him. I need to before the wedding. I've been trying to tell him for ages, but he doesn't want to know.'

I thought of how he shrugged it off every time I brought it up, claiming my problems were normal.

'But you're trying to get rid of it?' she asked. As if I could banish it, or at least medicate it away (I couldn't – I'd tried).

'Yes, of course I am.'

She nodded sagely. 'I hope that goes well.'

I was being truthful; I had to tell him.

In the end, I bared my soul to Harry a month before we got married. We were back in a restaurant, a different one to where he'd proposed to me. I knew we would never go back to that one; it was the proposal restaurant and that was that.

This time, it was a small Italian bistro that looked romantic from the outside, with condensation on the windows that turned the diners into a smudge, illuminated by the haze of a candle on each table. Inside, it was not so charming – all huge plastic-backed menus that covered our faces when we held them up. Two-for-one offers on the meals, watery cocktails and Wi-Fi details. We hadn't chosen well.

I did not mind this; Harry seethed.

The waiter put us at a table next to the window with a view on to the crowded street of people shopping in the spring evening. Perhaps he did it because we were nice-looking customers that would attract people to come in, but we didn't laugh or talk much – we didn't hold up our end of the bargain, and the waiter seemed a little annoyed.

I took my coat off because it was very warm in the restaurant, then Harry took his off, and then I went to the toilet, and then he did.

He asked about getting something to prop the table up because it was wonky, and eventually he folded up his napkin into small squares and did it himself.

We were self-conscious with each other at first. Harry sat fiddling with the seam of the tablecloth. The other diners all looked older than us either by a little or a long way, apart from one couple: a woman who leaned across the table and a man who fed her a forkful of pasta messily. She laughed, leaning further towards him; she wiped tomato sauce from her face and the whole thing happened so naturally that there was barely a pause in their conversation. The contrast was clear: Harry and I were so stiff. But I told myself we just needed a little time.

He forced himself to look away from the phone, placed it screen down on the table and ordered for us when the waiter arrived because the menu sat in front of me unread.

Two bowls of creamy ravioli, two glasses of wine.

I wasn't adding much to the dinner. I forced myself to drink the wine; Harry took hurried gulps and asked for another.

I snuck glances at the couple near us, imagining what it would be like to talk and touch in a way that just felt natural.

'Do you know them?' Harry asked.

'No.' I peered down at the sauce on my ravioli, which was thick and grainy.

'Well, stop staring.'

'Sorry. I thought I recognized them.'

The night before, I'd dreamed that I had killed him with a knife, pressed it into his throat.

At night, I was the kind of person who would kill a man.

I had to tell him.

In retrospect, it wasn't the best time. The phone fixated him – he had it back up again, his face a smile then a frown, responding to it. His hand was on mine. Managing me and multitasking.

'One minute,' he murmured and, dragging his eyes away, he placed the phone back on the table.

When I explained, he looked confused.

'Lucid dreaming?' The tone was prickly. Not faux concerned like Siobhan, just annoyed. I had been wrong to bring it up. He wasn't really asking me to explain any of it even though I was ready to tell him more, had a whole story prepared.

He picked up his phone and stabbed at the screen. I watched as he scrolled. You could see that he didn't absorb one thing before he flitted to the next, from article to listicle to summary. Scanning valued sources instead of asking me.

Harry looked up rapidly, cranking his neck, like he was trying to catch me out. 'But I thought you said you *couldn't* sleep?' He was slightly aggressive.

'I can't,' I said. 'Often, I can't sleep, but the dreaming has made it worse, the dreams are bad.'

'What do you mean?' he asked.

'Like, I wake up and there's someone pinning me down, holding on to me. But it's more than that. *I'm* bad when I'm in them. So, I'm scared to sleep.'

I assessed his reaction. He seemed wary, but *he knew*. He'd seen me getting worse, how I was in the mornings.

My dreams: Harry as a gecko; Harry with cuts; Harry, Harry, Harry.

Surely he knew.

'I can't move,' I said. 'I'm convinced I'm being crushed to

death. Like my ribs are cracking, but I can't pull away. I *hate* what I dream about – that part I can't control. It seems crazy, I know that.'

He raised an eyebrow. He thought that I was possibly mentally ill. I don't think Harry knew anyone with such problems – he tended to avoid those kinds of people, and so I'd tried to hide so much from him as I listened to him talk about his five-year plans. But I couldn't do it any more.

His head was down again as he read more about lucid dreaming, the stories from people who taught themselves, the associations it had, and the way it could cure or help manage other things: depression, anxiety.

I waited, and he let go of my hand to expand something on the screen with two fingers.

'It's not my fault,' I said.

'It's not that I think it's your *fault*,' he scoffed. 'But it changes things. You don't want to go to sleep. You're scared to sleep. But we can get you help? Let me help you.'

The offer sounded good, but he never did try to get me help, and it would all get worse before the wedding.

33.

Elise walked away from us and went back inside; I left the other two, ran in to face her.

'What the hell was that?' I asked.

'You're starting to see it, aren't you? You didn't feel bad in there. Look at you. You're changing. You feel a lot better?'

She sounded like Abigail.

'What are you doing to me?' I asked.

She mulled it over. 'I have always managed to make people feel better. It's not one thing here. It's a mix of many elements. The healing touch, I suppose, various select pharmaceuticals, nutrition of course . . . Anyway, I facilitate it all.' She shrugged modestly. 'It's a skill. I realized when I started helping people that there are certain girls who are just . . . right.'

'Who were those men?'

It didn't faze her. 'They came to see you,' she said calmly. 'They like you; they help you!'

'How?'

She sighed. 'I heard you there, Betsy, I heard what you were saying to the others; you've been piecing it together from the very beginning. Which is *good*. That's how it's supposed to work. You're a leader, you see. Your dreams have become a sickness to you. I understand that. And I'm willing to help you with them to an extent, but to me they are also something to be prized.

'At Carn, you're taken in and watched. It's an exchange. They watch. And they help you to become better. They . . . provide.'

Provide.

I didn't understand what *provide* meant.

They were funding this place, those men?

She examined me. 'Darling Betsy . . .' she said. 'I know this all sounds a little complicated, and it hasn't been so smooth, but it will all unfold for you if you're just a *little bit* more patient. Come.' And she gestured for me to follow her into her office.

I'd never been into Elise's office before, it was a hallowed space. And it was there that I found the dead girls.

I had intended to ask her so many more questions, but my drive vanished when I saw them: tidy corpses. They were all in black and white, which made it hard to tell if the photos were of girls from a hundred years ago or from the present day.

The girls were captured in carved oval frames made of thick wood. The glass was tinged with yellow, casting a sepia effect. No smears or dust, so either Elise or someone else must have cleaned them most days.

They lay on single beds, and when I got closer, I saw they were younger than I had initially thought.

'Why do you have so many pictures of dead girls?' I asked, and as I listened to the words come out of my mouth, I realized how absurd it all was. I almost wanted to laugh.

'What do you mean?' She was sitting at her vast teak desk with paper everywhere. A tiny silver laptop lay in front of her, and she started to tap away at it, giving me half her attention.

'The dead girls on your wall.'

She laughed and leaned back in her chair. 'They aren't *dead*, Betsy!' She shook her head in delight.

I saw that they were not old photos. The bed sheets were faded, but they were printed with modern Disney-style princesses, thick-lashed ponies and dancing deer. The effect was grotesque. I peered at the largest picture and saw something that looked shiny like plastic had been removed and sat next to the girl's cheek.

What was that?

Elise knew what I was staring at.

'It's a nasogastric feeding tube,' she said, her voice filled with admiration.

You could see the veins on their foreheads. Brushed hair fanned out over the pillows. I could almost smell the rooms they lay in – the stale stench of an inactive body lying for too long. But maybe that was too extreme. They were attended to; you could see by the neat beds and the way they were tucked in.

'But why?' I asked.

'These girls took to their beds. They are in a state of prolonged slumber, I guess you'd call it. They've done all sorts of tests on them, but little has been found. Some think they're faking, because they're not in a coma. It's more of a lovely long sleep.'

'So what . . . caused this?' I asked, transfixed by the pictures.

'The way I see it is that the outside world was too much, just as one might say it is for you?' she said. 'Too much animosity, too much sensory input, too much . . . drudgery. And there was conflict too, in their countries, terrible trauma. So, they retreated into an internal world. Who can blame them? You could probably visit them if you'd care to?'

Why would I visit a group of sleeping girls that I didn't know?

Once I was told they were sleeping, their bodies changed for me. The context clarified, it was easy to imagine a flutter of a breath if you moved close to them.

The girls' lips were just slightly parted, like they might speak or moan or sigh. I thought of the way they could move and turn under the covers, expected one of the photographs to change in a second, for me to be able to summon the girls from their slumber.

'I took these photos,' Elise continued, and I could hear the pride in her voice. 'I went to visit them myself, for weeks on end. They are abroad. I was – I still am – very interested in them. Their parents and the people who care for them did not find my interest . . . appropriate, which was such a shame,' she said. 'If they'd been here, if they'd let me take them here, we could have helped them, I know we could have. Anyway, don't you love them?' she asked. 'I think they're divine.'

'The whole thing sounds sad,' I said. I wondered how the parents must have reacted when Elise 'visited'. I had grabbed at her company in the hospital when we first met, and her solutions had seemed so appealing, but looking back it was because I'd been desperate. There was no denying she was creepy. They must have found her interest in their children unnerving.

'I can see why you'd say that,' she said. 'But I don't think it's sad. There's something beautiful about it. A conscious extraction from society, or an absolute refusal to partake in any of it. Then a period of deep restoration? Remember, they're not ill as such, there are many states that I do not consider to be illnesses; they are simply reacting to a world that doesn't make sense.'

'Do you really think that?'

'Oh yes!' she laughed. 'You three are the same. I see it, and you see it too. It's a reaction to society, an allergic reaction. I try and remove all the minutiae of life, show you your talents, show you the coin.'

'The coin?'

'On one side, the *illness*; on the other, skills that you are allowed to nurture. We dial down the parts you find difficult but keep the parts that make you special. So many people want to help you. You see that, don't you? I've shown you how you can be. Strong, dreaming. Absolutely perfect. If I could just get to them, I could help them too.' She gestured to the girls on the wall. 'Feed them up! Wake them up!' Here, she laughed. 'I can't believe you thought I had pictures of dead girls on the walls!'

She rose, so I stopped looking at her and noticed a picture frame on her desk. It was fanned outwards: a tanned girl in a striped swimming costume. She stood on a beach, somewhere with grassy dunes in the background, the wind blowing through her hair.

Elise put her hand on my shoulder to comfort me. 'I'm very happy with how you're coming on, Betsy,' she said.

There were so many lies about what Carn was, but regardless, I couldn't help it. I was glad that I was making her happy, even though so many questions remained unanswered.

A scream.

It was the first time I'd heard the night-time scream in the day, and it rose from somewhere down below. In the light of day, there was no explaining it away as a fox, and the scream was undeniably human.

Elise froze. 'I need to go, but we'll talk tonight. Get back to your dreams.'

She dashed out of the door, leaving me there alone. I considered following her, but I decided against it, though I didn't leave straight away.

I was taken with the frame on her desk; there was something about the photo. The girl with her windswept hair and her easy smile. She seemed dissimilar to us – we were tricky, Abigail and me, and the sleeping girls in Elise's office, and certainly Sally. We tripped up on all that life threw at us. This girl was simple and easy, and I was sure it was Elise's daughter because who else would she have framed on her desk?

And then, it felt like I was slipping away from reality: the men, the daughter, the dead girls. I needed to tether myself, to feel something in my hand. This was something I often did when I was trying to escape a dream. The little bone had worked well for this purpose and when I rubbed it, it brought me back into the present, but it was under the bed now. So, without overthinking it, I grabbed the picture of the daughter. There was a box of matches on the desk too, and I took those. I rushed out of the door with my stolen items and went up to my bedroom.

The photo was mine. I slid it under the bed, to join my bone. All these things seemed to be helping, more parts of Carn for me to try to piece together.

34.

The next day, Sally wouldn't get out of bed. I could hear her from my room, refusing to get up, until she must have finally given in, as she came downstairs looking awful. She ate breakfast when she was given it with Abigail and me, but I heard her retching afterwards. The helpers were sniping at her for the rest of the morning, telling her she needed the nutrition. Later, I caught her inspecting her ears in a mirror, then her gums, prodding at them insistently until after a while blood pooled at the gumline, red smears against the white of her teeth.

'A thermometer, please,' she said gravely to Smiler Helper at lunch.

'Why?' Smiler Helper asked. I still called her this, but her smiles were very infrequent by this point.

'I need to see how I am,' Sally said. 'I need to check my temperature.'

It was the most doctorly I'd ever seen her.

'A pen and paper too,' she said. 'So I can log it.'

Elise was called in, and she agreed to give Sally what she wanted, but she didn't seem happy about it.

None of it helped, and at lunch Sally was snarling at the helpers instead of eating, poking at her food. The helpers reminded her that she'd promised to eat while at Carn. But she wouldn't take a bite. And the helpers whispered away about her, and I could gather a fair amount just by following them and listening in. Although they tried not to talk in front of us, they slipped all the time.

'She's not right,' I heard one of them say as they rushed out to get Elise. 'She's stopped eating. She's not *right* for here.'

'I can't believe Elise would bring a *doctor* here,' a helper said.

I shifted my weight, and the creak of the floorboards made the helper spin round. It was Smiler Helper. She realized she'd messed up and I'd heard it all. But it wasn't really her fault.

'You weren't meant to hear that. You're okay, though,' she said encouragingly. 'You're right for Carn.'

I nodded and walked away, considering it. My thoughts lingered on the phrase, 'not right'. I thought I understood it, or at least I was starting to. That ideal level of illness and skills was not something I could define. But perhaps Abigail was right, and I was right. Sally could have been wrong for it all.

Sally lingered at the bottom of the stairs that afternoon, staring at an empty wall. I approached her with caution. She looked at me with a worrying blankness, a resignation to our situation that made my stomach flip. She still wore too many clothes, and I could see a line of sweat above her upper lip.

'How are you getting on?' I asked.

No reply.

'Maybe it's time to see if you can go? Back to your family?' I said tentatively.

She let out a snort that was very out of character.

I persisted. 'You could be around people who care about you?'

She was still looking past me. 'They talk about medical conditions all the time,' she said absently. 'My family. They can't stop themselves, even when I've asked them not to. They say I'm overreacting. Well, they used to anyway. After I started . . . to fall apart, they didn't want to know.'

'Are they not worried about you?'

'They don't stay in touch,' she said. 'They're embarrassed.'

'But now, surely. If they saw how you were struggling?'

She shook her head vigorously. 'Don't you get it? They don't want to know. They have the others, so if something goes wrong, they just get rid of the defective ones.'

It would have been a good time to say, yes, I understood quite a bit, because my brothers had always been the easy children. It could have been a chance to bond with her. But before I could say anything of comfort, she was looking at me with the most unnatural expression, lifting her eyebrows high, her mouth open in a silent scream. She brought her lips back together.

'They probably think I'm dead,' she said finally. 'Maybe I am.' She observed her hands as if she couldn't connect them to her body. Then she waggled her fingers experimentally. 'Maybe we all died here and we just didn't realize it?'

'I don't think so,' I said firmly.

She leaned in close. 'I think they're poisoning us.'

They could have been poisoning us, but she needed reassurance.

'I don't think they are. And you're real, alive. We're okay, but I'm not sure you should stay here. Just ask to leave,' I said. 'You can do that. It's not making you better being here any more, not at all. You need to get out of this place, so ask.'

She fixed on me with watery eyes. 'Why don't *you* ask to leave?'

I couldn't answer her question or explain the need I had to unravel Carn myself.

'I'm just trying to help,' I said.

'I don't need your help,' she replied. 'I don't need any of you. All so perfect.'

'I'm not perfect at all,' I said, and I felt the urge to open up to her. 'I can't swim, you know.'

'Really? I'm not a great swimmer either,' she said. She gave me a weak smile. 'Perhaps I've died,' she repeated, and then she looked straight past me and walked out of the front door at Carn into the sweltering day.

'Are you sure it was a human bone?' I called after her. 'The bone I showed you, you thought it might be human?'

I hadn't believed her at the time, but maybe she had identified it correctly. She didn't turn around to answer my question.

35.

I retrieved my treasures from under my bed, and then I went to see Abigail. I wanted to show her the photo frame that I'd taken from Elise's office, and I found her sitting by a window in her bedroom, staring outside.

'Look,' Abigail said.

I went over and we both peered out at Sally, a blonde head bobbing over the lawn. There was little logic to her movements; she staggered.

Abigail sighed. 'To be honest, she's losing her mind,' she said.

'Yeah. I was with her just now,' I said. 'She's not doing well.'

'Hmmm.' Abigail was only half listening.

'I have something to show you,' I said.

'Go on, then.' She was still looking out of the window at Sally.

'I was with Elise. She has these pictures in her office.'

Abigail turned when I said Elise's name and smiled like she knew.

'This.' I passed the frame over to her.

She took it from me. 'Why? Who's this?' she asked, still distracted by Sally outside.

'Her daughter,' I said. 'I don't know, I just thought it would be useful to have. I guess it must have been shortly before she died.'

Abigail whipped her neck right round. Sally was forgotten.

'Her daughter's not *dead*,' she spat at me with such venom it made me freeze.

'What do you mean?' I asked.

'I mean exactly what I said. You must have got the wrong end of the stick. We discussed her in my sessions! She's like . . . a surfer or something. Lives on some remote commune in

Cornwall.' Abigail sounded a little wistful through her rage. 'She tells me about her all the time.'

'I didn't get the wrong end of the stick,' I said.

'That *could* be Cornwall,' she said, peering at the framed picture.

My mind spun. 'Sally . . . I wonder what Elise said to her. Why would she lie to us about that?'

Abigail smirked. 'She wouldn't lie to me.'

She held out the picture and we both scrutinized it for a moment.

'She really said this was her daughter?' Abigail asked.

'Well . . . no.'

I had been so sure it was Elise's daughter, but I could see why Abigail was questioning it. The girl in the picture didn't look like an addict. Maybe this was the daughter before things had got bad?

'It just matches what she told me,' I said, but I felt the conviction start to drain. It was all based on a hunch. 'She had it on her desk,' I added.

Abigail held the frame close to her face, her nose almost touching the glass. Then, she turned it over. Deftly, she removed the frame and unpeeled the back section. I saw how thin the paper was as she handed both parts back to me, the picture and the frame. It was shiny. I turned it over and saw the fragment of a recipe page for 'Easy Cajun Chick'n'. A clipping from a magazine. A model.

My head spun.

What was she doing with it framed on her desk?

What had all that talk of her dead daughter been about?

'Her daughter?' Abigail said, triumphant. 'Really?'

I was moving the parts around in my mind. 'I don't know. I guess she told us different things. I think the daughter was a way to manipulate us. Elise just told us what we wanted to hear,' I said, half talking to myself.

Neither of us seemed to know what to do next. I was willing

186

myself to make a suggestion. With so many discoveries, I'd been thinking about it for so long, and I finally said it to Abigail with as much confidence as I could muster. 'We need to ask to leave.'

'Ask?'

'Even if we don't intend to go. Say we're not comfortable any more. I need to know if we're trapped here or if she'd actually just let us walk out.' I raised my head to get a better view out of the window at Sally, who was still swaying around on the lawn. It didn't look good.

'She lied,' Abigail said dully. 'She said she'd never lie.'

I didn't want this. Abigail's eyebrows no longer crawling with amusement, just a dead kind of expression at Elise's betrayal. I wished we could rewind because I wanted her to light up again, and for us to talk about our medical problems. Go back to the beginning to who we were when things were easier.

We both watched Sally. She seemed to teeter, and her wail cut through the air. Both of us flinched at the sound of it.

There was so much I hadn't told Abigail. It was time to tell her about the peephole, and possibly about Caroline, and how I was convinced she was involved with Carn. I had the bone in my pocket. I kept fingering its smooth bump every time the jitters started up. The words were there on the tip of my tongue. But then I thought of how Caroline had told me not to trust Abigail.

'I'm going outside,' Abigail said.

'Please, we need to make a plan,' I said. I had a few ideas already. I had noted the fire alarm, barely visible in the corner, and I thought I could use it in some way.

She shook her head. 'We'll talk later.'

I was surprised that she was going out to deal with whatever was happening with Sally. She had never shown much interest in Sally before.

Abigail walked out of her room without another word. Outside, the helpers had arrived, and one looked up from the lawns and saw me watching. They were losing control of us. Even from far above, I could sense panic.

Driver Helper raised her hands high over her head in some kind of signal, and within seconds I heard footsteps on the stairs. One of them came into the room and pulled the shutters down over the window.

'Stay here,' the helper said, as if I had a choice.

A click; they'd pressed a button and then I was locked inside Abigail's room.

I sat down on her bed and realized that Abigail had never said she was going to save Sally. She was off on her own.

36.

I waited to be released. I banged on the door to see if they'd let me out, but no one came. The whole place was quiet for a while, and then I heard muffled shouting outside.

Perhaps Abigail would return? I just needed to wait it out. A jitteriness ran through me like I'd drunk too much coffee. My brain wouldn't shut off. The house began with its usual noises in the background, and I was not scared of them. In the end, I lay down on Abigail's bed with the magazine picture under my cheek. I curled up into a ball.

The gong. The click of the door opening.

Abigail hadn't returned, but Bruise Helper was there, looking dishevelled. She spoke the same as always. 'Come down soon, please.'

I did, and when I walked into the dining room it was the same as every other night, candles lit, helpers to the side, but the room was so empty without the others. I wondered if this was how it had always been going to play out in the end, just the two of us: me and Elise. She was a mess with hair unbrushed in a wild mane and no jewellery. Where she usually sat up straight at the table, now her neck was hunched.

'Where are they both?' I asked in a whisper. It was Sally I was most worried about.

Elise did not answer. 'Let's eat,' she said.

The helpers had trays filled with aubergine and spears of asparagus swimming in puddles of oil. They didn't serve me any vegetables; they stood there with the trays. Fish for Elise – the spine a long twist of grey sitting in white flesh. For me, a very small steak that appeared to be barbecued. My body clenched when I took a bite, and it tasted quite unpleasant. I nearly spat it out, but I managed to push through and keep chewing. The flavours changed, and I found myself enjoying it. Despite everything, I savoured those minutes before I asked. I could pretend I was back on that very first day, filled with hope that I would be healed.

I broke the spell.

'I want to leave,' I said.

Elise was surprised. 'Are you not enjoying your meal?'

'I want to leave.'

'You can't leave now.'

'Why?'

And she pressed her hand to her forehead like I was causing a headache. I saw her face change, fill with annoyance.

'I give you it all,' she said, and she gestured to the dining room and the food. 'I give you everything you could possibly want. I know it's tough for you, but I try so hard to help you, guide you through. We've all been more than happy to hand it over, Betsy, for free – you didn't have to pay a penny. You come here, and you feel so much better. I *see* it, and then you want to . . . just leave? At this point?'

'You said we could leave whenever we wanted.'

She muttered something and I just caught the end: *recoup investment.*

'What do you mean?' I asked.

'We did a first reveal and they agreed that you're special. You're right. It's all been happening.'

She wanted me to understand, but the word 'special' made me clench all over.

'You felt good in that moment, didn't you?' she said. 'When they watched you?'

No.

Good wasn't quite right, but I'd experienced something, and I was sickened by that.

It was the medication. My feelings were manufactured by whatever drugs she was dishing out.

I think they're poisoning us, Sally had muttered to me.

'You can't leave,' Elise said.

37.

She'd said no, but she did excuse me from dinner. Back in my room, I had more time to think. I plotted it out in my head. She knew I couldn't get past the body of water on my own. I couldn't swim; she knew that. Really, I hadn't ever thought she'd just let me go, too much had happened and they were watching, people were watching me, and knowing it made my skin prickle.

I should have been scared – if they weren't going to let me go then crossing the water would be very hard, conceivably impossible, but the fear was fading. Instead, a strand of something ran through me, dark and insatiable – far stronger than fear. In the reflection of the window, I was fatter in some ways, but still somewhat hollowed out in the face. My eyes seemed set back in my head, the sockets too deep. My joints clicked when I moved closer to the window and there was a deep stretching sensation. In my mouth, there was a metallic kind of taste that I enjoyed. My hands had a weird hardness to them; fashioned from steel. I was inching closer to something incredible, unstoppable.

I waited, alone in my room, for at least an hour, and eventually they came: Elise with the helpers flanking her. She handed the pill over.

'Do you want me to wait?' she asked.

'No.'

I thought she'd argue with me, but she just watched me swallow the pill, and then she left.

I could have spat it out after she'd gone, but I didn't. In the last few days, when the pill hadn't worked so well, I'd noticed the return of old impulses. There'd been a particularly repugnant dream involving a blind octopus. One featuring a man with no mouth. Torn limbs and old skulls. But I wasn't affected like I had been in the past.

I didn't want to sleep, and so I considered my options. One thing I knew I could rely on was that Carn had lots of tech, with motion-sensor lights. Surprisingly, no cameras that I could see, but lots of other parts appeared to be automatic, like the smooth click of the door – an expensive locking mechanism. I had a strong suspicion the house would be sensitive to threats. I didn't have much of a plan or many resources, but first I retrieved the matches I'd taken from Elise's office. I scooped them out from under my bed.

The first match. One strike, and I watched the flame burn until it reached my fingertip; I blew it out. With the second match, I set fire to the picture I'd stolen, because the daughter was a lie. It had changed things.

The smoke was bitter, and it spread quickly. I lit another match and let it burn all the way along. Then, I knelt down and pushed everything together into a pile on the floor. I lit the pile to create a small fire with some other bits of paper that I'd gathered under my bed over the previous days. I topped it off with the folded card that I'd found on my quilt when I'd first arrived at Carn:

Breakfast – eight.
Lunch – twelve.
Dinner – seven.
Burnt.

The smoke drifted up. By the time I struck a fifth match, the fire alarm had started.

It was loud: the click of not only my door, but the faint clatter as many, many other parts of Carn unlocked. I had a wet towel under the bed too, and I covered the fire up so it went out.

This was how I'd hoped it would go, though I couldn't believe it was actually working. Slight chaos, that was what I was aiming for. I knew someone would probably come and get me; I dropped to the floor and slid under the bed.

194

'Betsy?' Make-up Helper came in, shouting above the alarm. She coughed and I could just see her feet. She didn't think to check under the bed for me, and then she was gone, rushing out of my room. She didn't see the residual smoke or seem to think the fire had started in my room.

There was a lot of other noise. Elise was directing everything in the corridor, and I heard the helpers go outside. With care not to make a sound, I eased out from under the bed and looked out from my bedroom window, staying low so they wouldn't see me. I tried the door and it creaked open.

So, I tiptoed down to the grand hall, and then went further, down steps and past the toilet where Patrick had ambushed me. I kept on walking, down and down to the basement kitchen. There was very little light, but reflections moved across the stainless steel. Was it designed to look like a lab? Or a kitchen in a restaurant? It was far bigger than I had expected.

I was unsure what I was even looking for. There was a pair of big chest freezers, and I walked over to the first one. I had a go at pulling it open, but it was locked with a chain and padlock. All the equipment was scrupulously clean, but there was just one thing there that appeared to have been left by accident. On top of the fridge lay a small scalpel covered in dried blood. I debated whether to pick it up, but I didn't want to touch it.

A bang.

I walked down more stairs towards the noise, aware that I surely didn't have a lot of time before they found me, and I reached a huge wooden door.

Another bang. Someone was locked in there.

I went to the handle and pulled at it, summoning every bit of strength. But this door hadn't automatically opened with the fire alarm like the others had.

A voice inside spoke, but I couldn't make it out.

'I'm trying,' I said to the door.

There was a keypad embedded into the wall. Seeing the shape and the style, something stirred in my memory. It was the same one as in the bookshop. I recalled going down the stairs to the basement. I'd wanted to see what Patrick kept down there, and then the unwelcome press of his cold hand on my shoulder as I'd reached the keypad, steering me away.

The voice behind the door was still speaking. I could just about make out what they were trying to do – give me the code to get in – but it was impossible to hear the numbers over the blaring alarm, and there was just no time, because Carn wasn't on fire, and they would be looking for me.

Silence.

The fire alarm stopped, and then I heard the front door slam far above me.

'Betsy!' someone called out.

I leaned against the door for a second, promising myself I would return. Then I raced upstairs. The lights buzzed as they came on, marking my passage. I went straight out through the front door, running on to a lawn filled with helpers.

Outside, the moon was bright and the pools of water from the sprinkler made my feet wet. The helpers stared at me. There would be questions, I knew that.

'Where were you?' Elise demanded.

'Toilet,' I said.

She looked at me with suspicion, but then she relaxed into a smile, and it was as if our tussle at dinner had been forgotten.

'You're not hurt?' she asked.

'I'm fine. Will you call the fire brigade?'

'Absolutely not,' she said firmly. 'Everything's fine. The fire alarms are extremely sensitive. I'm almost positive it's a false alarm.'

I had gathered that Elise would do anything to avoid having outsiders come out to Carn. It made sense – if someone came from the outside, it would be hard to explain what the place was. She didn't meet my eye, just looked searchingly at the house. It was white in the moonlight, the pink dialled down.

Carn was our pearly castle with the sheen that came off the bricks making it appear other-worldly.

'There's no fire,' she said, almost to reassure herself. 'There can't be. I'm almost sure of it, but you should stay out here for now while we work out what happened.'

A smidgen of assurance, and then she tore away from me to go back inside, the train of her silk dressing gown dragging behind her. The helpers stayed with me.

'Where are they all?' It was my last attempt. 'Abigail and Sally and Caroline? *Where are they?*'

The helpers didn't respond, they just stood there blocking my way back in with their bodies. It probably wouldn't be too long until they discovered the matches and worked out that the smoke had originated in my room.

I tried to put it all together while I waited.

Were all the girls down there? Locked away from me?

How could I get them out?

How could I get *myself* out?

Cold dread spread through me, reaching every limb. Elise and the helpers didn't know it wasn't a real fire. They had been looking for me, but there was at least one person in the cellar. They had all been willing to let whoever it was stay there and burn to death. As far as I could tell, they hadn't bothered to try to get them out.

Elise came back out, grabbing me. 'It's time,' she said. 'Come on.'

They used force; Elise pulled me inside, dragging me back up the stairs with the helpers assisting. I resisted as much as I could, scratching at faces and holding on to banisters with a strength born of desperation. I was lashing out, biting at them, until there was a bag over my head and I couldn't see a thing.

38.

'This isn't the ideal timing.' Elise, her voice wavering with uncertainty. 'Usually, it would be . . . a little less coercive? Are you absolutely *sure* they're ready for her now?'

'Yes, they said now . . .'

Someone else, a helper.

'So I think we should . . .'

And then a hand in my armpit and one down digging into my ribs.

'*Careful* with her.'

Driver Helper.

They were still pulling me upstairs. I stopped trying to fight back, and I let it happen. I couldn't have fought when I couldn't see a thing, and there were three of them and they were strong. They manoeuvred me on to what must have been my bed, and then they let go. The bag came off and Driver Helper produced two large pills from her pocket. They weren't the same as the ones I'd had every night before; they were oblong capsules, red one side and white on the other.

'What are they?' I asked.

'These will help with what comes next,' Driver Helper said.

'I hate this,' one of the others piped up, upset.

They were behaving differently to how they had before, but we were all different.

From the very first day I had treated them like they were maids until I realized they were our guards. If I looked at how old they were, and the fragments of conversations I'd heard over the weeks, I didn't think they were so dissimilar to me. In another life we might have known each other, working together on the freckle problem, drinking espresso martinis, going to barre classes. In another world, where I was normal and well, I could have been friends with girls just like them, with Driver Helper or Smiler Helper. That was something I could use.

'You could help me,' I said to Driver Helper. 'If you wanted to, you could. I won't tell anybody what happened here, I promise. You could help me get out.'

Pathetic, with tears running down my face. I was dizzy with the impossibility of it. I was shaking, and they saw it, but it made no difference. Driver Helper looked at me without sympathy.

I took the pills.

I lay there and I think she stayed with me until I drifted into unconsciousness.

When I woke up I was somewhere else, and I thought I was alone. I was lying at an uncomfortable angle with a nasty ache in my head, the inside of my throat scratched and raw.

I couldn't move. Everything was very heavy.

What had they used on me? A date-rape drug?

Wherever I lay, it was cooler than before, like the barn where we'd done the photos. I could hear the buzz of an air-conditioning unit, and it smelled different from the rest of Carn: old fast food and carpet cleaner.

I thought I might be positioned on a sofa or a low bed, but it was hard to tell because it was extremely dark. Black fabric had been hung up around me. Behind me was a glass window with darkness beyond. I peered down. I could just about make out my body as my eyes adjusted. They'd dressed me in something I didn't recognize; I craned my neck to take a closer look but it was too dark. My hand was resting on the fabric, and it was almost papery like a hospital gown.

When I could control my body a little more, I could feel how the gown was more revealing than I had thought. I was practically naked. I let my hand fall over the side of the sofa to test what worked. It seemed fine but shaky. I was regaining my ability to move.

The lights came on; they were dim, though.

Elise emerged through a door to the side of the room with a restlessness to her. She seemed nervous as she came up to me. There was a snap of pain when she gave me a hard pinch on the cheek. I tried to pull away but I could only move an inch.

'Stay still, please,' she whispered in my ear. 'You can just . . . breathe.' She took a long breath in and out to show me, and I took her advice because I found I'd been holding the same breath bottled up for too long. The knot of pure panic lessened. And she pulled the gown from me so I was naked.

Elise said: 'Are you okay if I take a little blood? I would never take it without your compliance.'

And I wanted to say no and push her away, but I was nodding. The needle went in. Was she taking blood or injecting me with something? It was impossible to look down, impossible to tell. Just pain, always, at Carn, with Caroline pressing her nails on Sally's wrists, and Abigail's sharp little teeth on my lip, and the man at the window falling to the ground.

I looked through the glass.

A different man stared at me.

A light in the corner came on, one of those motion-sensor ones. Those behind the window watched me – there was more than one of them, I could hear them. Thick panting.

I would not survive this. The end had arrived, and Elise was going to come back in. She would kill me, probably. Plunge a knife into my heart right there for these men to watch, lock my body in a big freezer where the rest of them probably were. It was over, and whatever they'd given me made it all seem bearable. I rose up above myself and tried to tune out. I managed to close my eyes. But it was not a day to die. At last, they lifted me. My angel helpers had finally decided to save me, with their hands on my arms and legs, so many of them as they took me away.

39.

It was a new day, and I lay in my bed. I didn't know how much time had passed, but it was light again. My room was lovely, just like it had been right at the very beginning. It was as if we'd gone back in time to those first days when it was all soft towels and ironed sheets. The floors were freshly scrubbed, and the air smelled of toasted almonds; sunlight bounced between the knots in the boards, and I guessed it must have been early evening.

Elise was there, hovering near my door with a glass of water in her hand, and she came in and stood next to me. She didn't speak. I guessed she was waiting for me to go first.

'The drugs,' I said; my tongue was heavy and foreign. 'So strong.'

She had said that she wouldn't drug me at the beginning, that everything would be *natural*, whatever that meant, and even though something far worse was clearly happening, it was still a great betrayal.

'I know,' she said, her voice level. 'I'm sorry. I had to do that.'

'Who was watching me there?' I was firm with her.

She handed me the water and then tucked the sheet up to my chin to cover me entirely. 'It usually works out better.' She wrung her hands together. 'And the girls are grateful to come here, truly. They react amicably enough. All the different parts come together. Because there are so many different parts.'

The phrase was familiar.

Moving parts.

That was what Patrick had said.

'None of it is supposed to come out like this,' she said, her voice cracking with frustration. 'The way it evolves, it really doesn't need to be so antagonistic between us, but this summer has been so very different, and I haven't been able to . . . explain it in the right way to you, so you understand, so you *get it*.'

'Tell me now, then?' I asked.

'I think it's because it's been so hot right from the start,' she said. 'Things have gone wrong in ways I couldn't have possibly imagined back in May, back when I first found you all.' She shook her head, mulling over the weather. 'I should *never* have brought a doctor in. Completely wrong; it contaminated the whole thing. But she seemed right at the time . . .'

'I want to leave,' I said. Still firm, but with a painful nest of tears in my throat.

'I can explain. If you give it a bit more time you'll feel on top of the world. It gets better, I can promise you that. Isn't that what you want?'

'No. I want to go.'

Her face split open in a pained attempt at a smile. 'Not yet. There's only four more weeks to go! A month! It's nothing, really, in the end. A month of being here so we can do what we need to do. You've felt the connection, I know you have, felt things you've never felt before. Only a little left to finish it all off.'

It was a stand-off. To escape, I would have to find a way across. Work out how I could make the bridge rise, or at least get through the forest to see how far it stretched back and bank on a gap in the waters.

I think she would have stayed with me for longer, but there was a wail. It was the same wail I'd heard in the night, that terrible scream always interrupting us. She rushed out of the room, pulled the door closed. She didn't even bother to tell me to stay there; we both knew that I was trapped.

40.

Special – the word is gold, a sticky-backed star peeled from a sheet. For the most part, I considered myself defective. Rusted metal rather than gold. Damaged. Abnormal, but sometimes passable. Able, with some encouragement, to drag myself through the days and be sufficiently human on the surface. Which is what I assumed many people did, anyway. Dredge up that muted sparkle with a forced laugh, the kind of thing that people expect from girls with shiny hair who work in marketing, who look *perfectly fine*.

Right at the beginning Elise had asked if I had any notable abilities, and I had told her *no, none*.

This wasn't quite true. There were my dreams, of course. Plus, I was good at climbing. Harry had decided we should have lessons, right at the beginning when we'd first met, but he'd abandoned the idea after a few sessions because I was marginally better at it than him. The instructor had complimented me, and I saw Harry's stony expression and realized we wouldn't be going again, not together. I kept at it, though, because it was important to be able to escape. Living in our flat high up, I needed to know how to get out in a fire, for example.

And the others? Abigail and Sally? I had seen their skills up close: Abigail's incredible hearing, Sally's memory. It hadn't been a trick, but they felt exaggerated at Carn. *They agreed that you're special.* That was what Elise had said. It seemed like fantasy – I didn't think I was remarkable.

As a child, I had been chosen to play Mary four times in a row in the Nativity, but you can read into anything if you try hard enough.

★

I'd explored Carn's farthest and widest reaches; finally got to grips with the sprawling floor plan. At the time I had marvelled over the fact that there weren't cameras watching us, but I had come to see they had never been too concerned about what I would discover. They assumed that if the door was locked, I wouldn't stray.

I lay there in my room. No one came to feed me, and soon it was dark outside.

I was filled with purpose. For luck, I retrieved the bone from under the bed and put it in my pocket. I pulled on some shoes and went to the window. It was a sash-and-case one, and it was easy to open. And so, I scrambled out. A warm breeze flowed around me. Falling wasn't an option; my foot curved for a grip that came naturally. I focused purely on the path in front of me. Maintaining my balance, I walked for a few metres along the edge of the roof. I kept going, even though I knew if I fell I'd break my leg, or worse, and there would be no ambulance.

I managed to get to the corner of the house where there was a huge tree. Overgrown branches clung to the sides of a drain-pipe, showing a clear path, and it was easy for me to shimmy my way down the pipe, and then let myself drop as I got close to the ground. The final fall was hard. My shoulder hit earth with a crack, and I lay there for a second, letting the ache fade away. Then I got up, brushed away the dirt. No serious injuries.

I walked down the main path first, towards the water that surrounded the house. It was far too deep to get across. I bent down and plunged a hand in – ice cold. I stood for a second to watch the pink algae as it swirled, and then I turned back to the house and went to the front door, fully expecting it to be locked. It wasn't, and so I went in and did a quick investigation for the box of phones. But they weren't there. Then, standing in the hall, I knew where I needed to go. I padded down to the kitchen, ignoring the freezers. I grabbed a knife from a block that sat on the side, and I held it close. Finally, I reached the locked cellar. There was a low wail; someone was moving around.

'Who's there?'

It was a voice that I recognized without the alarm blaring over us as it had before.

'Betsy,' I said. 'I've come to get you out, but I don't have the code.'

The keypad glowed angry red as I tried a random string of numbers, just to see. It emitted loud pings.

An intake of breath from behind the door. 'Stop.'

She recited a strip of numbers and I typed them in.

The screen lit up green. There was a long, satisfying beep as the lock released. I was ready to see what was down there. I pushed on the handle to open the door.

41.

A low ceiling, and I had to duck so as not to bang my head. It was slick and dark up above, with foul water dripping down. The stench of sewage and rot made me close my mouth tight, and I pressed my fingers to my nose to stop it seeping in.

I kept my eyes open, so they'd adjust.

A pile of clothes in a heap.

No, it was more than that. Then I saw her hair and her arm stretched out to the side.

Sally.

The smell of her was beyond belief. But it didn't stop me scrambling to get to her. Her eyes were all clouded and her mouth was a little puckered, like a fish. I'd never seen a dead body before, not in real life. Even with the girl who had drowned, she'd been taken away so quickly, and no dream, no nightmare, however terrible or violent, could possibly prepare me for how it would be. How the essence of the person I'd known would be gone. All that was left was flesh, blood and bones, and that horrific smell. A carcass. The pallor was some colour that I couldn't describe. Nothing of who she'd been remained, even her expression looked mangled; there was no peace in her.

I pulled at her shoulders; I couldn't help it, I shook her hard like it would do something, like she'd come to. My heart was pounding with shock and anger; she'd been discarded. She was a piece of rubbish, dumped in a corner.

Her body was cold.

'Betsy.'

I spun round.

Caroline.

'They did this to her,' Caroline said. 'This is what Carn does.' She gestured to Sally.

Caroline looked down; she had seen my knife, but she didn't back away from me, she just held out her hand. She had some kind of sway over me; without thinking I passed her the knife like she wanted. After placing it on the floor, she put her hands up, so her palms faced me in a conciliatory gesture.

'We need to leave,' she said. Her voice was reedy, as if she'd had no water for days. She smoothed down her dress; it was dirty. In fact, she looked terribly dirty all over.

'You've been down here this whole time?' I asked.

'Yes. We need to get a move on.'

I couldn't take my eyes off Sally even though I hated the sight of her. It was like a compulsion. 'I don't understand. What happened?'

'She was trying to get away. She drowned,' Caroline said.

My stomach dropped.

Was I to blame?

I had told her to leave. Had I planted the seed in her head that had led to this?

There was something wrong, and I scanned her body for what it was that jarred, tried to assess her injuries, but I couldn't make it all fit. I needed more time, and, according to Caroline, we didn't have it.

'Come on,' Caroline said. She pushed past me to the open door.

'And leave her?' I asked.

Caroline closed her eyes; she was gathering strength. 'There's nothing we can do for her. We need to think about ourselves now. We can talk about her later.'

I didn't really know whether or not to trust Caroline, but what else could I do? She had always been capable, and I had to get out.

'You have a plan?' I asked.

'I can get us out of here.'

Of course she could.

We left the cellar. We couldn't take Sally with us, couldn't carry a body out of this place. Still, though leaving Sally's body felt wrong, to leave Abigail was something else entirely. They'd dumped Sally, but Abigail was still inside, and I couldn't abandon her as well. The thought made me feel sick. But Caroline was too quick, racing away from me before we could discuss it.

'Abigail,' I shouted at Caroline's back as we approached the main door to leave the house. She ignored me. I chased after her across the lawn, and I was out of breath when I got to the water where she stood looking down.

'Algae,' she said, shaking her head. 'Still there.'

I didn't know why she was mentioning the algae, but I needed to get her attention. '*Abigail*,' I repeated.

Caroline whipped round. 'She. Got. Out,' she said. 'She got out without you.'

Hearing that was a punch in the gut.

I couldn't believe it; I was so certain she was still in there. I thought of her face when she'd learned about Elise's daughter.

'She's gone,' Caroline said firmly. 'And now we need to go too.'

At the bridge, Caroline bent down, grappling with the reeds to find the keypad. She tapped in a long chain of numbers.

She turned to me. 'I can swim,' she said. 'But you . . .?'

'No,' I said.

'You wouldn't want to swim through this anyway. The fish didn't make it, then?'

I thought of the koi, thick bodies writhing, then still. A sudden coldness eased its way up my spine. 'You did that?'

'Bleach,' she said with a wince.

'But why?'

Caroline's face screwed up. 'I didn't mean it,' she said. 'I didn't think it through. I was sick of that red water. It was supposed to be a final fuck you to Carn, to the whole place, and it didn't work of course, it just killed the fish. That was completely unintended, believe me.'

This was not the Caroline I recognized from before. She was more open, less controlled.

The bridge rose through the water while the red masses swirled.

'Come on,' she said to me, as if it was nothing and leaving was the easiest thing in the world. She walked ahead.

I considered what I knew about her.

She was involved.

She wasn't a good person – she'd killed the fish!

It was mad to trust her.

I looked back at Carn, with the morning light falling over it. One of the most beautiful places I'd ever been to and, despite everything, there was a rugged little pull deep inside telling me to go back, to find Abigail, to take her with me. But in front of me was beauty too as Caroline glided across the bridge, over the red water like a biblical scene; there was a shocking splendour, with the water below. The sky lightened above us, the wispy cusp of a sunrise visible. Her skirt lifted in the wind, billowing as she crossed.

I made my decision. I followed Caroline across the bridge.

We reached the other side, and she knelt to find a button concealed in the ground. When she pressed it, the bridge retracted in front of us, and we both watched until it had gone and the waters settled, making sure the route behind us was closed. There was no grand chase with Elise in pursuit. No one followed us at all. And so, I left Carn for the first time.

After Carn

42.

It should have been horrible after everything that had happened, but the morning was actually a slice of heaven as we walked away down the road. Huge leafy trees sat either side, swaying in the wind. Soon, the sun rose properly, and we reached a rocky path. It cut through the fields, winding and dappled with faint green-tinged sunlight.

That was our route. I took it one step at a time, trying to shut my brain down and just exist, just walk away. I had no idea where we were or what the plan was.

Caroline strode onwards with purpose. 'Come on.'

I raced to keep up with her, and at first I was sure that Elise would appear, just waiting to hear the telltale sound of a car approaching, because they'd track us down.

'You don't think they'll follow?' I shouted to Caroline as we came to the outskirts of a field full of gangly sunflowers.

'No,' she called, racing away from me.

'Why not?' I asked. 'Elise wouldn't let me leave. She said that. So why wouldn't she try and make me come back?'

Caroline slowed down a bit though she still didn't turn to face me. 'That makes sense. She wouldn't have let you leave early. You're a good source of income, but now you're gone . . . she won't want to do anything that would cause a fuss, involve the public. She hates attention.'

I pondered on that.

Source of income.

I needed more.

Caroline clambered over a low hedge, gesturing for me to follow.

'Stop,' I shouted, catching my legs on the brambles as I went over the hedge.

'In a bit,' she said. 'Not too far now.'

'No, *now*. I know you're involved. You work there or . . . something? What's going on?'

She upped the pace. I could tell that she knew the way, but she was also limping, and one of her legs seemed unstable.

I caught up with her, grabbed her shoulder. 'I'm not going any further with you,' I said.

She pulled her arm back from me. 'So many questions. You were so probing back there at Carn,' she said airily, rubbing away at her shoulder. 'Prodding at us all. I don't think you even realized how you came across?'

'I didn't like you much either,' I said, but hearing my own words, it hit me that I actually did like this new version of Caroline a bit; she was still condescending, but at the same time she was refreshingly blunt in a way I appreciated.

'Well, I didn't say I didn't like you, did I?' she said. 'I liked you fine. It was just an observation. You were actually a bit better than the rest.'

'In what way?'

She thought about it. 'You didn't really buy into it all so much. I heard the helpers talk about you, down in the cellar, and that's what they said. They were quite surprised by you because girls usually feel so . . . right at Carn. They love Elise, and they believe her, but you pushed against it all in the end. You grew more of a backbone, but it was annoying at the beginning, for sure. Mooning over Abigail too.'

Had I been like that with Abigail? Had everyone seen and laughed at me?

She softened. 'None of that matters. I want to help you,' she said. 'So fine. You're right.'

'You work there.'

'I work there,' she said simply. 'Well, *worked*. Not any more.'

It was what I'd thought. We'd stopped playing games and something like relief rushed through me.

'But . . . why?' I asked. 'Why pretend?'

She leaned on one hip. 'Well, it helped to seem like I was a guest, when people were kind of . . . flighty, like Sally was. There was *always* one who needed a bit more attention. I'd done it with lots of girls before, with other cohorts. Carn's happened at different places you see, and there's been different ailments and different girls.'

I wanted to ask her more, but she was speaking too fast.

'– anyway, Sally was a particularly loose cannon. To be honest, we nearly didn't take her. A doctor!' She shook her head ruefully at the idea. 'So, I worked there in the way you saw to make sure things . . . ticked along.'

'Why?' I asked, incredulous. Why would anyone work at Carn for a long time? Terrible things seemed to happen there.

She hesitated, like she was considering how to phrase it. 'I guess it helps to understand that the helpers are smart,' she said with a shrug. '*We're* smart. Really fucking smart, Betsy. There are lots of Oxbridge graduates, lots of medical students.' She rolled her eyes to show what she thought of that. 'But those set paths aren't enough for people who are genuinely brilliant, you know?'

She pondered on it. 'Life becomes dull after a while. A bit of novelty is too much to resist. You hear about a woman who can heal people, and you want to be around her. You spend your life being the best, rising to the top in everything you do. And then you find out about this exciting, secret place. There's the money too . . . Whatever you're thinking, it's more. It was easy to justify the training. Whatever's needed to do the job – costume make-up, cordon bleu cooking, minor surgery . . .'

Minor surgery.

She said it offhand, but it sent a chill through me, as I scanned my body for an indication that someone had done something, even though, surely, I would have known. But time was blurry at Carn; our bodies were not our own and we were bruised like soft fruit, all papercuts and sunburn. If we'd been cut open in some way . . . well, it kind of felt possible.

Caroline was speaking again. 'As helpers, we were implicated. Elise, Patrick, the helpers, we all became part of it,' she said with a joyless smile. 'It starts with Elise, and she's a pro at identifying the girls. You're all so delicate, so easy to contain. You don't like swimming, don't like driving, blah blah blah.' She was on a roll, ticking off a list on her fingers. 'All different girls: tall, thin, fat, short, Black, white. Rich girls, poor girls . . . Terrible things have happened to some of you. For others, nothing much has happened, but you all come looking for something. You are all *not yourselves*; can't keep jobs, can't stay in relationships. Something missing in life, and then you meet her, and you come to Carn.'

She sneered. 'You get there and what you find isn't good; you make a fuss, but so many of you do recover to an extent, or change in some way. A lot of girls accept it for what it is and go back home after Carn. They never tell anyone about it. They're ashamed, you see. They don't like that Elise has the pictures. She says she'll use the pictures, that she'll sell them.'

I understood, but only a little. It was terrifying how a picture could be manipulated. I thought of my old job at the cosmetics company, and the way we'd instructed designers to remove freckles or add more and more and more. But the photographs the man had taken in the barn, with the make-up. Well, they weren't that bad. Weird, yes, but not terrible. Also, they were not appealing. Who would she sell them to?

Caroline turned away, squinting at something. She set off ahead of me, and we reached a small clearing. The real world was encroaching with the distant grunt of a car engine, but despite that, she sat down on the ground with her back against a tree.

I sat cross-legged next to her. The spike of adrenaline had gone, and I was left with heavy exhaustion.

'We should take a breather here for a few minutes,' she said. 'We need to pace ourselves until we get to the train station and then we'll jump on. I reckon we'll be able to get away without paying. Are you okay?' she asked finally. It was one of the first questions she had asked me.

It was hard to make sense of it all. Trying to balance everything I knew and work out what I didn't, and all the while the image of Sally kept coming back into my head: her skin with a horrible slimy film to it, the terrible smell of death. Something had been wrong there, but it was all too much to interrogate. I leaned back on the tree trunk, keeping my eyes open so the image of Sally wouldn't return.

'I don't understand how you ended up locked down in the cellar?' I asked.

'Well . . . I was trying to expose them. I was sick of it all. Of course, I knew what we were doing was wrong . . .'

I thought of the man at the window, and then the other men, watching.

I thought of the way the man had grabbed at my cheek.

I felt stupid saying it. 'Is it a . . . sex thing?'

She wrinkled her nose up. 'It's not that. Well, that's part of it, I guess, but not in the way you think. Last time was different, last year another group of girls and . . .'

She paused.

'And what?' I pressed.

'Someone died . . .' she said, and I thought I could detect sadness but also anger in her voice.

'Sally?' I said without thinking.

'No, not Sally,' she spat. 'Like I said, it was *last* year. Keep up. Anyway, all of you, you were not responding in the usual ways.'

'The usual ways?' I asked.

She was calmer. 'Everyone was pretty compliant most of the time. The drugs were good, usually. I needed more evidence, but I had to do something. Honestly, I really did try. I put the bleach in the water, which was a bad idea, but I was angry.

'Then, I went to her office because there's things there, documents and stuff.' She raised her hands in defeat. 'I wasn't careful enough. She was spooked. She got the rest of them to lock me down in the cellar until they could figure out what to do with me. But the other helpers were kind of lax, and they chatted away when they came in to feed me – they weren't sure how to treat me or what to say.

'I was able to keep track of what was going on upstairs. The night they caught me, I was trying to get photos, or letters, or contracts, or anything that would paint a picture of what we were doing there and who was involved, because some of the people that come are actually quite well known. But she caught me in the act.'

So, Caroline had gone down to Elise's office. That had been the last thing she'd done before they'd found her.

'Honestly, she was genuinely shocked when she saw what I was doing,' she said. 'She trusted me.' Caroline shook her head and let out a hard laugh. 'For me to *betray* her like that. The funny thing was, she didn't want to believe it at first. She wanted there to be a good excuse. I could have lied. I think she would have swallowed it, but I told her I was going to the police, going to tell them what she was doing. Elise had no idea what to do, so she locked me down there.'

I observed Caroline closely as she spoke. There were things she was holding back. And when it came to what she was telling me, I didn't know how much of it was lies. She paused and then she was saying something else about the heat, but I had stopped watching her and tuned out; I was thinking of Sally's grey face.

'Now what?' I asked.

'This is your out,' she said. 'Go back to your life and pretend it never happened.'

'But Sally!'

She flinched. 'I'm going to sort it, I promise, but we're done for now.'

'No,' I said.

She laughed at me. 'No?'

'No. Tell me what was going on in that operating theatre?'

She didn't respond.

I thought of the scalpel with blood down near the cellar. My hand went to my pocket and it was there, the bone. I rubbed at it. I enjoyed the smooth surface; it calmed me.

Then, I tried again. 'The operating theatre. You haven't explained it. What is she trying to do?' I asked.

Caroline closed her eyes. 'You don't want to know,' she said. 'I'm doing you a favour. It's much better if you just go back to your life.'

I should have pushed, but in that second, I agreed with her. Maybe she was right. The recollections were actually too much; too fresh for me to bring up again.

All I wanted to think about was Elise's hand on my shoulder, and the constant sense I was being healed. It had been so right for a while. I had been transformed. I still was transformed.

'There's no sense in you getting caught up with this,' Caroline said. 'Anyway, it all needed to stop.' She was speaking with more and more force; a fire had been lit within her. 'Like I said, I was trying to expose them. It was out of control.'

I gave up and looked at where we were, a peaceful place, but surely we couldn't rest for long. 'How far?' I asked.

'Just a bit further.'

We got up to continue the walk, this time side by side.

'I know a little about you. It's your sleep? That's why you agreed to come to Carn?' she asked mildly.

'Yes, my sleep.' As I admitted it, I was so tired I could have lain down right there and passed out.

'You must have been desperate,' she said. 'Everyone's desperate by the time they get there. Were things really that bad?'

I trusted her in some ways, not entirely but enough. The conversation had been horrible but also invigorating after all the swampy misunderstandings. There were still so many parts of Carn that I needed to work out, but we were back to talking about me.

'Yes, things had got very bad,' I said. 'Before I got married they were bad.'

43.

Are you sure you're okay? How are you feeling?

Those are normal questions you ask someone, but Harry seemed accusatory in his interest.

It started so perfectly with that first Christmas – burnt lasagne and abandoned Monopoly – but the whole shape of our relationship had shifted over time, with more outwardly violent moments that came about when he asked me how I was. After so long enjoying his attention, I couldn't bear the pity or the focus on me.

The acts began.

He didn't even know about the acts because I did them behind his back. I walked into the bathroom one day and went to our toothbrushes. I took his and dipped it in the toilet. There I was, squashing the bristles under the blackened rim. Immediately, I felt dirty, and spent at least ten minutes scrubbing away at the brush. In the end I threw it out and bought a new one and he was none the wiser. The night before, I'd fashioned him a tooth-brush in my sleep, a brush of tiny little razor blades like ones made for a mouse. He was compelled to use it, cutting into his gums as he moved the brush backwards and forwards.

I could control my dreams. I was aware that I was dreaming, but I couldn't change the kind of person I became in them. The worst one featured the girl in the swimming pool. I pushed her down and she struggled against it, and I dreamed it so often I questioned the reality of that day. Had I jumped into the pool and hurt that girl? Had no one told me? I did not know, but the more it came to me at night, the more real it was. Always, I woke in a cold sweat. I could never change the outcome, and I replayed it again and again until I stopped myself sleeping.

When I drifted off, it came: the smell of chlorine and then the feel of her skin and her wet costume hanging there.

Harry preferred to pretend nothing strange had happened. *Insomnia*, he insisted, even after I'd explained to him in the restaurant that it wasn't that.

Two weeks before we got married, I decided to make him dinner. It had not gone well telling him about my dreams, and I was trying to make amends. The plan was that we'd eat together as a couple. I chose a spaghetti dish and got to work. First, a visit to the Italian deli on Leith Walk to buy everything I needed. I chose a bottle of red wine and picked up ingredients, settling on the most expensive options. Striped red onions and a lumpy bulb of garlic; a comically large bunch of basil. I bought stock and bay leaves that smelled like the back of the cupboard but seemed to be integral to the recipe.

After my shopping trip, I cooked, and I thought how sad it was that this was so *notable*. To do what other people do all the time. But I was so, so tired. That night I was able to push through, though, like everyone else did.

The main thing, I thought, was not to let it burn and stick to the bottom of the dish, turning bitter. I stayed stirring, and it thickened and thickened to the point where I wasn't sure if the sauce was *too* thick. By that point, I was experimenting with abandon, adding salt (ill-advised) and sugar (helped a little with the balance).

I wasn't using my phone much, but I dug it out to send a picture to Harry, who sent me back the least emphatic of the smiley faces. Then I sent the picture to Siobhan too. I wondered if she'd comment, but there was no response.

I let the thought of the two of them sit in my mind for a second too long, and then I pushed it away. If I did not think of them together, I could keep my world intact.

I had suspected something between them for a while. I couldn't even say how long it was before the wedding, but certainly it had been months. It was a wariness about the two of them that lurked below every group activity, but I never let it develop further. I thought perhaps it was my own insecurities, but I knew for sure that Harry responded to Siobhan in a way that felt kind. He smiled at her, and he was always amicable with her. He wasn't really like that with me.

I decided to break my no-drinking rule and have a glass of wine that night, and then another one. Harry walked in from work, and he was shocked to see me cooking, even though I'd sent the photo, and he'd sent me the smiley face. It was reasonable for him to be surprised, as generally I pulled something together from the freezer, and it wasn't always successful.

He put his bag down and approached cautiously. 'Smells brilliant,' he said, but then he was concerned. 'Are you sure you're okay?'

'I'm fine. It's just pasta.'

I walked over and kissed him. I was rising above my body, observing an unknown woman kiss a man I'd never seen before.

'Sounds good,' he said, and he perched at the kitchen island, but only for a second; he rose to get a glass, taking his time deciding on which one to use. He settled on a wine glass that matched mine, and he pulled the bottle over and poured, basking in the light of the early evening.

He watched me as I cooked. I stirred the sauce with a final flourish and made a big deal about tasting it. Strained the pasta, ran some olive oil through it, and then piled the sauce on top, adding a handful of aged Parmesan I'd grated earlier.

He knew this was a peace offering. I passed him the plate. He took it and smiled at me. A dashing smile that made me melt a little inside, even though really it was simply a result of excellent dentistry. Handsome, caring Harry.

I couldn't smile back. I sprinted to the toilet and splashed my face with cold water.

'Are you coming?' he called from the kitchen.

When I returned, my face was red and wet. I grabbed my

bowl, and then I went over to sit next to him. He hadn't waited for me, and he was shovelling pasta into his mouth. I picked at mine because I wasn't hungry now I'd made it. But I ate anyway, to show willingness.

Harry didn't speak at first. His face twisted in a grimace, and he lifted his hand to his mouth and pushed his fingers between his lips. From his teeth, he pulled out a long strand of hair. The whole thing was kind of funny because it looked a little like a magic trick, like a magician pulling scarves from a sleeve.

He held it up and let out a little groan of annoyance.

I put my fork down. 'I'm sorry,' I said. 'I didn't tie my hair back, but I didn't think it would fall out.'

He pursed his lips. 'It's fine.'

He placed the hair next to his plate. It was horrible to see a strand of my own hair in that context. For a start, it was coarser than I would have thought, and it was longer too. He took another mouthful, digging in with vigour, but he then frowned again and reached into his bowl. Another long, dark hair, and this time he let out more of a growl. He pulled it out of his bowl and laid the hair alongside the first one.

'This is disgusting,' he announced. He wasn't aggressive when he said it. He stood up and put the bowl in the sink without scraping the food in the bin, and then he picked up his gym bag from the floor.

'I'm going out,' he said, and he left.

Then I picked up his bowl and poked about at his portion. Hair threaded through his dish. Spaghetti, spongy and beige, sitting against black strands.

I kept on eating mine (which was hairless) down to the last mouthful, and at the end I held the bowl up to my mouth and licked it clean.

Delicious.

In my dream the night before it had gone down a little differently. I had poisoned him with a viscous green liquid. In real life, of course, the meal was harmless. I could not remember doing it, but I must have added the hair. If I forced myself, I could just about see myself pulling it from my scalp, laying it in, stirring it through.

Later that night as I slept it came to me. The hair in my mouth. In my throat, there was a huge knot of it, and I woke up and touched his side of the bed, my body coated with sweat. But he was gone, and the sheets were cold on his side. And so, the closer we got to the wedding, the less normal I behaved, but he was not willing to back down; we would get married.

I did not tell any of this to Caroline. The story sat on my lips, starting with the sleep deprivation to justify it. I wanted to tell her some of it at least. Tell her that Harry liked me a certain way, just like Elise had. But there was no way to relay these stories in a way that made me look good.

'He turned me into someone I didn't want to be,' I said.

She nodded. 'Sometimes all we need is a change because we've been living in the wrong way. We all live in the wrong way sometimes.'

Bland advice.

I had a horrible urge to return to Elise, a desperation for her approval over everything else.

'I thought she was curing me,' I said.

Caroline just shrugged.

44.

The train seemed to falter as it drew in, like the driver had seen us and was unsure whether they were going to choose to stop. This was not how trains worked, but it would have been fair: I knew how we looked – far from respectable, wild hair and no possessions.

I lingered on the platform, below the trees that formed a cool canopy overhead. The shade was welcome. When the train did finally come to a stop, I followed Caroline's lead, because she jumped on without a second thought as soon as the doors opened. We discussed what to do in the quietest part of the end carriage, sitting close and whispering to each other. We hid in the corridor when the conductor came.

A woman asked if we were okay and I was impressed by how well Caroline fobbed her off, politely but without encouraging any further conversation.

'You said you had a plan,' I pressed Caroline once we'd settled.

'I told you, it's best I do it alone,' she said. 'With the police.'

My main concern was telling them about Sally. We had to. It was vital to do it as soon as possible. I thought of Abigail too – I knew I needed to find her and make sure she'd got out safely. I wondered about her journey, if she'd been sitting on this train the day before, and if she'd managed to find the station on her own.

We arrived at Waverley. There were people everywhere, which was brutal after the peace of Carn.

Caroline dodged them. Then she ran up to the desk, but she was back in minutes with a biro, flailing it at me.

'Your number?' she asked and stuck out her arm.

I wrote it up the whole of her inner arm, even though my phone was in a drawer somewhere in Harry's flat. The scratchy zeros disappeared upwards into the crook of her elbow, and it made me think of her nails on Sally's wrist forming an 'x'. How shocked we'd been. The memory was uncomfortable and the thought of them in the cellar gnawed at me.

I finished writing and we stood there.

I didn't want Caroline to leave. She had so many answers, but I could see she was desperate to get away from me.

'I know what to do,' she said, and she was forceful and bossy, just like she'd been when she'd protected Sally in those early days at Carn.

I nodded.

There I was again; I'd regressed, perhaps temporarily, to the meek hamster incapable of doing what needs to be done. I couldn't call the police. Would Caroline even call them? By doing that she would implicate herself.

She read back the number to me, and then she was off, dashing to the taxi rank. I wondered where she was going.

My head was pounding, and I was so grubby in a white dress that I was desperate to rip off as I walked through the streets from the station. The mess of my hair made a ratty halo around my face, but Edinburgh was busy, and no one gave me a second glance.

I wasn't walking in any particular direction. The thought of turning up at my parents' house was unbearable because they wouldn't have understood. I could imagine their pity, and I just couldn't take it. My father would be confused, and my mother, she would kind of shake her head and blame me for the whole thing. Whatever she said, deep down she would think it was my fault.

I'd need to go back to the flat. At no point in my life had I ever felt so utterly alone as I did in that moment. Even though I was back, there was no one in the world who cared about me, and I had nowhere else to go.

*

I asked the concierge for a key, and he handed it over, no questions. Then I let myself in quietly. I'd picked up the habit from Abigail, who'd moved stealthily, toes to the ground first with her heels soft.

Inside was different. There were plumped cushions, new ones decorated with embroidery. I didn't actively dislike them, but I never would have chosen them myself. The flat was cleaner too, and it smelled of tea tree oil. I noted a few new pieces of furniture slotted into the existing layout. On the coffee table sat Siobhan's ornamental elephant in pride of place. It was an ugly thing, made of a shiny metal and studded with jewels. I knew she'd bought it online, but to others she'd always been enigmatic about where it had come from. Never outright lied but hinted at some faraway travels. Seeing it in the flat was deeply offensive to me.

She was there too.

The hole I'd left, filled by her. She lay on the sofa looking relaxed with her feet dangling off the edge, snacking on a family-sized bag of crisps. The TV was on – American women in leggings shrieking at each other. She saw me and frantically tried to turn it off, pressing every button on the remote and eventually silencing them. They kept on screaming in mute.

Then she rose from the couch. 'You're back!' she spluttered. 'I was just helping out. Holding down the fort.'

I ignored her, and I was about to go to the bedroom to get my things when Harry came out with headphones in. It was then that I realized it was a Saturday. He had a routine that didn't change, and he looked as he always did on a Saturday – well exercised and damp from the gym. I noted a tension throbbing through him; I could see the rising impatience that I was so used to. He was holding his phone, and he didn't look up. It was a shame that he was still tetchy on a summery weekend morning, even when it was her and not me.

Our eyes met, and then he looked to her. The two of them shared a glance that was closed off to me. I wanted to demand what the look meant, what their secrets were.

'Betsy . . .' He trailed off.

I thought I'd want to know everything about how it had begun, exactly what had happened.

How long before the wedding?

I had expected to sit down and make them tell me it all. I was always questioning – I had been at Carn, I was here. But in the end, there was no point.

Something needed to happen, and I felt a surge of rage so intense I was carried by it. I went towards her, and she edged to one side. I picked up the elephant and threw it towards the glass table. The elephant was effective, smashing through the table in a satisfying crash.

Siobhan screamed. Harry was surprised but did not make a sound.

Tears. Hot down my face. Salty. Sweat in my armpits. That look flicked between them again. It killed me because it showed such closeness.

I went into the toilet and locked the door. It sounded as though they were trying not to raise their voices; I could hear that they were on the verge of a fight though I couldn't make out the details. There was a knock on the door.

'Betsy.' Siobhan's voice. 'Betsssss.'

She wasn't going to leave. I opened the door, and she slunk in and sat on the floor in front of me.

'I'm so sorry,' she said. 'We didn't want it to happen like this.'

We.

'It started later,' she said. 'I promise you. After you'd gone.'

Liar.

'I don't want to speak about it, not to you,' I said.

Her whole demeanour changed. She stood up awkwardly and crossed her arms. 'Really? Do you really not want to talk about it?' she asked. Everything about her was crisped and hardened. She flipped her hair over her shoulder.

'I have things to say,' she said.

Things to say.

232

'We were just *chatting* at the wedding,' she said. 'Nothing had happened, but you freaked out, and so he suggested you go up to the room.'

But that was not how I remembered it. He'd practically dragged me up there.

'He locked me in,' I said to her. 'You know that, don't you?'

She shook her head. 'Um, I don't think so. Whatever, Betsy. I mean, what you did . . .' She was expectant, waiting for me to fill in the gaps, forcing me to hold up the scraps of the day. They were a gluey mess, but she wouldn't leave until she'd prised them out, and I think she was the only person who could force me to do it.

I had not forgotten what had happened that day, but I forced myself to push the thought away whenever it bubbled up.

She raised an eyebrow. 'What *you* did to him that day,' she clarified. 'It was quite something.' There was a defiant grimness mixed with dark glee at my downfall.

45.

In the weeks before the wedding, I'd struggled. Every time I thought of Siobhan and Harry I felt a little bit of sick rise in my throat, and I told myself that that would explain the acts: the hair, the toothbrush, all those things. I had pushed my thoughts of them away and told myself I was paranoid. Part of it was that I refused to lose Siobhan as a friend. I'd pinned so much on her, and I didn't want to give her up. But as the wedding approached, my acts were growing worse. Still, we pushed on. And so we did the final fittings and the final tastings, and I did well to never think of them together.

Then the big day. It was one of mirrors, reflections in sunglasses, reflections as I saw myself in the window. The dress was huge. The icing, pink.

We had the cake-cutting ceremony with the knife that Harry picked up. He pushed down through the different flavours and the cake bent like a living thing. I was overcome with a terrible thirst, made worse by the sight of food for some reason.

Why were we cutting the cake so late, when everyone seemed so drunk?

After, Harry slid his hand away from my waist. Then there was a flash of orange as Siobhan left the marquee; I saw the flaps to the side open and close again.

Skip to me standing with the cake, alone, because Harry had gone. I peered around, looking for the chartreuse suit. I pushed through the guests. I saw the two of them outside, and it was impossible to ignore. There was a terrible tightness in my chest. This was the truth. I knew it, knew that everything had been a lie.

Harry noticed me and offered a tentative smile, and he did

have the loveliest smile, but guilt lurked beneath. It was filled with the suggestion that I should look away and ignore what seemed so clear. He walked over to me and grabbed my arm, leading me through the crowd. Away we went, past my brothers, all ruddy. One of them was fighting with the bartender.

We walked past them and inside to our room. Harry nodded at the staff as we went upstairs to show them that we were absolutely fine.

Will you need anything? the staff said. *No, we're great, thanks so much for everything,* Harry responded smoothly.

It dawned on me that we were going to our room.

'Stay there,' he said, and then he was gone. I rushed to the door, but it was locked. I didn't think to try to get out. I didn't know what I'd do if I got out.

Eventually, he did come back, later, when it was dark outside, but I could still hear people and music.

'I brought you a slice of cake.' He handed over a sticky cocoon of napkins.

'Where have you been?' I asked. 'What happened?'

'You needed to calm down for a bit. I could sense you were about to go off on one. You seem more relaxed now?'

The hamster has its rest in the nest, wakes up sleepy-eyed.

'So, you locked me up here?' I asked.

His expression morphed into disbelief. 'B, the door's been unlocked this whole time,' he said. 'I wanted to bring you up here for a break away from it all. I genuinely thought you were going to freak out down there.'

I had no idea if he was telling the truth or not about the door. Maybe I'd jumped to conclusions, assumed it had been locked, maybe it had just been stiff? It didn't matter.

The hamster cannot pass the bars of the cage, clicks its jaw, works out how to approach.

'You and Siobhan,' I said. 'She went for you.'

'Went for me?!' He laughed and it was cruel. 'What on earth do you mean?'

236

'I saw it. She was going to kiss you. You pushed her away.'
Would he deny it?

He considered the accusation for a second. 'Ah, but, Bets, if I pushed her away, what's the issue?' he asked, triumphant.

'So, you admit something happened?'

'How much have you had to drink?'

'You know what I'm talking about! Together. The two of you.'

'For fuck's sake! We were joshing.' He hummed like he was trying to remember. 'She was teasing me about God knows what. I pushed her away. We were talking because she's . . . she's part of the fucking wedding party!' He shook his head at me. 'You see that, right? You see how ridiculous you're being?'

'You looked guilty,' I said.

'Really? You're actually losing it,' he said, very gently.

I knew what I'd seen. Even when things were murky in my mind, that exchange was so tender, and I was so sure.

I growled. The words that were meant to come out, *I saw*, didn't really sound like words at all, and I hardly recognized the sound I was making as I jumped up off the bed and went for him, flying across the room.

The hamster is enraged, at the bars of the cage, scuttling, biting.

I clawed at his face, breaking through the skin, and he let out a howl. He tried to back away from me towards the door, but I was quick and I grabbed at his hair, going for the fringe. I think I would have gone for his eyes, but he had my wrist tight in his hand, and then we were entwined. With my free hand, I picked up the cake and pushed it into his mouth. He was groaning, and outside they must have heard, surely, with the windows open to let the air in. The noises he made were horrible. I went at him again, and he pushed me backwards on to the bed. He tried to restrain me, held me down by my wrists on the bed. He lay on top of me, and eventually I stopped struggling, because I was spent and my arms were jelly.

'What the hell!' he spat in my ear. He was much stronger than me; he could have done anything, and he pushed his weight down for a second before heaving himself off. He lurched from the bed and wiped the blood from his face. 'You've lost your fucking mind,' he said, incredulous. 'I can't go back down there like this.'

What would they have thought?

That's what he feared – the shock and pity of our guests. I understood because sometimes I hated pity too.

He came to our room the next morning, and we drank our coffee from those little white cups, and I played with the sugar sachets again, fiddling with them, but just me, no Siobhan there to fiddle alongside me. I didn't need to say a word.

In the morning, I didn't fully blame him for any of it. I knew that I'd pushed him further and further, lashed out knowing we'd both break. I was a damsel to him. He liked me to be a little ill, a little meek. He had from the beginning. But not *too* ill. Just the right amount, wherever that line was – I had no idea. But we fed from each other. If he was better, harder, more ruthless in his goals, I got worse – softer and madder. With Harry, it was all unmanageable. He tried to force me back into a more acceptable form of illness. He made me into someone he wanted me to be, but we had turned each other into the worst versions of ourselves.

The sun streamed into the room and the clothes on the floor were stained. I had to look away from the state of his face, and he didn't speak to me.

'You remember!' Siobhan said, voice rising in a tense delight. 'Of course you remember! You hurt him badly. I thought you might have fractured something because his face was super bruised. Those scratches were *terrible*.' There was a hyper kind of elation in her chatter.

'I remember parts of it. I shouldn't have hurt him.'

She pursed her lips, sour, the glee gone. 'You know, he wanted to make a go of it with you. Even after that, can you believe it!'

'Hmmm.' I didn't know what to say, but she was probably right.

He had tried with me. He'd returned after the hair incident; he'd come back after the wedding, even after what I'd done, and we'd gone on our honeymoon.

She knelt on the floor in front of me. 'He was like, angry about it, obviously, but we all knew you had problems. We knew about the dreams. We knew you weren't well, but we didn't know how bad it was. You kept breaking down. It was why he moved out for a bit, and then, when he came back, you didn't want to talk about any of it. We had no idea what to do! Anyway, like I said, nothing happened between us until afterwards.'

I couldn't think of a response. All the conversations I'd planned in my head seemed pointless. Did it even matter when it had begun?

I think the story of Harry and me had always been set to come to an end. Long before we'd said our vows in the heat, before I'd hurt him so horribly. Years later, Harry and Siobhan would get married, and I would not be invited, of course, but I would see pictures on a friend's phone, flicked in front of me to prove it had happened. The friend didn't know the full story and they would hide their delight in digging up the past – *Poor Spencer! He didn't deserve that! And you, of course, you didn't deserve that either.* A few seconds of contemplative silence, and then the topic of conversation changed. It would look nothing like our wedding. No marquee. You could see in the pictures there was a distinct lack of sun. It would take place on a drizzly Friday, and there would not be any sprawling rhododendron bushes, no flowers at all. I guess such elements had been snipped away at planning stage, and they'd surely tried to avoid every single thing Harry and I had had at our wedding. Perhaps that's a normal reaction when you plan your second wedding.

I walked past Siobhan, back to the living room, where Harry was scrambling about for phone chargers and stray socks. It was clear he would not talk, and he just wanted to be away from the situation. I watched as he buzzed around.

'Your car,' I said to him before they left. 'I need to borrow it.'

'You don't drive.' And, 'You never drive.' Harry and Siobhan spoke over each other.

'Where's the key?' I asked.

It was a relief when they left. I had expected Harry to throw me out because it was his flat really.

'Do whatever you need to do,' he said as he handed me his car key without any jibe about scratching the paintwork or remembering to lock it, although I could see him struggling not to add rules.

He said I could stay in the flat until we sorted things out. I should have been drained from the conversation, but I was wired for whatever would come next.

46.

I swept all the glass from the broken coffee table, popped the elephant ornament in the bin where it made a loud clunk, and brushed away the crumbs of crisp from the sofa. Then it was time for a long, hot shower. I shaved my legs and moisturized them with care. I poured myself a pint of water, added ice and drank the whole thing in one, letting the cubes rumble around my mouth until they melted into a cold ache that spread into my jaw. When the ice was gone and there was nothing left to distract, no sensations to pull myself away from my mind, I thought of Sally, Caroline and Abigail. There was no blocking them out, especially Sally. *Call the police.* Sally's voice in my ear, and I hated it. Such strict instruction burrowed into the back of my head, and I tried to do as it said, but every time I went for the phone, I couldn't make myself dial.

It was so *selfish* of me; I knew that. To push thoughts of the police away was absurd after what I'd seen, but I can only justify it with the fact that there was a lot I didn't know about Carn.

Minor surgery.

Moving parts.

Recoup investment.

Special.

I wasn't ready to hand it all over to the police even though I wasn't sure what to do next.

So, I ended up doing nothing much, and the guilt at my inaction subsided a little. It became easier as the days passed, because if I pushed that churning unease to the side, I felt very good. I was just on the edge, with pain at the forefront, like at Carn: needle sharp with bright colours in my peripheral vision. Agony that was almost moreish. I chewed on ice; experienced static shock from metal doorknobs. It was a brilliant feeling.

It was time to begin a new life. I had returned home to many changes – no Harry; no job, even if I wanted one, because I couldn't work in the bookshop. Tentatively, I eased back into adulthood over the week that followed with a huge food shop delivered early in the morning. I unpacked it with sad films on in the background. And then progressed to horror films, the dead girls plastered against the screen. Now I had seen a real dead girl, these appeared fake. The colour of their faces was wrong, and you could almost see the laugh in their eyes, ready to spill out when the cameras stopped rolling. They were not dead, and I thought of them as I lay in bed.

Those first nights were long because Carn hadn't cured my sleep entirely, though I don't think that was ever on the cards. I dozed in random stretches, with street performers strolling outside the windows. The persistent staccato from a demented snare drum disturbed my long naps on the sofa, but my dreams were quieter mostly: songbirds instead of knives.

Two more weeks passed of much the same.

I rooted out my bank cards, wondered how much money was left in my account. My and Harry's shared card still worked, and I figured it was something to sort out later.

Call the police, the voice said.

I decided to take Harry's car out. I sped through the streets with the windows down, blaring out music. I wanted to be in it all – the Fringe had begun and the crowds were inviting. Acts wandered the streets with flyers, and the bars and restaurants heaved. I was alone in the city, and so I walked around watching. I paced through Edinburgh's suburbs, past rows and rows of bungalows. But walks felt too slow, and I was too fired up. Running was better, and I managed a shaky ten km.

On my second attempt at a long run through the Old Town,

I turned a corner and nearly tripped up over a bunch of girls looking at a phone.

'Sorry,' I said. 'Did I hurt you?' The one I'd come close to hitting had tousled blonde hair, and she nodded, accepting my apology without interest. She didn't look terribly like Sally, but the hair brought Sally back: the view of her on the lawn, kicking off at the helpers.

I stumbled away from the girl. My feet slapped against cobbles, nearly turning my ankle at each step, and I practically welcomed the hint of an injury to knock images of Carn away.

Browned avocado and pink bacon served at breakfast.

A shining candelabrum, and Elise presiding over it all.

I sped up, ran until my lungs hurt, right into the middle of a busy intersection with so many people – buskers and bagpipers and cyclists all fighting for space – and then I stopped.

One of the men from Carn.

He looked at me. It was him, the one who had twisted my cheek between his fingers, pressed in with his nails. He stood there in the street, hovering at the kerb, frozen. I stared at him, heart beating madly, and people walked past the man, not registering his presence as an inconvenience, perhaps because he appeared spectral amongst the bustle. Sally's question returned to me. *Maybe we all died here, and we just didn't realize it?*

I was shaking. Was it fear? I couldn't even tell. It was something, certainly, a fizzing kind of feeling.

Surely he would approach me?

But, no. He showed no intention of getting any closer.

When the lights turned green, I ran as fast as I could across the road towards him, willing him to stay put. As I approached, people coming the other way over the junction bristled and tutted as I weaved between them.

The man remained still. He wouldn't come to me, but would he flee? He let me advance until I was a few metres from him. He grinned at me.

The crowd was thick in front of us, and then a group of children flocked below him. He was some kind of terrible Pied Piper. He looked down at them with little interest, and then he turned and drifted away into the crowd. It was a magic trick, in a way, as people swarmed in his wake and blocked my sight. There were too many of them for me to battle through, and I gave up running, though I tried to see where he had gone. But he'd disappeared.

The fizz eased away. I thought of the euphoria that Caroline had described: her nails on Sally's wrists and then the calmness that followed. I wanted that stillness, but as I walked it started as an itch at the top of my shoulders. I abandoned the idea of continuing my run, and it built and built like burrowing ants in my clothes. I couldn't scratch it away – I tried but I could tell it was beneath the skin.

I had experienced a change within myself.

I was hungry. I felt horribly, sickeningly empty as I got closer to the flat. Though I had lots of food at home, I stopped in front of a butcher's – a traditional kind of one with a white-and-red-striped awning. The smell of meat coming from the shop was strong but also compelling, and I went in and ordered the first fillet I saw, pressed against the glass at the front of the counter: pork. Back at the flat, I unwrapped it from the plastic bag. I needed to eat, a desperate, all-consuming craving that took over every part of me. It had to be the meat.

I took out the pork and seared it in the pan, and then I put it in the oven, willing it to cook quickly, and the drum was beating outside again, and it formed an endless loop that made time stand still. Then, I cut the fillet into neat sections, ravenous for the first bite. I chewed, but there was no taste. The second bite I took was even worse.

It was all . . . wrong. The texture was quite abnormal, like munching on something manmade, and I thought the meat had gone off, but it was more than that. It was not rotten, just . . . nothing. And so I added salt and pepper and then chopped-up chillies, jamming the seeds into the flesh, fried up garlic, golden-brown, but it didn't help.

Something was wrong with me. It crawled within me and couldn't be made still. It squirmed, morphed into an urgent thing, moving upwards into my throat, became hot acid, but it wasn't reflux; in fact, it was nothing I recognized. A hunger, I was sure of it, but eating had become impossible.

I tried to calm myself. A drink would solve whatever this was, wash away the rot. So, I rattled around the flat, pulling out twee cartons of premixed cocktails that Siobhan must have brought over, leftover spirits and finally the dregs of old port. I took slugs of them all and the texture of each one seemed too thick in my throat, like phlegm, and I gagged. I rinsed a glass with vermouth and added gin. The result was undrinkable. In the end I reached to the back of the cupboard for the kind of drinks we'd had at Carn. I pulled out dusty bottles to make negronis, mimosas, trying to bring back some of the magic, but it all fell flat. Every single drink had a lumpiness to it. It was my imagination, surely? Everything tasted full of my own spit.

I could not solve the hunger. Food had become unbearable. In a last-ditch attempt, I ordered a takeaway, but I only managed a bite before it went straight in the bin. The chow mein was rubber, and I spat it out and brushed my teeth to get rid of all remnants.

I sat down, finally.

Panicky.

I tried to approach it analytically. It wasn't that my taste buds had been destroyed by Carn, more that the mere concept of food didn't seem right any more, and paired with the hunger, it was a strange, torturous combination. Something was knocked out of alignment. The voice was still there, but it wasn't telling me to call the police.

That evening, as I sat surrounded by bottles and plates of food, the message had changed. The urge was to see Abigail – she was still alive somewhere, and I needed to find her. This time, I didn't block the voice out. I went to her.

47.

Abigail lived in the basement flat of a tenement building on an extremely busy and noisy road, which seemed like an awful choice for someone with her afflictions. Outside, there were two stinking bins overflowing with cardboard and old food. The door was the colour of dark cherry skins, the paint glossy.

When I rang the bell, I expected her to be out, or to ignore it, or for it to not work at all. I waited, poised to walk away, but after a few minutes she was there, standing in front of me looking shocked. She was about to slam the door in my face, but she recovered.

'You found me!' she said with a small smile.

It had been hard to track her down, but not impossible, because I was a decent online sleuth – I used to spend whole days at work trawling for updates about minor freckled celebrities.

I had quickly discovered pictures of her from university, drunken photos from a pub crawl: Abigail covered in face paint, a beer bottle in her hand, leaning in, smiling. She had long hair and looked nothing like the girl I'd met at Carn. I worked out the town she'd grown up in by virtue of elimination. From there, I learned her surname and tracked her down online in a list of entries, her name weaved through them: boldened and underlined in the minutes from a residents' association meeting, titling an old biography from a job not so dissimilar to my old job. She'd lived an unremarkable life, like me. It lurked on the internet, easily found. She seemed to have no reason to scrape away her digital presence, but at a certain point, it just stopped.

I was relieved that she'd answered, but I instinctively pulled back. I wanted to see her better, but it was dark in the flat. She asked me to 'Come in,' and so I did.

I closed the door carefully behind me even though it had a noise softener. She instructed me through a convoluted routine – taking my shoes off, hanging my bag up and my coat too.

I followed her. The place was gloomy. I noticed that she'd done something to the walls, clad them in a beige material, and it made the corridor seem narrow. I reached out and pushed at one wall; it was springy and damp.

'It's soundproofed,' she said to me as we walked through on cold wooden floors. 'I did it myself. Not as good as Carn, of course. But still, it does work. The landlord doesn't know, but he never visits anyway. Listen . . .' She tailed off with a finger in the air.

We'd reached the kitchen at the back of the flat, and although we were metres from a busy street, the flat was silent. I could hear a faint and persistent ringing in my ears that I never heard in the city. I'd heard it at Carn because it was very quiet there too.

Big windows framed a dank garden, full of dark green bushes that cast a witchy light upon the grubby cabinets. There wasn't much there: unpacked boxes, an old kitchen table.

'Hardly any noise. And there's no one in the flat above, hasn't been for years. If I stay here, I can pretend,' she said with a horribly forced smile.

'Pretend what?'

'Pretend I'm *normal*, of course,' she replied in the same bright tone. 'For a while. It only lasts a while.'

The life was drained from her. Now we were finally, properly looking at each other, I could see that she was putting on a good show. She was trying to be the Abigail who had blossomed initially at Carn, but she wasn't able to pull it off. Even her tattoos seemed dull.

'Sit.' She gestured to a chair.

I did, and she sat opposite me, maintained a distance.

'I'm surprised you found me.' She cocked her head. 'Why are you here?'

'I needed to come. I wanted to make sure you were okay. You left without me!' I knew I sounded angry, and I was, but I still cared about her.

'Sorry,' she said, but she didn't sound it at all. Then she got up and turned her back to me, filling the kettle. The noise of the heating element cut through the quiet, and she shivered.

'I don't understand how you did it?' I asked.

'I left,' she said dreamily, though I could not see her face. It was like she was remembering something a long time ago. 'I came back here. I left for the last time.'

'For the last time?'

She turned to face me. Her face was pinched. There was so little of her left.

'I've been to Carn before,' she said. 'Many times.'

48.

She wouldn't say a word more until she'd finished with her preparations; 'Tea, tea, tea,' she sang, sliding around her kitchen and delaying the conversation. Finally, she sat opposite me with a steaming cup.

'Well, I say I've been many times, but it's always a different place,' she said in a disconnected kind of chant. 'They set it up, move it around, so no one can go back, apart from me. She's built me all kinds of things, all kinds of rooms! Once it was cabins in the Borders, once it was this old church. I've been again and again. Different groups of us too. A girl who had terrible eczema came once.'

Irrationally, one of my first thoughts was that I was not her closest friend. I had imagined our connection to be unique, but I now suspected this wasn't the case. Perhaps Abigail had a routine at Carn, and she always found someone to cling to.

'Why would you keep going back?'

'Because she helps me,' she said, like it was obvious. 'Every single time I feel so much better. I'm not stupid, I know she tells me what I want to hear. She finds me, she tells me I'm her favourite. She makes me remember how it is to go there, to be treated, to drink, to eat . . .' She shuddered. 'I say I'll never go back, but I always do. Anyway, I think I'll be able to stay away this time because I know it's wrong . . .'

'Why is it wrong?' I asked.

She ignored the question. 'You feel it, don't you?' she said. 'You feel better.'

She had said the same phrase to me so many times at Carn. I didn't say yes or no, but she was right, I had felt better at Carn, and upon my return I'd felt wired with a chaotic kind of energy that wasn't unwelcome.

She rubbed at her arms, and I saw how hard she pushed down; she was still bruised, just like I'd noticed in the library. Rows and rows of marks down her arms now, but it was *her* causing them, pressing her fingers in. I realized that there was no mystery assailant hurting her.

'You've lived it all before,' I said. 'You know about the peephole . . .'

She shrugged. 'They want to watch as it happens.'

'As *what* happens? They're taking things from us?'

Elise had taken blood from us, right at the beginning and then again.

Whole chunks of time were blurry. Extracting something from us? I was running through different scenarios.

'Leave it,' she said. Echoes of Caroline's words. They all wanted me to leave it alone.

She sipped her tea, exhaled loudly with pleasure at the taste. 'I'm actually glad you came.'

I was ready to push her, more than I'd pushed Caroline, and I tried another tack. 'You've been before, you know how messed up it is, so why run away?'

'She said she'd never lie to me,' Abigail said. 'But she *did* lie. She told us different stories about the daughter. Anyway, you're being coy. You must know everything because you're out! You know it all.'

'I don't think I do. I escaped,' I said.

She spluttered on her tea, and she placed her cup down carefully. 'You *escaped*! They're going to be looking for you.'

'With Caroline,' I continued. 'It's just, I thought we'd leave together.' I was embarrassed. I tried to swallow the lump in my throat away. 'You and me. But Caroline helped me.'

'Caroline?' She was staring at me in wonder. '*Caroline* got you out?'

'You knew she was a plant.'

'Yeah, I knew. She's a helper, has been for ages. She's decent at it. With weirdos like Sally. There's always one who goes psycho. Can't handle it,' she said.

'Caroline wants to go to the police; she wants to report them. They were keeping her in the cellar, that's where she was,' I said. 'And Sally too.'

'The cellar!? So where are they now?' Abigail asked. She looked at me expectantly.

'Sally's dead.'

'No.' She shook her head. 'She can't be. They wouldn't do that. They would *never* . . .'

'Abigail, she is. I saw.'

'But how?'

'Well, you were out there,' I said. 'That afternoon when I think it must have happened. Can you remember anything about her getting hurt?'

She was slow to speak as she forced the recollection. 'God, I don't know. There was all this commotion. They were holding her down, I remember that. They were so focused on her. To be honest, they barely registered I was there. Then . . .'

She tapped at her head as if to bang the memory out. 'Well, I think one of them went to check on you too. They moved to the other side of the house, I guess, and I left. I was so angry.

'They don't mind me leaving because I always come back. I do as I please when it comes to staying at Carn as long as I don't interfere with the other girls. But this time was different. We talked more, we shared more. I was so angry with *Elise*. I couldn't stay there any longer, and I just . . . left. I jumped in the water and left. I could hear them, all of them shouting. Sally was pretty noisy, and then I started running when I got over the other side.'

'She drowned,' I said. 'She tried to get over the water and she drowned.'

Abigail looked like she was about to burst into tears. 'So, what now?' she asked.

'The police.'

'The police,' she repeated. 'Sally.'

Neither of us spoke, but we were possibly both thinking the same thing. It was probable that no one would be looking for Sally. At least not for a while. No one would report her missing, and it would need to be us who sorted it out.

'I wouldn't trust the police,' Abigail said. She turned to focus on the garden. 'It's beginning again. I can't *bear* the noise. I really need to try some new protocols. Some new therapies. I'll go back to the doctor, I think. Nothing feels right.' She stroked her cup. 'I always hate the sounds they make,' she said. 'When *they* watch us.'

I was glad in a way that she'd brought the conversation round to *them*.

'I saw one of them on the street,' I said.

She let out a choked kind of sound. 'They watch,' she said. 'After you come back. They still like to watch.'

'I don't understand who they are, why they come? You can tell me,' I said. 'You can trust me.'

She shook her head. 'You should go,' she said.

I didn't get up. I waited.

'Go see Patrick,' she said. 'If you want answers. But don't mention me. Promise you won't? You can say Caroline sent you.'

'I promise.'

My heart hurt to look at her.

She smiled sadly. She'd left me, and I wanted to forgive her for going because I had cared for her so much.

Me and her against the world. I almost wanted to lean in and touch her, but I was scared she'd push me away.

I rose and walked to her front door. We stood there on the doorstep. She gave me her number, but even to look at it, I was almost sure it was fake. I suspected I would struggle to see her again. I was already thinking ahead to Patrick.

'Be careful,' she said.

'Caroline said someone else died there,' I said.

She was about to close the door on me.

'You know about this?' I pushed.

'In the last cohort,' she said. 'Ask Patrick.' And she practically shouted it, but it was more frustration than anger, and I couldn't help but go in closer, smell her and feel her, my fingers on her sides as I gave her a hug and the bones in her ribs pressed against me. It was at that point I saw the ear plugs she wore. They were subtle. Her lips were close to my ear; they always seemed to go there. 'It's not what they took from us,' she said. 'It's what they gave us.'

Before I could say another word, she'd pulled away and slammed the door so fast I jumped at the suddenness, and the door was a slick of red like the inside of a scream.

49.

I went to the bookshop straight away. It was the afternoon, and the city was filled with smoke, like bonfires and charred meat from BBQs. I smelled the aftermath of a rain shower in the steamy streets, and that soft fuzz of summer light seemed drained, even though it was still the middle of August.

When I arrived and the door came into sight, I saw the hand-written sign – *Closed* – in Patrick's scrawl. The door was locked, but Patrick had given me a key which I'd kept in my purse. I pulled it out and opened the door to let myself in.

Inside, the bookshop was just as I remembered – dusty, cool and dark. I touched the books on both sides as I went further in. They were Patrick's books, his pets. I was waiting for him to appear, because although the door was locked, his presence was everywhere: used coffee cup next to the till, piled-up Tupperware. It all seemed recently abandoned, but I couldn't see him anywhere on the shop floor and so I went to the back of the room and down the steps to his basement.

Like at Carn, the journey ended with stairs. There was the keypad at the bottom, and I tried the code that Caroline had given me. As I expected, it lit up in green and so I walked in.

Elise's office had been a fairy-tale of a place, sleeping girls taking centre stage in an airy, light-filled room. Patrick's was the opposite: stuffy and cramped, with piles of books everywhere, stacks of messy paperwork and two overflowing filing cabinets. Deep under the shop, there were no windows, but dark curtains made of thick velvet hung around the walls. In the middle of it all was Patrick on a chaise longue. He was dressed in a greying vest that dipped low and barely covered his nipples, with a pair of tuxedo trousers, his arm flopping out. I heard a light snore, and I coughed, unsure of how else to get his attention while staying near to the door. I didn't want to get any closer to him. He looked up and smiled at me dozily and heaved himself up with a groan.

'Well, hello, Betsy. I suspected you'd turn up at some point. You escaped!' He sounded delighted; no hint of his former tetchiness.

'Caroline helped me.'

'Did she now?' He walked over to me and stuck a finger out to prod my face.

I darted back from him.

He withdrew.

A truce.

'Abigail told me to come,' I said. 'And I guess . . . I wanted to see you. You tried to save me.'

I thought of his offer to take me away from Carn. I hadn't wanted to see him at all, but I found myself buttering him up, so he'd tell me what I wanted to know.

He seemed confused, but then he burst out laughing. 'Save you? Did I say that? I think I said I was going to bring you back here. Keep you for myself.'

I thought of his words to me at Carn: *Because this does not mean that I'm on your side. Be quite assured, I am not.*

'I have little interest in it now,' he said breezily. 'Now you've got out, you seem somewhat tainted.' He inhaled. 'You smell different. You move differently.'

My stomach clenched. There was no way to be further away from him in the room because my back was up against the door.

'Now, the question is, what do you want?' he asked. 'Why are you here?'

'Tell me everything about Carn,' I said, fighting the urge to run from the room.

'Sit.' He gestured to a chair.

I shook my head.

'Suit yourself. Everyone's truth is different, of course, but I'll tell you mine. My truth is magnificent, Betsy.'

He sat back down on his chaise longue, stretching out with a contented sigh. 'It starts with Elise,' he said. 'But you knew that already. Lovely Elise. A collector of people and a remarkable talent in the art of selection. She scoops you up from all over the place. AA meetings in town halls, from hospital beds, from anywhere, really. But I found you, and you were mine.' He stared at me, willing me to deny it, but I didn't say a word.

He continued, 'Before that she was a nurse, you know? That's where I met her. That was when she became interested in illness, with these people who are broken. She says it makes them powerful, and I took a little convincing, but once I saw it, God, I *saw* it! I saw what you were. But I opened her eyes to how it could be so, so much more. How we could push it further, make it more spectacular.'

He sounded very proud.

'What did you do to us?' I asked, heart racing.

'No need to rush. You asked for it all. So, I have the contacts, of course. They frequent the bookshop,' he said, lying back down. 'They have money to spend, but this is a kind of wealth you can't imagine. These men, they like illness, if you make it sound clever. Wrap it up for them with words they like. *Hysteria. Neurology. Beauty. Pain. Death.* We have a waiting list, you know. Nothing is off-limits. Especially when it comes to the women, the girls.'

My skin crawled at the way he rolled the word on his tongue, *girls*.

'We came to see you, and we understood you were special. The things Elise saw in you? Well, we saw them too. We liked the pictures of you at the beginning – the illnesses manifested visually.' He smiled encouragingly. 'We really do enjoy the pictures a lot. I have them here. And money. That was at the heart of it, of course. There was so much profit in it. Elise sold the pictures to different companies for marketing; she can sell anything. Even the ones where you look ill, they like it. Pharma companies especially like it. They found that the pictures always did well for adverts and things because the girls are so special. And I sold them too as art, to go on the walls of houses so fantastic you'll never see the insides. Limited edition pictures. A story for a dinner party.'

I thought of the pictures of us, the repulsive make-up that had shocked Sally.

Here he lowered his voice so it was almost a growl. 'And the richest men come to watch.'

'Why, though?'

He laughed. 'Well, we can help cure you! We can impart something to you. We are rich, erudite. We are the best of the best. Excelling in our fields. We give and give, and we watch you transform at Carn, your talents even better and brighter. It is truly the greatest gift for us.' His voice went low. 'We watch as we go further. We're inside you.'

An inkling of comprehension. I didn't want to understand. I squirmed. He stretched on his chaise longue and stood. He lifted his vest up very slowly like this was a game, leaning to the side, and there wasn't much to him underneath, all skin and bones. A dressing covered his entire side, stained but still taped on tidily.

Patrick did not break eye contact. He ogled me as he reached down and peeled off the dressing, starting with where it sat at the top of his ribs. Once the dressing was off, hanging below all pink and wet, the stitched wound was visible to me. I don't think it was infected. It was tidy enough, you didn't need medical knowledge to see that, but still, there was bruising all around; it did not look like it was healing well. He let go of the dressing and ran one finger lightly over where the stitches pulled at the skin. This should have been painful for him, and I expected some kind of reaction. I flinched, but he did not, and his hand moved freely downwards until it settled on his navel. He finished with a sudden jab at himself. No reaction. He seemed to experience pain selectively.

'Oh, I'm not sure you got any of *this*.' He grabbed at the flesh. 'After all, you left.'

He nodded. He was urging me to understand but I couldn't get there, and then he spoke. 'We feed you,' he said, exasperated. '*Feed* you.'

Feed
  You.

My heart battered at my chest. I didn't want to understand. He wasn't being obtuse, but I had to force myself to accept what had happened. I could feel vomit rushing up into my throat. I pushed it down.

A crowd of cracked recollections, of the frail man at the window, of Caroline's words – *Minor surgery*, she'd said. The bloodied scalpel, and the man on the street watching me when I'd left. I had felt *sorry* for them, for those injured men who were mutilating themselves for us.

Patrick did not seem upset at my reaction. He lay back down. He stretched and yawned, all curled up. 'It's a privilege,' he said as he snuggled into himself. 'That's how I see it, and how the helpers see it, and of course how Elise sees it. Everyone takes a while to come around. We feed you and we watch you. The connection is simply unreal. The process is sublime. A mere sliver of abdomen, some buttock. You eat it right from day one at Carn, and we watch, we feel the connection grow; we feel stronger and you do too.'

I needed to get out, but my mind was racing so fast.

It hit me. Caroline knew. She'd only eaten fish.

But it was Abigail who I couldn't stop thinking about. Abigail who had eaten it all; her face as she'd picked up her fork on the first night. Her grimace as she chewed on a long sausage. I'd misread her disgust and thought she had an eating disorder.

'Abigail knows . . . and she keeps going back?'

'Ah yes . . . Abigail,' he said, like it was a distant memory. 'I remember Elise finding her at some ghastly audiology clinic. She thought Elise was there to get hearing aids! Imagine! Abigail can't stay away; she loves it really. That tells you something. Elise reveals all at the end usually, when they feel better. She didn't get a chance with you.'

He was looking at me keenly. 'I mean . . . perhaps you feel the connection between us?' he asked me. So earnest.

There was no connection. I shook my head. He pointed at something I hadn't noticed because it was tucked away in a particularly dark corner of the room. A wine fridge stocked with tiny vials of blood.

'You gave it willingly,' he said gently. 'For us to have a little sip. She always asked you, didn't she? Every single time. We'd never take anything from you that you didn't want to give, that would defeat the point.'

I was repulsed, but I pulled myself together. There was the question I had to ask. I needed to understand if Sally had been the first.

'Caroline said someone else had died.' I edged back, hand on the door, ready to make a run for it.

He let out a deep belly laugh.

'Yes, Rory. He went a little far with one of the surgeries. Too generous. Let's just say he wanted a little too much removed . . .'

He laughed and laughed.

I had no idea who Rory was, and so the name had no effect on me, but I could picture a man in his fifties in that makeshift operating theatre. Nervous, excited perhaps.

It was nothing like I'd thought. When Caroline told me someone had died at Carn, I'd assumed it was a girl, but I'd been wrong about it all. They'd done it to themselves, and this Rory had died.

I turned to open the door.

'You're going so soon?' Patrick asked. He was putting his dressing back on, applying the tape tenderly. He was less interested in me after his reveal.

So many thoughts, and I'd tried to hold them at arm's length. But it was impossible to do it any longer, the effort was too much.

I was thinking of Carn, of course. What I'd eaten: buttery pastries, thin slices of steak, mince in all its forms and burgers too. Pushed on me, but I'd wanted them. A taste that I hadn't recognized. I'd eaten virtually nothing in the last few days, so when I threw up at the door of Patrick's office, it was mainly liquid rushing into my mouth, all acid as my body seemed to purge itself without me having any choice in the matter. I was hollow afterwards, all of it expelled on to the floor.

50.

The responder coughed first and then read off a script. 'Hello, 999. Which service do you need?'

'Police.'

'I'll connect you now.'

Almost immediately. 'Police, what's your emergency?'

I kept it simple. 'Someone died.'

'Okay, where are you?'

'I'm not there any more. It's a place called Carn.'

'Carn. Hold the line, please.'

So brisk. Like it was nothing. And I had to hold for far too long.

The hold music tinkled on and on and on, and finally they came on to the line.

I told them about the train station, about where I thought it could be, and they said they would go there and find it, and that they would be in touch. They said I didn't need to go back myself, but I was always going to return. I had to. The thought of Sally's body was gnawing at me.

I had told the police I wasn't sure where it was, and I was telling the truth. But I hadn't actually tried to find it. After the call, I poked around, and, despite my sleuthing skills, I struggled to find Carn online. Someone had done some work to hide it, and even looking it up on the land registry hadn't worked. But I found a rough area where the house could be, tracking back to the train station I'd arrived at – where Caroline and I had walked on that early morning.

I decided to go alone.

What would happen when I arrived?

The police would meet me, and perhaps Elise would be there. She'd be arrested. They would see where we had been kept. So much could go wrong, but I had to go. I wanted to throw up again. I had felt a deep nausea ever since Patrick had revealed the truth.

I sped out of the city in Harry's car. The truth was unbearable if I held it in my head for too long so I skidded round the corners to forget, immersing myself in the road. I tried to follow the signs – they were unfamiliar to me – *Braemar, Auchallater*. Periodically, I reached down – pressed next to my thigh in the car seat was a knife, a long, thin one with a wooden handle, purchased to make sushi, though we'd never got round to it. Harry had missed it in his knife-collecting round before Carn, and I had planned to hand it back to him when he picked up the rest of his belongings.

My heart rate slowed down about halfway through the drive. I had committed to returning, and I had my knife. I reminded myself that the police were coming, but still there wasn't really a plan. Could I even tell them about the true purpose of Carn? I hadn't thought it through properly, and I suspected I had committed some kind of crime.

Eventually, the road became familiar. I pulled over, got out of the car and walked a little way. A curve and the path became gravel. The house came into view, and I finally saw what Carn had become.

Carn, Again

51.

I'd had a deep belief that you could not remove that grand house from the earth. If you destroyed it, the foundations would work their way back up through the soil, fanning out, pushing upwards through the ground with roots meshing to create those flesh walls drilled with peepholes.

You could not remove it, but when I returned, Carn was transformed.

The water was the most noticeable thing. As much as it had been a necessary tool for containment, it had also had a certain beauty. Now, the water was gone, and the hole that circled Carn had been filled with what could have been sand or impacted mud. I'd be able to cross if it took my weight. The walls were a yellowish white, and the clematis was gone. I noted the pitted tarmac, replacing the curved driveway, and the surface appeared sticky in the sun. A *careful* ugliness. So much work.

The forest had been chopped to stumps and there was smoke. A bonfire in the distance.

I walked across where the water had been and on to the grubby lawn and up to the front door. I pushed it open. Inside, it was not the same either. The expensive wallpaper was gone; it was all painted bright yellow. The floors were lino, and there were a few small touches – battered fire extinguishers and tatty signs with a jumble of fonts and instructional messaging: *Do not play With the Heating!!*

It's hard to emphasize just how thoughtful the transformation was. In some ways, it was *too* well done, and it struck me that perhaps the place had been restored to a former, extremely shabby version of itself. It was like a rundown community centre; somewhere institutional and unloved. I knew this was all Elise.

I was standing there in the hall when I heard footsteps.

A police officer.

He walked straight in, and I was flooded with relief for a second.

But then he just stood there. He stared at me.

It didn't feel quite right with only one police officer. I'd thought there would be more of them, a whole squad or something. I was surprised that he was here so soon after me as well. Had he followed me? Or maybe he'd been here for a while.

It was okay. I tried to reassure myself: the police were here, and they were going to investigate. Still, something was off. He stood there without introduction when surely he should have taken the lead and spoken to me straight away.

Then Elise came out of her office. A chill ran through me and I edged away, my back hitting against the front door.

She was almost unrecognizable: she wore no make-up and her hair was scraped up into a ponytail, straggling locks hanging down the back of her neck. She sported a pair of cheap glasses with thick plastic frames and another pair sat crookedly on her head too. Her dungarees were covered in paint and, underneath them, a faded T-shirt. She held a mop, and she leaned against it.

Nothing made sense.

She looked at me with disappointment. Despite myself, my stomach dropped to see that there was no admiration or love.

The policeman smiled.

'Hello.' Elise greeted me like I was a stranger, then she turned to the policeman.

'Hi, Greg,' she said with a nod, and then she tilted her head to the side, simpering. 'I'm just cleaning this place up,' she said to both of us. 'I know it's a little . . . unloved. Groups of walkers use it; it's the only low-cost accommodation in the area.'

The policeman nodded; he seemed bored. He sneaked a peek at his phone, at a game he was playing, and tapped away. There was a beep and a rattle from the screen – the tinny sound of sweets falling.

It clicked.

I recognized him.

'You were there,' I said. 'Watching me, in the drawing room.'

He looked up from his phone and grinned at me almost cheekily.

'They say the girls at Carn are really something. If you can find the place,' he said, wringing his hands together earnestly. 'If you can finally see them for yourself. They say if you do all that, you'll be struck by what you can give them. You'll be connected to them forever. It's life-changing.'

Elise nodded encouragingly.

The act was over; he wasn't even going to pretend any more that this was any kind of investigation.

'Don't let the fire get too high,' he said to Elise, and he came towards me. I stepped to one side, and he walked out of the door without a backwards glance.

She gave a coy little wave and then turned to me. 'Betsy,' she said. The disappointment was still there, and her brow was furrowed. I thought she was about to ask me how I was, but her face went blank.

'This is what we do afterwards,' she said to me. 'This is the boring bit, the clean-up.'

I heard footsteps. A voice asking a question.

'Are we keepi–' The voice floated, became louder, then broke off.

Elise spoke softly. 'Well, here we are. Betsy, this is my daughter – you know her as Caroline?'

And Caroline stood there in the hall, staring at me in horror.

52.

Gently does it. Elise was cold to me upon my return to Carn, but she still smiled a little at this revelation. And she was gentle with me as she handed me the final piece of her puzzle.

The daughter with the knee injury.

Elise had cherry-picked the parts she liked when she drew a picture for each of us.

Offered me an opiate addict.

Given Abigail a surfer in Cornwall.

Perhaps parts had been true? It is, after all, so much easier to create someone from morsels.

I rejigged what I knew about Caroline. Although that wasn't her name, she would always be Caroline to me. This was the missing part. She'd been trapped in a cellar, that's what she'd said. Elise had punished her for her betrayal.

I had believed her.

Caroline looked broken. 'You shouldn't have come,' she said. 'I told you to leave it. You got away, but you're back.'

They were alike when viewed next to each other, though I hadn't noticed it before, and it made me realize I'd never actually seen them stand side by side. They had a similar nose and both of their eyes were green with the same heavy lids.

'Why are you here?' I asked Caroline.

'She's here to help,' Elise said, as if that was obvious. 'Carn moves on. Now we have to move and that means we need to hide it all.'

Elise appeared relaxed but Caroline was beside herself, and I'd never seen her this way.

'I wanted to tell you everything,' she said, and her voice splintered with tears.

'Did she actually lock you down there?' I asked.

'Yes! I can explain. This isn't what I want. I'm still on your side.'

Elise had been letting our conversation play out, but now she jumped in. 'Oh, don't be silly,' she said to her daughter. 'You had a bit of a wobble. But you're back now.' She turned to me. 'I knew she'd come back.'

The knife was in my hand, edging upwards to defend against whatever might come next. They could see what I might do if pushed.

Caroline walked towards me. 'Hand it over.'

She was so like Elise when she chose to be, and I saw it now. She could switch in a second: calm and able to steer me. When she spoke, it could be hypnotic. I couldn't believe I'd never seen it before.

Then, as she came to take the knife from me, I didn't quite comprehend my actions. I was watching the whole thing from above, and my hand just passed it over.

'I'm sorry,' she said as she took it.

Elise seemed fine with Caroline having the knife. She pushed her full weight on the mop. 'I do hope you're happy, the two of you. All this work destroyed. And when there was so much potential. I thought this house would be more of a long-term set-up, and now look what we've had to do to cover our tracks!' She let out a snigger as she admonished us. I think she expected us to fight back.

'All of it gone because you ran away, but you just had to come back,' she continued. 'The thing is,' and here she looked at Caroline, 'I *know* you. I knew you'd come back. You're young and you don't understand what needs to be done or how to get there. It's a shame we had to dismantle so much of it, but it's all fixable in the long term. And as for you –' she turned her attention to me – 'we cannot have people like you coming back.'

There was a vacant chill to her; the warmth had all gone and this was what was underneath: cold logistics. Her face set in a sad frown. 'There are parts that are flawed. But it is what it is. You do what you have to do, and when you have money, you can do anything. We've always been able to make a lot of money here. Money flows to us,' she said. 'It pools at our feet.'

Elise came over and stood next to me. She held my hand in hers. But it all felt wrong. I wanted her to stop. I couldn't bear it.

'How could you come back and be on her side? After what happened, after what she did to Sally?' I said to Caroline, because I needed to understand.

Elise looked confused, and she twisted to me. There was a change in the air, and I sensed that Elise was about to ask me something. But she hardly had a chance to get it out because Caroline was speaking too. It was like all the words were travelling through water and nothing made sense.

Caroline was coming for me, her face a mask of fury.

I backed away.

No room. I was trapped, with the wall behind me, and there was nowhere to go; she was too fast.

A guttural roar filled the hallway.

She charged forwards with my knife.

I was calm, just blank acceptance. And then it all slowed down so I could see her in her entirety; she was so clear to me. Where her hair had seemed like fire, everything softened, and I could observe her freckles and take her in. She was enraged, a warrior.

She swerved.

Elise hadn't expected it. She was still trying to speak and explain. Both hands went up to protect herself; they went to her face, which was the wrong decision. Caroline was too quick. Elise let out a choked kind of gurgle as Caroline struck out, once, twice, jabbing. Then, a final grunting stab, right in the belly through the denim. Elise lurched backwards and fell to the floor.

The knife was in Caroline's hand and blood was everywhere, so much of it. She looked at me in horror, tossed the knife to the floor and sprinted to the door. I ran after her and called her name until my lungs burned. Tarmac stuck to my shoes, forcing me to go slower, and soon she was far ahead of me. She was so fast, despite her knee. I couldn't keep up as she ran into the maze of stumps and, eventually, I had to stop. Where the remains of the forest began, I collapsed, panting for a second, trying to get my breath back. I could see that she'd stopped too and she stood amongst the cut trees.

She screamed. A flock of blackbirds spread when they heard it, the same scream that had come from the cellar, rising through the floorboards and entering my dream. I stared at the birds as they scattered in dark scrawls against the sky that stretched blue and endless.

The sky here is different. That was what Abigail had said.

53.

I was close to Caroline, and I could have gone closer still, but I didn't want to speak to her.

I went back inside the house and sat on the floor, staring at the fire extinguisher until it blurred and doubled. I watched Elise's body like it was a job assigned to me and, if I took my eyes off it, she'd rise. Then, the door opened with a creak, and Caroline came into the entrance hall.

We both looked at the body lying there on the floor. Caroline let out a high moan that clotted in the air. Her cheeks were blotchy and red. I'd seen so many changes in her that day – the quick descent into juddering rage and her face on the edge of tears.

Without discussing it properly, we moved Elise. Caroline led the way, and it was awkward, even with two people. I had to find reserves of strength from somewhere, but the sheer physical force required meant that I could block out what we were doing and concentrate on getting through the task.

In the end we got her outside, and we dragged her across the tarmac. The surface stuck to her skin. If I thought about what we were doing, it was overwhelming. So, I focused on the route and on the landscape as we went down past the herb garden, which was now set up as a derelict play park.

Finally, we got to the woods, to the bonfire. Rubbish melted in the flames but I could still see furniture from Carn: Elise's desk from her office hacked to pieces.

54.

Caroline prised every single ring off her mother's fingers, and then we heaved the body into the fire. This final thrust summoned a strength from within. I'd expected the body to harden, but she was still soft and moveable. Her limbs flopped into the heat.

Both of us jumped away as soon as we could see she was going to burn. The fire was so strong, and it would take her soon enough.

Caroline sat on the ground. She was too close to the fire, and her face must have hurt with the heat. Tears fell, fat and heavy, down her cheeks, but she didn't wipe them away.

'I went to see Patrick,' I said eventually.

Her face warped. I think she knew where I was going with this.

Patrick could have been her father.

It tied it all up. Patrick – when he'd ambushed me in the toilet, he'd said that he had come to Carn to make a delivery, and now I understood what that delivery was. Meat.

He'd also mentioned a visit: *I was here to see someone, but they don't appear to be around.* It would make sense if that person had been Caroline.

'I don't want to talk about Patrick,' she said flatly. Her face was shiny with the trails of tears, but the crying had stopped. She took a few deep breaths. She was real – so emotional and alive and much more fragile than I'd ever seen her before.

'I should say something about her,' Caroline said. 'Some kind of send-off.'

I nodded. 'You should. She told people about you.'

'Really?' she asked, and my heart kind of hurt hearing how excited she was, and how she tried to hide it by forcing her voice to stay level.

'In a way,' I said. 'She told people she had a daughter.'

She nodded.

'You wanted to say more about her?' I prompted.

Without looking at me, she spoke. 'When I was ten, she told me she was glad I was a girl. She said she would have killed her-self if she was having a boy.'

I winced.

She shook her head. 'No, no, you don't understand. It sounds like a bad memory, but even the ones that are bad were . . . remarkable.'

'Did you believe her when she said that?' I asked.

'I've never really thought about it. Maybe. Anyway, she said when she found out she was having a girl, she was delighted. I'm saying this not to make her sound like a monster. I want you to understand that it was actually incredible to be spoken to in such a way, to be confided in with something so raw, so terrible. Would your parents be so . . . honest?'

'No,' I said, straight away. 'Definitely not.'

'Right? They just don't usually speak like that, but she did.'

Caroline was back in the good times, but I needed her to move away from that, back to Carn. Because there was one final part of it all to discuss. The words were there on my lips.

'I want to tell her that, at one point, I loved her,' she said. 'Very much.'

'But what she did . . .'

She looked at me with pity. 'She wasn't the same as she is now. She was the most glamorous, exciting mother you could imagine.'

'So, when did it start?'

'We travelled about before she trained as a nurse,' she said. 'We spent a lot of time together, the two of us. Before we had money, before any of this.' She gestured around. 'Even then, she liked illness. It started with me. She liked it when I was thin, feverish. Well, she liked certain aspects, but she hated others. Like vomit, for example, she found that repulsive . . .'

280

'That's horrible.'

'It wasn't that bad,' she snapped.

I realized I couldn't criticize Elise, only she was allowed.

'My mother has, or had, strange beliefs. You've seen what she began to believe in.' She smiled sadly. 'As did Patrick. They were bad for each other. I wanted to please her because I was never enough for her by the time I was a teenager. Maybe because I was . . . robust by then. I wasn't swooning around, unwell. I loved her, but it was all too much. I got away as soon as I could, but I was messed up.'

'Painkillers,' I said.

She did a double-take. 'Yes. I had some knee issues, and then I was in a bad place for a while. She decided I should come work with her. It saved me.'

'You saw what was happening?'

She nodded. 'Taking on these places, old hotels, old manor houses, anywhere really, and setting up these temporary retreats and loving it, loving all these sick girls. Kind of curing them, kind of making it worse. Saying they had special powers. The men Patrick brought in . . . The meat thing . . .' she said it almost shyly, like she was checking I knew too.

I gagged. But I hid it and nodded.

'I knew I needed to stop her. I was the only one who could do it. I had this whole plan,' she said.

'You should have told me in the forest when we got out,' I said. 'You told me about the helpers. You should have told me it all.'

'Seriously?' She shook her head. 'You wouldn't have understood. I *did* come back to confront her. I was biding my time. What I told you was all true. About the girls and about the helpers. I haven't *lied* to you.'

'I don't think that's true. They locked you down there with Sally.'

This was it – the memory that rubbed at me. There was something else I'd seen in that cellar.

There was nothing accusatory in my sentence, I'd been careful to keep my voice very neutral, but Caroline turned to me. We were past discussing Elise's motives, their relationship.

We were back in the cellar, or at least she was. I had taken her there, and it was a horrible place.

'Elise *loved* Sally at the beginning,' she said. 'She was so beautiful, and Elise was into that. But you have to understand, a doctor was never right. Never right at all. Too medical.'

'Okay,' I said, waiting for more.

'You know,' she said, very simply.

Did I?

I thought I might.

It was swirling around, a muddy puddle of a thought that was growing, becoming intermittently sharp, battering at my brain. It wouldn't go away. Such a terrible bleeding memory that was inextricable from the smell of Sally's body. You see, the sense of unease had begun when I'd seen Sally's wrists in the cellar. I had said nothing, because I'd hoped there had been an explanation for it. So dark, so hard to see clearly. I'd been in shock when I'd realized she was dead. I hadn't thought to question Caroline's story of drowning, because that was such a prescient fear for me, and it was very believable. But while Caroline had done her best to make me leave the cellar quickly and stay away from the body, I'd seen the gashes on Sally's wrists. They had looked deep, far deeper than the light marks made by Caroline's nails on that first morning. It had stuck with me at the time, but I hadn't interrogated it any further.

And then . . .

And then I'd seen Elise's confusion. She had been about to refute the accusation that she'd hurt Sally, it hadn't been her, and it hadn't been the helpers. I suspected that Sally had died later.

'You claimed she drowned,' I said to Caroline.

'I did say that, didn't I.' She rubbed at her jaw, looked exhausted. 'It just came out.'

'So, what happened?'

'She was so desperate. You should have seen her. I was trying to calm her down, and she screamed and screamed. I wanted to help. I did the nail thing.'

'The nail thing,' I repeated.

'It usually worked! Elise did it on me when I was younger. There's something to it. I never meant to hurt her,' she said. 'I . . . I cut her too deeply. She was clawing at where I'd pushed down on her wrists until there was blood all over her from the cuts, and then I went for her neck, to stop her. I squeezed.'

'You killed her,' I said.

She flinched. 'Well, she died,' she corrected me. 'But yes, I'm the monster. Killed the fish, messed up the surgery on Rory, hurt Sally.'

She thumped her fist across her chest and said it again: '*Monster.*'

Was she a monster?

She didn't really look like one to me; she never had. Green eyes, coppery hair and an unmemorable face.

It was instinctive to jump in, to say *you're not a monster*, but I didn't.

'You know what I couldn't stop thinking about when I got out?' she asked me. 'If I hadn't done it, they would have let Sally go eventually, released her to the world. She would have gone back to her life. Maybe she would have recovered completely and got another job or something.' She picked up a stick and poked at the fire.

I believed she'd tried to stop Elise, and I believed things had gone wrong. I watched the flames and thought it over. I wondered about where Sally's body was. It had seemed so important when I'd been driving here, but I didn't know why I'd been so concerned, because she wasn't coming back, and I had helped. I was part of it all, now.

The fire burned. I stood up and walked away.

Epilogue

Five years passed with no word from them. Then, one day, the postman arrived and the swoosh of mail falling on the mat kickstarted an unpleasant surge of adrenaline, made worse because of the exhaustion. The night before, I'd had some trouble sleeping. This was common enough and it didn't bother me too much any more. I'd spent the night doing what I did quite often when the urge to check was too strong. In the depths of an online forum, I went back to some of my posts, clicking through to them without even thinking and scrolling down.

Anyone know what happened to that doctor? Can't remember her second name. I haven't seen her on TV for years and I just wondered if anyone knew her?

I was waiting for someone to bite, because surely there were friends and family out there who cared.

My post resulted in minor speculation. Some people remembered Sally; someone said they'd bought a second-hand car from her, and another said she'd gone out with their cousin's friend. I could see that no one missed her.

After I'd gone through the posts, I found some old daytime TV episodes. I sat on the sofa at three a.m., the cruellest hour of darkness, when it feels like no one else in the world is awake. I watched Sally, her hair combed neatly. She was unrecognizable. I found her to be confident and charismatic as she answered the medical questions from viewers, reassuring some teenager about an embarrassing skin condition.

It gnawed at me as it always did when I watched her. I had wanted to go to the police for quite a while, even knowing what had happened and what Caroline had done.

Perhaps Caroline had been telling the truth and it had been

closer to an accident than an attack, but Sally still deserved closure.

That morning, I went to pick up the mail, and there was a letter with my address handwritten on the front. I opened it carefully, and the smell of strawberries hit me: Abigail's vape. The envelope contained a thick piece of card. It was an invitation with my name, and a time, and a place. There was no option to RSVP.

I dressed entirely in black, wrapped up in a huge coat, and took my time walking there late on a Friday night. The event – whatever it was – seemed to be held at a gallery, down a narrow side street on the outskirts of the New Town. I turned up with my invitation in hand, and the man at the door shuffled in front of me to block my way. He asked for my ID, and then he squinted at my passport for too long. I could feel myself blushing. It was like he knew me, but I didn't recognize him.

Eventually, he let me in. 'It's a bit of a trek,' he said, gesturing up the stairwell; many flights loomed above.

I walked up. The first set ended in a small landing, and there was a large photograph of a man. I realized it was a memorial when I saw the dates below: a date of birth, a date of death. There was a small card under the photo. Candles dripped below, lighting him up. I went to read the name: Rory.

He was ordinary-looking. It just seemed like a snap from the office with his wrinkled shirt in-frame. A modest shrine to a man I'd never met.

I dug my hand into my coat pocket for my bone. The incus. It was well handled by that point, and I wondered if it belonged to this *Rory*.

There was a woman stationed at the next landing. She checked my invitation again, asked for my passport and cross-referenced it against a small black book. In front of her was a door and a keypad, the same keypad, always. She walked ahead of me, and the swish of her skirt reminded me a little of Elise, and then the woman input the code, opened the door and stepped to one side to let me through. She averted her eyes to the ceiling as if I was harmful.

I was allowed to walk up the final set of stairs without my identity being checked again. At the top, I entered the gallery space. It was large and echoing with a photography exhibition set up alongside the far wall, between the windows. The walls were that same white as Carn.

Lashings of double cream. Fat clouds.

The lighting was dim. I wandered closer to the centre of the room. There were lots of men and some women, and all were dressed in tuxedos and dresses in dark tones. I was underdressed, and I tried not to draw attention to myself. Luckily, when I took my coat off, I looked a bit like the servers who circulated, drifting around the room with trays of wine and canapés. I made my way over to the exhibition, past men in small groups of two or three. Sliding alongside them, I snatched a look at their faces. I thought I recognized a few from Carn, but I wasn't sure. There was certainly no one my age there. No one was paying me any attention.

I walked around the perimeter of the room before I reached the photographs. Huge portraits, blown up five or six times larger than life, and all were severed under the clavicle. I recognized the make-up – the exaggeration of the unwell, with the mix of greenish pallor and lines of age. Shadows under the eyes, a visible film of sweat.

It was strange to see them all like this, expertly lit. The photographs were of many girls I didn't recognize, but these were the girls of Carn. Some had little red stickers on them, indicating they were sold.

I stood for a minute or so and peered at those pictures – trying to find whatever it was that made us so desirable to Elise, to Patrick. Symmetrical faces that spoke of some equation for attractiveness? Certainly not conventional beauty.

And then there was me. And Abigail.

People stopped and stared at the photo of Abigail. A small group congregated in front of it.

I'd actually seen an advert featuring Abigail on the side of a bus stop a year before, smashed glass around her head. It had been taken at Carn – her lips slightly open so you could see the gap between her teeth. A model pose for shower gel. Neon bottle with a chaotic jungle scene imposed behind her body, all greens and yellows. She wasn't naked, but she had some skin on show, an arm to her chest and her hand against her face. She looked unnatural in the way her shoulders and collar had been smoothed out – an easy click of a designer's mouse, or perhaps it wasn't her chest at all. The image had been manipulated so much. I hadn't understood it, because she looked ill. There were still some vestiges of the make-up and it had made me focus on her more. Was this what people wanted? Was this what they liked?

I walked over to the corner of the room. I did a double-take.

A picture of Elise.

Elise was quite a bit younger in the photograph, but she was made up, just as we'd been. Dead eyes, skin rubbed and stretched. Maybe she was the first one, the guinea pig. Maybe she'd tried it all out for us. That would mean she knew what it felt like. And I considered this. I wasn't sure how it changed my feelings about Elise.

A group noticed me; they turned and looked, their interest piqued. They froze. If this was the connection Elise and Patrick had talked about, I hated it. The air was a thickened rope.

How could I leave?

I had scoped out the exits, and I knew how to make my escape, but then I saw Patrick, dressed in a tuxedo like the rest, and he spotted me too. He left the group he was standing with and moved towards me.

'You came,' he said.

'Yes.' I looked past him to see Caroline; she was there somewhere in his features. I was glad that she didn't appear to be in the room. There would be no photos of her, and she was not part of this. Perhaps she had made her escape.

Patrick was closer to me than felt comfortable, his eyes roving up and down my body. He smiled. 'They're marvellous, aren't they?' he said, raising one hand to the exhibition. 'People can see. The process can begin again. This is how it all starts.'

He snapped his fingers, and a girl dashed over with a tray. Tiny little tarts crafted from pastry, filled with raw mince and finished with a smidgen of egg yolk sitting on top. A surge of feeling rushed through me, the anticipation of the taste. He took the tray from the girl and he held it out; the mince looked pink. He didn't force me to take one, he just waited.

Acknowledgements

With thanks to my agent Emily and DHH Literary Agency, the team at Viking: Rosa, Vikki, Lydia, Harriet, Ellie H., Georgia, Juliet, Karen, Ellie S., Charlotte, the UK and international sales team, the rights and the audio team. Thanks also to the debut community for their wisdom, Niamh for her sage advice, to my friends and family for all their support over the past few years. Finally, to the booksellers, reviewers and readers who make this such a rewarding job.

Liked this?

Read on for an excerpt of the beautifully
dark *The Things We Do To Our Friends* . . .

France

Three girls dance in front of him.

One of them has set up an old stereo, and tinny music blares, blocking out the sound of the cicadas that sing relentlessly at this time in the evening.

The garden looked beautiful when he first arrived, extending back to meet an old farmhouse where delicate vines stroke the white walls. There is grass that feels comforting – a damp rug under his feet. But things are not right, and the smell is a little aggravating. It makes his nose itch and his eyes water. When he focuses, the place looks like it has been left to become wild, and the fruits loaded on the trees are overripe. The garden has the heavy, sweet smell of the monkey enclosure at a zoo.

He struggles to concentrate on his girls, because of the sun on his face, perhaps, but it's enough to summon the tangled beginning of an urgent lust, deep in his gut. Two of them hold hands high above their heads to create an arc and the third shimmies and then dives under. There is a screech of excitement as she does so.

He remembers that kind of frenzied joy. When he was their age, summer seemed to go on forever. He would get up to all sorts of things, unsupervised. Now, these months are oppressive, caked to his life like dry mud on a car. Summer means foreigners clogging the roads, children everywhere and the slog of work. Supplier events, tastings, factory rounds: in this part of the country, none of it stops because of the heat. It all becomes more tiring the older you get, and each summer is more difficult to tolerate than the last. An itch on the sole of his left foot. A gurgle, and a cranky, more than irritable, bowel. Each shadow of physical discomfort is worse in the evening heat, but these girls know none of the pain that comes with age. The girls are life itself, and things seem easy for them. They are too young to feel a pinch near the hips or the pull in the lower back as their bodies contort to the music.

They certainly hadn't a care in the world earlier in the day. He'd seen them outside the shop on the bench in the car park, waiting for a lift that hadn't come. When he picked them up, he could barely tell them apart. In that delicious way, the girls were preferable in a collection, a flick of hair, a flash of a smile. Tumbling in confidently, like it was their right to be taken to wherever they pleased. Their grimy knees up, pushing against the back of the seats in front with no consideration for the upholstery, something he would never have let his daughters do, and the smell as they'd chewed on strawberry-flavoured gum – a horrible habit – and chatted away to each other, ignoring him.

Now, hours later, he sees how different the girls are as they peel away from each other in the garden. That stack of limbs jumbled together in his car has parted to make way for three separate identities, and it seems fitting that he gives each of them a name.

There's the one who's tall and blonde and the most classically beautiful, with straight white teeth and a face that is perfectly symmetrical. She's bruised all over her tanned shins, but not in the way that you'd associate with abuse. A healthy, monied type of injury that he imagines might be from playing a gruelling game of lacrosse or falling in a photogenic pile when skiing. Each limb looks taut, her calves clearly defined and ripples of muscles in her forearms. He can tell she's the one in charge, as she issues directions to the others. He'll call her Blondie.

There's the one who has black hair braided into a complex arrangement and then pinned high on her head. He can see her shoulders, and he notices that they're sullied with a thread of sunburn. Braid will do for her. Staring at Braid, he feels a pang in his loins for that dark hair, those dark eyes, and an idle thought that he might like to slit her throat, to slice across the

298

neck where the sunburn marks it and cut her head away. He imagines hacking at her to separate her sweet face from the unsightly mess of those bodily scars inflicted by the cruel sun.

The final one in the trio looks like a child dressed up as a belly dancer. Her body still has that lovely, almost dripping layer of fat that jiggles as she moves, and she appears to be swaddled in a full-length velvet floral gown. She blows him a kiss, and her eyelid dips into a theatrical wink. He nods back, acknowledging her but declining to invite her further. There'll be plenty of time for that later. He'll call her Winky.

The sun is so low in the sky. A scarlet flare that bleeds more across the horizon every time he treats himself to a long blink. The brightness sears his eyeballs when his eyes are shut, forcing him to reopen them and refocus. He assesses the situation. He's sitting at the centre. The star of the show, a treasured guest. He tips his head back and breathes in, realizing how deeply, deeply thirsty he is. The thirst is crunchy in the back of his throat; dry air hurts his nostrils. Everywhere, his skin seems tight and parched, like every drop of moisture has been sucked out.

A grubby metal tube lies on the table next to him. He recognizes it. There are many tubes that are very similar at work. He shakes his head in wonder, and beads of sweat run off his face and down on to his suit. Yes, he's still in his suit.

Could that be true? The tube is from the farms? Perhaps. Perhaps not. Suddenly, it's important. What detail! What sensitive *curation* of the experience.

It explains things, in some part, but the whole picture won't quite form properly.

He tries to nod for water.

Winky ignores the gesture, but she saunters over and pours a glass for herself from the pitcher on the table. She takes a deep glug and slams it back down. The other two have stopped dancing, and the mood has changed. The music is louder. Some kind of horrible rock music and he can't escape it. Something is happening; the sense of relaxation has disappeared.

Everything changes.

Braid and Winky have gone now, and it's just Blondie. He sits straight and tugs at the handcuffs around his wrists, tentatively pushing his ankles apart to test the restraints there. They're far too tight to budge. Blondie unfolds a white cotton napkin and lays it out in front of him.

Winky and Braid emerge from the house, and Braid has an enormous platter. It's antique silver, far too big for her, like she's in a school play. She lifts the top off the platter and reveals a dish, holding it under his nose with glee. A deep bowl of mushroom risotto, the rice hot and steaming. The aroma of stock and fresh porcini.

Winky picks up the serving spoon. She shoves it into his mouth while Braid secures him for the feed – her fingers dig into his gums. They ignore the fact that the food is escaping and spilling down his front. He barely has a moment to think; all he can taste is mealy rice.

Blondie is laughing quite madly.

No, he wants to shout out, *not me*, but there will be no words to phrase an impassioned plea to the girls.

The mushrooms become warmed slugs and they stick in his throat, but there's no time to chew, so he gulps, hoping to push the chunks down. The next course is a ratatouille served by Winky, and again, she feeds him, spooning the food into his mouth, forcing it down. She does so alone and the other two watch. Then corn, fried in butter and laced with herbs, ripped from the cob and forced down his gullet. He pulls at his wrists, but there's no point.

He can only measure time by the food that arrives. Vegetable stews, creamy cauliflower gratin, a yolk-yellow soufflé, then pasta coated in cheap American cheese that you use to top burgers on a barbecue and should never, ever be used in a pasta dish.

They manoeuvre the implements with ease, ramming the courses down. The metal of the spoon is painful against his palate, like a dental instrument, and then, later, further and deeper into his throat.

He is choking.

The food congeals, turns to grey glue as night falls. His body convulses and the music plays on.

PART I

I.

Edinburgh

I've decided to look back and make some kind of sense of it all, and the initial idea of starting to put the pieces together in one place was because Tabitha's mother asked me to write it all down so she had something of Tabitha's – a tangible record of her life for the extended family – but I couldn't quite bring myself to cobble together a fictional account where we were normal students who did normal things, so I ended up giving her a vague excuse, and she didn't ask again. But the idea wouldn't die down once she'd brought it up, and I thought, why not? Why shouldn't I go back over what happened for my own purposes?

Then the question was, where does the tale begin, and although there are other places that may seem more logical, September 2005 feels right.

My arrival.

How very dramatic that sounds! But it felt dramatic at the time.

September is a month that has a special anticipation associated with it. As the leaves turn and the nights darken. The first time you open a book, cracking the spine and smoothing down the pages so they can't spring back up.

It's a month that means fresh beginnings, and that only happens a few times in life, when the slate is wiped clean and the story is ready for you to begin and tell it how you wish. The first day of a job when you're cautious and rule-abiding, or with a new partner when you share appealing parts of yourself to test the reaction. At university, it is even more of an opportunity. Nobody knows who you are; there are no expectations or preconceptions. How you answer each question and how you position yourself is entirely up to you. But it needs to begin somewhere, and for me it was Edinburgh, at Waverley Station.

I was ready to move, so desperate to leave Hull for good, but it was hard not to feel a little discouraged when I stepped off the train and strode out into the city. I was expecting post-summer blustery days with the warmth still in the air, but the weather was particularly bad that year. I thought of my granny and what she'd say in that scornful tone: 'It's just a few hours away, Clare. I don't know why you expected it to be so *different*.'

How grey the Old Town was. It was magnificent, but there was an underlying sense of squalor below it all. Steps led to alleys, weaving with possibility, where you could just as easily find a grand square as you could a dead end and a seagull gnawing on scraps of cold chips. I remember the magnitude of scale when I walked along to Queen Street and stared down to the New Town. The views went all the way to the Firth of Forth, a glimpse of water, but the winds were quick and soon a dampish fog obscured it all, like a bundle of laundry pulled dripping from the washing machine, then pinned up. I ignored the weather. I was determined to stay optimistic about the whole thing.

Enough wandering. I had a map printed, tucked in my bag, showing where I was staying. My new home was under a mile away, so I decided to walk. It was a battle through the streets alone with two suitcases, which contained everything I owned, and on the way I encountered a group of confused tourists. They blocked the entire road and craned their heads to take pictures of St Giles' Cathedral with bulky cameras hanging from their necks. Then there were the other students who bumbled alongside harried commuters. What a mix of people to get lost in!

I was a bubble of nervous energy, and I could have screamed out loud, right there in the middle of the street, but I held it in.